WHERE D'YA PUT YER WILLY?

Jeff Kristian

A Mr Binks Media Book

Copyright © Mr Binks Media 2012
Cover design © Mr Binks Media 2015

Second Edition
Edited by Robert Ingham

British Library Cataloguing in Publication Data.
A catalogue record for this book is available from the British Library.

ISBN 978-0-9928456-3-6 (Paperback Edition)
ISBN 978-0-9928456-4-3 (eBook Edition)

Mr Binks Media
mrbinksmedia@jeffkristian.com

I DEDICATE THIS BOOK TO
CHARLIE B

"My life has found its meaning
since you came along."

www.jeffkristian.com

CHAPTER ONE

'Fakakta phone!' yelled the plump, agitated man on the curb outside the newsagents. Perhaps it was the crippling September humidity and sunshine buggering up the signal. Whatever, the high street was so busy he probably wouldn't be able to hear anything if he did get a reception. Pulling a hankie from his Nike joggers, he removed his baseball cap and wiped the sweat from his shaven head and face. He looked at his watch and glanced fervently up and down the street. He was in the right place at the right time.

Wiping a large dewdrop from the end of his even larger Jewish nose, the sound of tyres screeching caught his attention. He turned just in time to see a car leave the tarmac and mount the pavement. It veered straight toward him in what appeared to be slow motion. His scream muffled slightly as his lips smacked the windscreen and he flew twenty feet into the air. His Cuban heel knocked the glass cover clean off the street lamp before tearing a hole in the top of the overhanging shop canopy on his way back down.

Head hooked on its steel frame, he swung lifelessly to the tune of I Believe I Can Fly from a passing ice-cream van.

As the car sped away, a little group of shoppers gathered around his swaying carcass, watching in awe as if it were a drama on television. Nothing quite as exciting as this had happened in the high street for some time.

'Where's his head, then?' said one old lady with glee, glancing around the pavement while popping another chip into her mouth.

'Through the hole on top of that new overhang. Mr Gupta won't be very pleased,' her friend replied.

It was still stuffy and hot a week later when a cackle of expectant drag queens gathered for the wake. Lewisham's Municipal Offices had not long had its annual summer overhaul. The smell of new paint and cheap floor polish coupled with the emanation from the open-topped luminous pink coffin at the front was almost too much for this fair and delicate collection of side show cabaret starlets to bear. It was only the slim possibility of redistributed worldly goods from the dead drag that kept them waiting so long.

'And she did have some lovely diamante bits that might be up for grabs,' continued one pseudo-Chanel crone.

'You won't get none of that, girl. Them two thieving bitches from Sugar Sugar will have it away before you can say lip gloss,' came the acid reply with an equally bitter glance to the two potential benefactors in the front row. 'Mind you, they need it stuck in that dive,' he added, running a black fishnet glove over his plastic pearl necklace. 'It's not as though they can get work anywhere else, is it?'

Finally, the Solicitor arrived. About eighty and looking half dead himself, he hobbled to a large flat screen TV at the front. As he glanced at the corpse, his own mortality flashed across his mind, as well as a little disgust at the absolute gaudiness of the casket and its outrageously costumed inhabitant. Turning to face the gathering - a sea of men in violent makeup, frocks, hats and stilettos was however a shock he hadn't prepared himself for. The glare from the jewellery alone was enough to make him try to remember where he had put his sunglasses. From his sensible grey flannel jacket pocket, he took a small tin and popped a heart pill. From the same pocket he retrieved his notes. He licked his fingers and repositioned what was left of his sweat sodden silver comb-over. He settled slightly when he noticed a man, dressed as a man and looking every bit like a man in a lumberjack shirt and blue jeans sitting alone at the back. He was relieved to see at least one other normal person in the room. Everything would be fine.

He cleared his throat, trying to regain his composure. The last job of a busy day in this ridiculous heat wave. Run this one off in ten minutes and he could be back in the car in time for David Jacobs.

'Good afternoon everybody,' he began deliberately and pronounced, 'and thank you for attending this, the reading of the last will and testament of Letitia Von Schabernacket, The Cunt-ess of Catford.' His nerves were getting the better of him. A knowing titter from the crowd didn't make things easier. Running a long bony finger around the inside of his ill-fitting shirt collar, he took a deep breath. 'I'm so sorry, I mean the Countess of Catford, as she, err, he was known in his, I mean her professional capacity as a... hmm, drag queen. Also known of course, as Mr Bernard Cohen.' So far so good.

'My name is Nathaniel Smythe, Letitia Von Schabernacket, The Countess of Catford also known as Bernard Cohen's Solicitor of Smythe, Saxon and Smythe, executors to his will,' he bumbled nervously.

'I know it's a little unconventional to do this sort of thing instead of a funeral service, but it was the express wish of Letitia Von Schabernacket, The Countess of Catford also known as Bernard Cohen, that matters proceed in this way and that she, erm I mean he, um Letitia Von Schabernacket, The Countess of Catford also known as Bernard Cohen, be present. Albeit in an open-topped casket.' Beads of perspiration began to form on his forehead as he fidgeted with his notes. 'Indeed he, I mean she...' He glanced around fervently for some kind of respite like a chair, but nothing was to hand. 'Letitia Von Schabernacket, The Countess of Catford also known as Bernard Cohen has recently recorded his or her own eulogy on video tape, which I will play for you now.'

He bent forward, painfully trying to reach the video player on the ground below the TV. It was no good, he would have to do it from another angle. With his back to his audience he tried once more, finally reaching the start button. As his finger made contact, he glanced briefly between his legs to see an upside-down Tallulah Bankhead parody in the front row, pursing his lips and winking back at him. Momentarily belying his arthritic condition, Smythe leaped back to his feet as the VCR whirred into motion.

'Hello Gorgeous!' screamed the outrageously coiffured drag queen from the TV screen. 'Yes, it's me! Speaking to you from Heaven. Isn't technology delicious?' The enormous glitter-edged eyelashes batted and the sparkle of the fake diamonds overloaded the video signal creating momentary little white blind spots on the screen. The room marvelled at the kitsch glamour of it all. 'I know some of you
8

are here just to check for yourself that I've really gone. Well you can. That's me in that clitoris-pink box over there. With the lid removed... so you can say it to my face!' His final audience already had scripted what they would say.

'A coffin's the only thing you've ever worn that you look good in!' came a shout from the back.

Lettie plumped the side of his huge matching pink wig with a smirk. 'Yes, I bounced off that car bonnet and landed outside the Pearly Gates in a swimming pool, right on top of Esther Williams doing an upside-down scissor-split turn. Gawd bless her!' His psychotic laugh echoed around the room. 'As for the rest of you, here to see who gets their vicious little claws into what... Well darlings, I'm leaving my entire estate of five hundred thousand pounds...' he paused, anticipating the gasp from his audience. 'Yes, that's what I said. Half a million, along with my fifty per-cent shares in the nightclub Sugar Sugar to...' Another pause, this time for dramatic effect and a drum roll. 'Mister Michael Small, *ta da da da ta da da!*' he sang to a trumpet fanfare.

'That's it, I'm off!' said one drag, gathering his Gucci bag to leave. Several others prepared to follow.

Lettie continued. 'Everyone, this is Michael. Ain't he just the cutest?' The room stopped to look frantically around for what could be so cute as to get the lot. As excited eyes settled on the man, dressed as a man, looking every bit like a man in a lumberjack shirt and jeans sitting alone at the back, moist bums settled back in seats. This was going to be good. Michael was mortified at this sudden unexpected attention. As if the shock of Lettie's eulogy wasn't enough, he was surrounded by twenty drag queens foaming at the mouth at the thought of what this ever-so-slightly gorgeous and soon-to-be rich hunk could do to change their lives forever. He became uncomfortable. More so when a simple toss of jet black hair from his crystal blue eyes caused an echoing, collective sigh from the desperate rabble.

'Michael honey, it's all yours,' continued the eulogy. 'But, there's a condition.' If there was one thing Lettie ever knew in his short life, it was how to milk a crowd. Suddenly a Jewish violin began to play and Lettie swung into full Yentl mode. 'Bubalah! What are you doing with your life? Sweetie, you deserve a new beginning. A shagetz more farklempt I've never seen! There's a purpose waiting you never knew you had.'

Michael was confused. What could he possibly mean? He had only spoken to Lettie a week ago and nothing had been mentioned about a purpose. In fact, he hadn't known him long and only came along today to be polite. His head was swimming.

Lettie was building the drama. 'Therefore, the condition of my estate is... that you be my successor. That's right, you will become... A DRAG QUEEN!'

Over Lettie's cruel pre-recorded cackle, Michael leaped to his feet and yelled at the TV screen, 'You what? Me? A drag queen? I ain't that fuckin' gay!'

The ageing drag in a zebra print jacket to his left also jumped to his feet grabbing Michael's arm, and in a voice as deep as a coal mine screeched, 'Honey don't tell me, just show me!'

Michael shrugged the old hag off and sat back down, a little shocked by his own impulsive outcry. He was far more comfortable in his straight-acting

10

world keeping himself to himself, the way he always had. This was all getting out of hand. He desperately glanced to Smythe as if for an answer, but the old man was way too focussed on his own rising blood pressure to notice.

Lettie wasn't finished yet. 'Yes, a drag queen in our glitzy little show at Madame Fifi's Sugar Sugar in Soho, safe in the more than generous bosom of The Sisterhood. Just for six weeks, then everything will be yours. Don't do it, and the money goes to all those little sick orphans. And nobody wants that, do they!' A murmur of understanding agreement filled the room. 'Mazel tov, baby! And Connie, Chastity… my beloved family. *I'll be seeing you in all the old familiar places,*' he warbled.

Attention suddenly returned to the two uncharacteristically speechless drags at the front. They had been Lettie's sisters at Sugar Sugar for years and everyone had expected this to be their show. Yet the drama of the lumberjack stud getting all the money had completely topped the bill so far.

'Oh, I'd forgotten all about them,' said the drag with the Gucci bag.

'How easily we forget when there's a Cowboy cock pendulously dangled before us,' came a reply.

'Girls, I bequeath you Michael. Trust me, you're gonna love this.' Already, a nicotine-starved Connie was loving this so much that steam was coming from his ears. Lettie continued, 'Give and you shall receive. So all that remains for me to say to you today is…' the finale. Every good show ends with a song. *'Consider me gone! Consider me gone!'* he sang theatrically, *'I'll be off then, bye-bye for now!'*

Without warning, from behind a sparkling curtain ran four flamingo-pink feathered drag showgirls with matching tap shoes, followed closely by two muscled, glitter-oiled go-go boys in matching Lycra shorts. With a crazed cackle, Lettie continued.

'Time for me to strap on, my little wings and fly. Time for me to go to that firmament on high. Gonna shoot off over the back of life, to that drag queen mansion in the sky... hit it, girls!'

With that, a choreographed Busby Berkeley tap routine ensued around the coffin.

'This is it, I'm on my way. I'm sure that you'll cherish the day. I'd like to say I'll miss you, but I WON'T! Time for me to climb the stairway to beyond. Consider me gone!'

'Oh, for feck's sake,' came Chastity's dry Irish retort. Michael sat open-mouthed as Smythe's body slumped to the floor, the trauma of it all finally getting the better of his ancient heart. As the song ended, there was a moment's dead silence, broken only by the click of the video machine switching itself off. The only movement was a slow zig-zag of pink rose petals dropping onto the coffin from on high.

Suddenly, Hell itself visited Lewisham. Amid shrieks and screams, flying chairs, a flurry of flamingo feathers and what was now a selection of dead bodies, Connie finally lunged violently at the coffin.

CHAPTER TWO

Dazed and confused, Michael found himself in the corridor outside. Under the echoing drone of activity within this huge Municipal building, he could still hear the screaming and shouting coming from the room full of pedantic drag queens. He looked up and down the corridor for support, as if perhaps Lettie would be there to explain himself and make sense of it all. But Lettie was dead and Michael was on his own. He looked once again at the notes he had taken from the hand Smythe had been clutching to his chest. It was there in black and white – five hundred thousand pounds and fifty per-cent shares in Sugar Sugar. All for Michael Small.

The doors from the wake creaked open slightly. Out stumbled the deep-voiced hag that had fought over the chair to sit next to him. In his hand, his luscious red wig and the zebra print jacket, dragging on the floor behind. Michael could now see his balding grey head reflecting the fluorescent lights above. In the brighter daylight of the corridor, his deep wrinkles noticed more. The dark makeup had smudged across his face but missed these rugged crevices leaving lighter stripes. His face now matched his jacket. He squinted up at Michael, sitting alone in one of the deep window bays backing onto the main road outside, and a brief glimmer of opportunity flashed across his eyes. Then he remembered the mess he was now in and abandoned any possibility of chatting him up. With a shrug, he removed his one remaining glittery earring, put his top set of teeth back in and hobbled away up the corridor.

Michael tried to clear his head. 'Hold on a minute, let me get this straight,' he murmured to himself. 'Some four-be-two that you've only known five minutes has left you half a million and half of this club. But why? It can't be to get in your pants, 'cause he's, well… kind of dead-like. And he can't be a long lost relative 'cause you ain't Jewish… you haven't even had the short back and sides down below. So what you gonna do?'

What was he going to do? He could just walk away now. Nobody but Lettie knew where he was from and nobody would know any different if he just disappeared. 'But half a million?' he mumbled. He'd never had that much money in his life. 'Six weeks in drag with two drag queens? How hard can it be?' Then he remembered The Zebra with the top set. 'I can't. No way. This just ain't gonna happen!'

His mobile rang. 'Hello? Oh hi, Tamara. Yeah, look can you cover me shift for me? There's something I've got to sort out. Yeah, I know Billy will go mad, but it's really important. I've got a plan to get the ten grand I owe him. Just tell him… tell him I'm sick. Yeah I promise, thanks sweetheart. I owe you.'

His dear friend Tamara had reminded him how serious and dangerous his situation back home was. His choices were limited. 'Looks like I'm wearing a dress!'

His train of thought ended abruptly as the doors from the wake flew back open, violently bashing against the wall to either side of the doorway. Out

14

stormed a tormented Connie. His painfully skinny frame made it hard to understand how he could support the weight of so much jewellery. As his stilettos clacked across the polished floor, Michael looked him over. He had a piled-high blonde Pamela Anderson wig, but unlike The Zebra, his makeup was impeccable. He wore a sequinned boob tube with a fake shag jacket, a Lycra mini skirt and thigh length PVC boots over fishnet tights. Head to foot in funerary black he looked respectful, though not too respectable.

Chastity however was a different story. Shorter, broader and older, he wore a very appropriate two-piece pencil skirt suit and jacket with a single string of oversized pearls. Black tights and five-inch court shoes were topped with a mousy bob brushing gently down either side of his experienced, worn face. A plastic cherry laden pill-box hat and matching leatherette clutch bag, both in scarlet by way of a touch of colour, completed the ensemble. While removing his matching red gloves, he followed hot on Connie's heels across the corridor to the next window bay.

Connie was close to hysteria by this time. 'Bequeath you Michael? Bequeath you Michael? Bollocks to Michael, give me the fucking money! Give and you shall receive? PISS OFF! Who the bugger is he anyway? She's never even mentioned him before, and in our show no less, our show! Can you believe it?'

'Connie love, calm yourself down before you burst something. And keep your voice down, he's only standing over there.'

'I can't believe she's left all that money to a total stranger. Now I know why Christina Crawford wrote Mommie Dearest.'

'Yes, but that was no reason to punch the corpse, was it? You should be ashamed.'

'She said we could check she was dead. How was I to know the coffin would fall off the plinth?'

'Her head jammed in the heating vent. We've just sent off our sister with a Lewisham Borough Council motif stamped into her forehead!'

Connie was having none of it. 'How do you get out of this place? Government buildings! You need a law degree just to find the bloody exit. I need a cigarette, give me a cigarette.'

'You can't smoke in here. Get yourself a fag patch.'

'Get yourself an ugly patch!'

Michael stepped up. 'Erm. Excuse me. Hello, sorry to interrupt but I err…'

'I can't do this!' Connie spun on his heels and stormed off up the corridor.

'Hello, Michael. I'm Chastity. You'll have to excuse my friend, she's a bit upset... in a deranged sort of way.'

'She's upset? It's a lot of money, but a fucking drag queen? There are limits. Oh, no offence.'

Chastity ignored his back-down. 'Our Lettie must have been very taken with you to leave you all that. I'm surprised she's never mentioned you. How long have you known her?'

'A month.'

'A month? But...' Chastity's bewilderment was growing. Connie meanwhile had been recognised as the instigator of carnage by Lewisham's two municipal security guards. They attempted to persuade him to leave quietly, but he was way too stressed to do anything at low volume.

'Any part of you that touches me, you're not getting back!' he yelled, as a guard each grasped a sleeve of his jacket. 'This is Donna Karan! Tear this and you'll be picking up your bollocks with broken fingers!' The guards lifted him off the ground and headed quickly for the nearest exit. With his skinny PVC covered legs splaying in the air, Connie's screams disappeared into the distance.

Michael looked on agog. Chastity had seen it all before.

'Oh, for feck's sake! Security's got her now. Sorry love, I'll have to sort this. If she doesn't get a nicotine fix soon her tits will fall off, and that's not a figure of speech. Do you know where our club...' He interrupted himself, suddenly realising the enormity of what Lettie had done. He took a deep breath and smiled politely. 'Let me re-phrase that. What I mean to say is do you know where your club Sugar Sugar is?'

'I could find it.'

'Come along about six-ish tonight. I think we need to talk!'

Chastity knew there was no point stepping straight into a cab with Connie in this state. He decided they should walk for a while and smoke a cigarette or two. Lewisham High Street was not the safest of places to parade in drag, but woe-betide anyone who challenged Connie in this mood. Besides which, it would be a good opportunity to discuss what was worrying Chastity so much.

Connie took a long drag on his fag. 'That's another death.'

'I know. I thought he'd just nodded off, I didn't realise it was a heart attack.'

'No not the Solicitor… Lettie! But now you mention it, I was surprised when he keeled over during that chorus line. Still, he was ancient.'

'It was the shock of that last high kick, straight into the dip. That drag queen on the left had no knickers on. Lettie's last laugh.'

'Yes, us drag queens are a dying breed.'

'Things won't be the same without her.'

Chastity was relieved things had calmed down a bit. After so many years working together, he was accustomed to Connie's hissy fits. It was always Chastity who had calmed the waters, although Lettie had been very good at defusing a Connie Tantrum by making him laugh.

'Do you feel better now you've had a couple of fags?'

'A bit. Did you see Valuptua was wearing the same hat she did at Kevin's funeral?'

'She can't afford a new one because she keeps snorting cash up her nose. That's why her septum fell out. And now she's hideous! The left side of her face drapes her shoulder and she's got a third nostril like Michael Jackson. So she's added the veil. Did you ever see anything like it without an admission fee?'

'Don't speak ill of the practically dead.'

A Marseilles car horn sounded. They turned to see a battered old green Ford Escort slowly pass. Full of laughing drag queens, it had a replacement orange driver's door and a wing mirror missing. A long fishnet leg topped with a leopard skin stiletto hung out of the rear window, waving at them as the car bumped the curb and meandered off towards Catford.

'Yes bye then, bye,' Chastity called after it. 'Back for your funeral, you rancid old poof!'

'Donna Kebab? I thought you liked her? You said she made you laugh.'

'When she got done for shoplifting, yeah. Oh, and falling out of that second floor window was quite funny. Though how she could do so much damage to the pavement and come away with just a broken hip mystifies me.'

'There's no justice in this sparkling little world of ours,' Connie mused, thinking about Lettie. 'Even your closest friends can stab you in the back.'

'Oh for feck's sake, nobody's stabbed you. There's something very wrong about all this.'

'What are you rattling on about now?'

'Lettie! It can't have been love, this Michael's not her type. She preferred that young Charlton Heston look. You know – hairy back, burning bush...'

'I don't care. That mad cow didn't leave us a penny after all we've been through together.'

'He must have had some kind of a hold over her.'

'She owned half that club and didn't even tell us? A lipstick short of a makeover.'

Chastity wouldn't be distracted from his train of thought. 'Why did she say, "you're going to love this"? Anyway, you've got no chance of getting your hands on any of that money unless you're at least civil to him.'

Connie thought for a moment. The drama of the day and the disgust of Lettie's decision to leave

19

everything to Michael had prevented Connie considering his shag potential. Usually it was the first thing on his mind. Nicotine-charged head now a little clearer, Connie imagined Michael naked and erect. 'Well, he is rather fit I suppose. That arse is so tight you could bounce a golf ball off it!'

'Don't even fecking go there! We've got to work with him for six weeks and then he'll be our boss.' Chastity took a hankie from his clutch bag and flapped it at a wasp that seemed attracted to the cherries on his hat. 'Just because you're running out of men to shag in London. Besides, what if he's a murderer?'

'Eh?'

'How did Lettie know she was going to be killed by a car before it happened?' Dabbing a couple of his chins, Chastity threw the hankie back into his bag and snapped it shut.

'She knew it was going to happen, but didn't stop it. Told you, mad, mad, mad!'

'And giving all this money to someone we've never even met… she's only known him a month.'

Connie stopped walking. 'A month? A fucking month? But we were her family! She had no one else. It should have all been ours.'

'In that case, it's our moral obligation to befriend him and find out what's going on.'

It was an awful lot of money thought Connie, and it should rightfully have been theirs. Think of the fabulous things he could spend it on. 'Well, I have seen a pair of outrageous pink diamond Cartier earrings that simply adore me. I could at least pretend to be friendly, I suppose. For a while. But don't expect me to like him.'

20

Chastity took Connie's arm and continued walking. 'We'll get to work on him. We'll need a week.'

'We'll need a fuckin' miracle!'

'Anyway, that's the least of our problems. The first thing we've got to do is convince Madame Fifi that this stranger should join our show. She's not going to be happy about this at all!'

CHAPTER THREE

Michael wandered around Lewisham in a bit of a daze for quite some time looking for a tube station. Finally realising there wasn't one, he bit the bullet and took a cab to Sugar Sugar. He only had thirty pounds in his pocket, but he figured he would still have enough for his train home that night.

He paid the driver and turned to face the entrance of the club. The frontage was black marble, above which grubby two-foot chrome letters spelled out the name. He walked apprehensively to a large framed poster to the left of the glass entrance doors, showing photographs of a stage show in progress. There was a shot of Lettie dressed as Snow White leap-frogging a dwarf. Another was a heavily pregnant Connie wearing a skin-tight red PVC catsuit pushing a matching pram. To the left was a snap of Chastity riding on a flower-entwined swing suspended just above centre stage.

Diagonally across the centre of the poster in bold red letters ran the title, "Madame Fifi's World Famous Sugar Sugar", next to which was a photograph of a petite, shapely chestnut brunette in a sequinned Ring Master's jacket with matching corset. She held a whip above her head, as if ready to bring it down across the back of the loin-clothed muscle men kneeling at her feet. Perhaps this was Madame Fifi herself. He wondered if this was a reflection of the woman's character. It intrigued him. If he was going to be a drag queen here for six weeks, she would be his boss. He looked closer at her face. He didn't recognise her from being at the wake. He tried to guess her age, but the photograph had been so heavily airbrushed that it was impossible to tell.

He looked at his watch. It was ten past six. Taking a deep breath, he pushed at the glass door and stepped inside.

The lobby was dark, lit only by the fast dimming daylight flooding in through the doors. There were more photos of the show on the cherry red walls and there was a tatty worktop across a recess, which housed several clothes rails holding empty wire coat hangers. A dank smell of stale beer and last night's illegal cigarette smoke hung in the air. As his eyes adjusted to the dark, he could see a matching tatty red-carpeted staircase disappearing down into a black abyss.

Arriving at the bottom of the stairs, he found himself in the main body of the club. Clearly some way underground, he was amazed at how large the space was. He was on a higher platform next to a dimly lit bar. Several yards in front of him across a wide expanse of red and gold patchwork vintage lino was a wide staircase down to a lower area with another bar and several small round tables and chairs. A young man in a white vest was restocking the back shelves of the lower counter with bottles from a cardboard box. The only other person in view was an elderly lady with a flowery old-fashioned wrap-around pinafore and a little hat, mopping across the skirting boards from a tin bucket on noisy wheels.

Enormous elaborate gold-framed photographs of various drag acts filled every space on the red velour

24

walls. There was Connie, one of Chastity, one of Lettie and two or three he didn't recognise. Pride of place above the upper bar was a portrait in oil of who he assumed to be Madame Fifi as Queen Elizabeth the First, complete with ginger wig and drop pearl earrings.

Right at the back of the lower area was an enormous stage, draped with hundreds of yards of red velvet and gold tassels. To either side was a giant gold statue of a drag queen's torso, complete with Stepford Wives roller-coaster wig. Each had an arm outstretched to the centre top of the stage, completing the proscenium arch. Suddenly, Michael realised this is where he would have to perform in drag. Intrigue turned to fear.

'Well Lettie, here I am. The world famous Sugar Sugar. Your Heaven, my Hell.' He thought for a moment and reality hit him. 'What am I doing here? This is insane! I need to get back to my own job before Billy realises I'm missing.'

'Hello... Hello!' He recognised Connie's voice. He noticed for the first time a partially open door at the other end of the upper level to the left of the stage area. Connie, makeup refreshed with a towel turban and wrap-around gown, was already half way across to him.

'So, this is our Lettie's little Michael!' he flirted. Here was Connie's opportunity to check Michael's shag potential.

'Err, yes. Yes I am.'

'Aah! Are you nervous, Dolly? He's nervous, bless him,' he called back to the door. 'Don't just stand there on the doorstep. *Step inside love, let me blow you today!* Lorra lorra la,' he warbled in his best

Cilla Black, pushing three fingers in and out of his mouth, imitating a blow job.

Michael was harassed but keen to connect. 'Err... I... err...'

Connie stretched out his hand. 'I'm Connie. Connie Lingus,' he winked lecherously, waggling his tongue to demonstrate his name. Realising his hand would not be kissed, he retracted it sharply. 'I'm here at your service, wearing nothing but this modest silk Versace dressing gown, sling-backs and a smile. I'm single, available and extraordinarily juicy for a Tuesday. You've seen how I do a blow job, and the type of cunnilingus I expect in return. You've even seen my Cilla... now there's a thing! Well, that's me all exposed and naked. Now, what about you?'

Michael was speechless. Thankfully, Chastity was on his way to rescue him.

'Don't listen to her, she's got her face on,' he warned, stomping across the lino in a white towelling dressing gown with matching mules and a skin tight wig cap. As he reached them, he spun Connie around by his arm and pointed into his face. 'Look, smacked pig's arse.' He batted his newly applied eyelashes at Michael before turning back to Connie with fake disapproval, as though scolding a child. 'And what have I told you about saying Cilla and cunnilingus in the same breath? Some things in life are sacred! I feel betrayed,' he cried with fake horror, ripping the wig cap from his head and clutching it to his heaving chest. Connie raised his eyes, plumping his turban with disinterest.

Michael could see that, like Connie, Chastity's eyes now seemed huge compared to how they had been a couple of hours ago at the wake. A rainbow of glitter sprang from each eyelid and rose to a sharp point just below the cropped greying hairline at his temples. Drama over, he turned to face his bemused visitor. 'Hello again, Michael. Welcome to Sugar Sugar. What do you think?'

'It's astonishing and a bit surreal. Like a pantomime? I don't really belong in a place like this.'

Connie was bitter that his attempt at flirting with Michael had been interrupted. 'Jeans and a lumberjack shirt, looks like you belong up Brokeback, love.'

'Shut up you! You are gay aren't you Michael?'

'She'll be coming round the mountain when she comes!' sang Connie aggressively. Chastity wasn't impressed.

'I'm going to smack you so hard in a minute!'

'Look, I'm gay but I'm no drag queen, alright?' Michael was feeling penned in and bullied.

'But can you sing, love?' Until this point, Michael had only been attempting to comprehend the enormity of dressing like a girl. The threat that he may have to sing like one as well hadn't even entered his mind.

'No. Well... what I mean is, I've never tried.'

'Oh, for feck's sake! This is going to be like trying to get spunk out of a stone.'

'I told you, it'll be tears by bedtime.' Connie wasn't being much help at all.

Chastity did his best to make Michael feel welcome. 'Where do you work?'

'I'm a barman.'

'Where? Heaven? G.A.Y?'

'Billy's Bar.'

'Billy's Bar? Where's that?'

'Southend.'

'Ooh, sounds very butch. Don't you think, Connie? Butch?'

'Losing interest fast,' yawned Connie.

Chastity continued, 'What is it, a leather bar?'

'God no! Homophobe Central. If Billy found out I was gay and working here, let alone as a drag queen, he'd fucking kill me. Literally. Concrete shoes off the end of Southend Pier!'

It all sounded a bit far-fetched. Chastity knew a few gay people from outside London. Having to pretend to be straight all the time because of their surroundings often made these regional queens paranoid. 'Well you might not be a drag queen, but you're certainly a drama queen.'

'Seriously, I got blamed for a rigged-up drug deal at The Kerzal. He thinks I owe him ten grand, I weren't even there!'

Maybe there was a problem. Drug deals and people after him for money. And who was this Billy?

'I'm not getting mixed up in all this!' said Connie.

This isn't what Chastity wanted to hear. He had to get to the bottom of Lettie's secrets and he needed both Connie and Michael on side to achieve this. 'Sounds like Billy's a bit of a drama queen as well. How ironic. Well at least you'll have no problem being gay in Soho love. In fact it will probably do you a favour.'

'Yeah, when the three of us are working the street corners after he destroys our fuckin' show!' moaned Connie.

'She's not really bitter! Why don't you sing for us, love? Do you know anything? Even Happy Birthday? Just to let us hear your voice?'

'No, I can't! I shouldn't have come.'

Connie agreed. 'The feeling's bloody mutual, Dolly!'

'Look, I should just go. Connie's right, this is madness! Lettie can't have been thinking straight.'

'Our Lettie didn't have a straight thought in her life!' Chastity could feel he was losing the battle trying to keep everything on track. Michael was in some sort of personal trouble, as if Lettie's will wasn't enough. 'Look, I shouldn't but I'm just going say it. Did you murder Lettie?'

'You what? You're all fucking mad, ain't you? No, the deal's off and so am I. Let the orphans have the bloody money before I'm murdered.' As Michael angrily turned to leave, Chastity ran to block his path.

'No, wait! Wait! Lettie wasn't mad and neither am I. Though, where Connie's concerned...'

'And your point is?'

'Something else is going on here and we've got to find out what it is.'

'Like what?' Michael snapped tetchily.

'Lettie predicted her own death. How did she know and where did she get all this money from, because it sure as hell wasn't from these wages? And what about the Sugar Sugar shares?'

'I don't care.'

'Yes, but why did she leave it all to you when she'd only known you a month? Why were you connected? Where did you meet?'

'Southend. He just turned up one day asking for me. Then I couldn't get rid of him.'

'But Lettie hated Southend. She threw a party when the Kurzal burnt down.'

'Really?'

'Yes. It was probably her that set fire to it! Why was she asking after you? And if she's done this to you in London, imagine what she may have waiting for you back in Southend? How can you go back?'

Chastity was making a point that Michael hadn't yet considered. Connie nodded in agreement. 'She was a manipulative bitch.'

Chastity took hold of his hands to make him focus. 'Michael, we've got to do this. It's the only way we can get to the bottom of it. All we've got to do is convince the old dragon…'

'Convince the old dragon of what? Who is this boy?' Without warning, Madame Fifi appeared as if from nowhere out of the darkness. Theatrically spitting every over pronounced syllable, her petite stature belying the ferocity of her demeanour.

Michael was shocked at her sudden arrival. He had only first heard of her earlier that day, but already she seemed like a living legend. She was immaculately dressed in a blood red two piece suit with matching shoes and a necklace of what could only be real diamonds and rubies dripping into the cavernous cleavage between her enormous breasts, which were made to look all the more large by her sharply pinched waist. Perfect make-up, perfect hair - almost unreal. Even her meticulously shaped talons had exactly the same shade of nail varnish. She looked like a miniature ageing Elizabeth Taylor but with a broad Eastern European accent.

'Oh, fu... Fifi! You're here,' Chastity stuttered. 'I was just saying... well we… that is, Connie and I…'

'Don't you dare involve me!'

'Pink diamonds…?' Chastity whispered.

'Fifi! Let me introduce you to, erm, Europe's biggest drag star. May we present... Lulu... Lulu...' Connie glanced desperately to Chastity for support.

'L'Amore.'

'Lulu L'Amore!'

'So, you are a big star?' hissed Fifi with a suspicious glare. 'Then why have I not heard your name?'

'Because... she's just arrived. Today. She's just arrived today... from the Middle East, and won't work anywhere else but London's famous Sugar Sugar,' bumbled Chastity. 'So, without Lettie…'

'So, you are now booking the acts at my club? Surplus to requirements, am I now?'

'We haven't arranged anything, we just thought that...'

'Perhaps you would like to find yourself another job without me, Chastity dearest?'

'Well we tried to…'

'And perhaps you, Connie darling, would prefer to find somewhere else to live without me?'

'What a bitch!' Chastity bit his own tongue for accidentally venting his anger out loud.

'And yet without this bitch you are nothing, but still you betray me and try to imitate me. Eve Harrington lives! Now let me look at you, boy. Stand up straight. My staff have the audacity to believe that you would be good for my club. Tell me, why would this be true?'

'We've got to do this Michael,' whispered Chastity desperately. All eyes and hopes were now upon the poor hapless heir. Beads of perspiration began to form on his forehead. His throat dried and his mind raced for ideas.

'Well, I've... err... I've worked right across Europe. And the Middle East. I can promise you, I'm the best there is.'

'Do I hear a promise?' Fifi hissed like a snake. 'And can you keep your promises to me boy? What delicious suspense! You will start tonight. If I like you, you can stay. If not, when you leave Connie and Chastity will be leaving with you! You have two hours. Now ciao!' Conversation over, she span on her heels and marched away.

'Tonight? But... I...' Michael was mortified. Chastity was a little shocked himself.

'Oh feck! Feck, feck, feck! What are we going to do now? The great Danny La Rue herself couldn't make Ragtime Cowboy Joe here into a world class drag act in just two hours!'

'Well you got us into this, you can get us out. I'm not losing my job over this!'

'Sorry girls, I'm outta here! I can't do it.' Michael turned to leave but Connie grabbed him by the back of the belt.

'Like fuck you are. If you're outta here then we're all out of here, and that's just not happening, Dolly.'

'Lock the doors, Connie. We need a miracle and we're going to make one out of sequins, glitter and glue.'

'What is this, Blue Peter?' asked Michael.

'No, Blue Rita,' replied Connie. 'Now get in that dressing room and sit the fuck down!'

CHAPTER FOUR

The dressing room was like an explosion in a sequin factory. It was overloaded with costumes, wigs, shoes and props covering practically every inch of wall space. Not a large room, made to feel smaller by a dressing mirror, which ran the full length of one wall. It was surrounded by lights, atop a counter littered with makeup and jewellery of every colour, size and shape. Even the backs of the doors had hooks adorned with clutter. Three doors led in turn to the customer area, to a small grubby toilet with a sink, and finally the scariest of the three, up some steps directly onto the back of the stage. Michael could not take his mind off this door and kept attempting to glance in that direction, though it wasn't easy.

'I'm not going to be able to wear these eyelashes much longer. It feels like my eyes are being squeezed,' he whinged.

'It's only because you're not used to them. Now look up so I can put this eyeliner on.' Connie's creativity was a welcome distraction from his fear of impending disaster. His own job was now on the line. At least if he could make Michael look fabulous it might distract the audience and Fifi from his inevitable lack of ability. Despite his warped mind, Lettie was a very hard act to follow. Although Michael did have one advantage over Lettie. He was beautiful.

Chastity meanwhile had his mind firmly on the enormous task of finding something for Michael to do on stage beyond just looking pretty. 'It's only another hour before curtain up, Michael. You've not done drag but you must know one song. What do you sing when you're in the shower?'

'Well you know, Achy Breaky Heart? Mandy?'

Connie's fears sprang back up from his stomach. 'This is wrong! This is so fucking wrong! She's up there laughing at us. I'd kill the bitch if she wasn't already dead.'

'Yeah, I'm beginning to wish I smacked her corpse too.'

'You'll have to keep still Dolly, or I'll get your eyebrows crooked. My hands are shaking enough as it is. You can look in the mirror when I've done your lips.'

Michael was in a panic. 'I'm going to fuck this up for sure. There's no way I can do it. Then it's bye-bye jobs, bye-bye inheritance and hello concrete shoes.'

It was all too much for Connie. Drawing back his hand, he gave Michael one almighty slap across the cheek. 'Pull yourself together. Men your age were at war!' Michael reeled in shock and pain. He hadn't seen this coming. A momentary numbness preceded suffocating panic.

'For feck's sake Connie, is there anyone you're not going to hit today? Now Michael, take some deep breaths. You're Lulu L'Amore and Lulu can do this even if you can't.'

'I'm Lulu L'Amore and I can do this... except I'm not and I can't!'

'Just focus on the money,' said Connie. 'Six weeks and all that lovely money's yours. But when that sparkly little diamond encrusted cash card drops onto your fluffy little doormat, just remember the two stressed out bitches that helped you!'

'I wish Lettie was here. She was good in a crisis,' remembered Chastity.

'She's the author of this crisis!' screamed Connie.

'Let's think. What would Lettie do?'

'Now, let me see. Erm... Drop dead? Leave her friends fuck all?'

'No, she'd shave her arms and armpits. I've got a Bic somewhere.'

'Armpits?' This was not just going to influence Michael's mind.

'There's no shaving foam, Dolly. You'll have to use some of that hand lotion. And keep your bloody face still!'

'And shave your chest,' continued Chastity. 'Remember love, professionally you're a woman now.'

'Otherwise you'll look like some old mooshmalt from The Balkans.'

'It ain't pretty.' Chastity screwed up his face at the thought.

Shaved armpits, shaved chest. Whatever next? 'Where d'ya put yer willy?' Michael asked innocently.

'Up yer arse love, make the most of it,' retorted Chastity with a wry grin.

Connie selected a wig from a polystyrene head on the shelf. He looked down at Michael sitting in the chair like a scared child. With a sigh, he pushed up the perfect black fringe from his face and slipped on the wig. Despite all his catty remarks, for a moment Connie actually felt sorry for Michael. He looked beautiful as a woman but he had been equally as beautiful as a man. It was odd how adding so much to Michael's face could take so much away. The moment was short lived as Connie noticed the time. 'Shit! Ok, I think you're about finished, Dolly. Ready for this? Look in the mirror. Ta da!' He spun Michael's chair into the great reveal.

He was stunned. His face was paler than usual, and his cheeks highlighted with flamingo pink and oyster made them appear high and pronounced. His crystal blue eyes looked massive, an explosion of silver and pink metallic glitter with enormous eyelashes, the tips of which reached his now pencil thin eyebrows. Atop his head, a huge fusion of red curls spilled down either side of his face and the whole ensemble was underlined with larger than life rose-red Clara Bow lips. His panic intensified. 'Fuck! Oh my God!'

'Have you ever been so gorgeous?' exclaimed Connie, proud of his masterpiece. 'But what's she going to sing?'

'Bugger! You'll have to pick one from Lettie's list.' Chastity bumbled amongst the piles of clutter on the makeup table. 'It's mostly old stuff, I'm afraid.'

'I don't know any old stuff!' Michael could feel his throat tighten, trying to push tears to his eyes as he looked at a long list of song titles he had never even heard of. It might as well have been another language. Suddenly, a line sprang out. 'Oh! But I know that one.'

'How do you know that one then?' asked Chastity, craning his neck to see which song it was.

36

'Lettie never stopped singing it on Karaoke night at Billy's Bar. It didn't go down too well, that's why I remember it. I got sick of the fucking song. The irony now is that I'd quite like to hear him sing it again.'

This intrigued Chastity further. 'But Lettie hated Karaoke! Still, it is a perfect debut number. Although, I'm afraid there's a bit more to it than just a song, Michael.'

Could it get any worse, Michael thought? 'What?'

'Connie love, it's time. Press play.' Connie pushed aside a piece of bright orange satin on the work surface to reveal a small CD player. Composing himself and taking a pronounced deep breath purely to heighten the drama of it all, he pressed a button on the top of the machine. But instantly, the moment was ruined by a burst of very loud wacky jazz music.

'Not that you dozy slag, track two!' screamed Chastity. Connie jumped and fumbled among the knobs and buttons until finally the desired effect was achieved, with the dramatic vintage Hollywood going away music from Casablanca.

Chastity regained his poignant composure. 'Remember! The most important thing of all about being a drag queen? More important than the make-up, the frocks, the eyelashes, the wigs... more than anything?'

'What, what is it?' asked Michael.

Connie and Chastity had his full attention. 'Attitude!'

'Think Minelli, Midler, Davis, Crawford,' began Connie.

'Deitrich, Garland, Swanson, Garbo.'

'I vant to be alone!' droned Connie in his best Greta.

'Mansfield,' Chastity gargled and choked, as if he were the dead star herself being decapitated in the car crash. 'Heyward. Sarkasian La Pierre.'

In an instant, Connie switched off the music. 'Who the fuck's Sarkasian La Pierre?

'Cher.'

'Well why didn't you just say Cher?'

'I thought we were doing surnames... Oh, and not forgetting Doris Day, Gawd bless her'

'What do they all have in common?'

Michael thought for a moment. 'Attitude?'

'Precisely!' Chastity smiled at Connie. Perhaps they were actually getting their point across.

'But don't copy!' Connie threatened.

'Oh no, no, no, no, no, you must become! Feel it running through your veins. Pulsating through your whole body with every beat of your heart.'

'Every nerve and every fibre.'

Chastity span Michael's chair back to face the mirror. They moved in behind him, positioning their faces either side of his to look at their reflections together. 'And with this my precious child, you may be crowned forever more...'

In stereo unison, as if to complete the brainwashing procedure, they announced, 'A drag queen!'

They had done a good job on Michael. His face was gorgeous and the auburn wig piled up on top with twenty-seven Kirby grips was magnificent. Even the ball gown looked fantastic. If only he didn't carry it all quite so much like a geezer.

Chastity fussed at the bust line. 'You know, green taffeta's a good look on her.'

'Matches the veins in her neck,' Connie bitched.

'And it's light too. Sequins can be a bit heavy when you've not dragged up before.'

'I can't quite believe you all get paid for doing this. It's insane!' Michael's adrenaline was rushing round his body, tightening his stomach muscles.

'Darling, you don't know the half of it!' Chastity put down his eye pencil and assumed the role and posture of a Catholic Priest he remembered from childhood. 'Welcome to The Sisterhood. By the grace of God and the holy Catholic Trinity, we welcome into the fold... Lulu. And may the boat that she rows never falter.' Connie had by this time taken the role of faithful Acolyte.

Despite the comic stance, Michael could sense this induction meant more to Chastity and Connie than just play-acting alone. The Sisterhood was about unity. Three becoming one – strength in numbers. He knew this meant they would be there for him, if only while he was in drag, and he quickly became determined not to let them down, despite the ever-growing terror of what was to come.

'Peace be with you my child, and may Mary, mother of the blessed drag queen, look down upon you and smile.' Chastity drew the sign of the crucifix over Michael's forehead. Then with Connie, stood before Michael, hands poised in prayer.

'Ahh, men!'

Becoming a member of The Sisterhood gave Michael a strange kind of confidence he hadn't expected. It was a good feeling but alien to him. He'd had one or two good friends like Tamara, his work colleague at Billy's Bar, but never before had he been a part of anything in quite the same way. He had no family, growing up in and out of an orphanage with no clue as to the identity or whereabouts of his parents. The closest he'd ever had to a sister was Tamara. From as far back as he could remember it had been just him against the world. Now it would seem, for the first time in his life perhaps he had a family, of a sort. Yes they were drag queens, but now so was he. With this sudden realisation, the feeling in his stomach abruptly changed.

'I think I'm going to be sick,' he gulped, desperately pushing past Connie to the toilet cubicle.

'That's it love. Get it all out and you will feel much better,' said Chastity supportively.

'Hmm. Those lips will need doing again.'

A million miles away from the sequins and glitter, Billy's Bar in Southend was rocking. Loud aggressive grunge music was attempting to drown out an equally loud and aggressive mix of tattooed bikers and their molls. Billy paced up and down behind the bar violently, his bulky overweight frame making the bottles in the beer fridges rattle. He took a Zippo lighter from his pocket, flicking it open to re-light his cigar while habitually pushing back his lank brown, thinning Brylcreemed hair. There were two things on his mind – his missing dogsbody Michael and his latest betting racket.

He rubbed a gold sovereign covered hand across his belly and belched loudly. 'Better out than in,' he laughed to himself, tucking the front of his sweat-stained wife-beater vest back into his trousers.

His attention focused when the phone started ringing. His small, shapely barmaid Tamara checked herself in the mirror behind the bar's optics before picking up the receiver. Fluffing at her bleached blonde hair and looking over her immaculately made-up pretty face, she pulled down the front of her pink v-necked sweater, making her ample bust pop forward as though about to burst out. She smiled to herself, remembering how this always made her dear friend Michael laugh, but her smile turned to a look of concern. He hadn't returned from London when expected and she was getting worried.

'Hello, Billy's Bar. Tamara speaking, how can I help you?' It was one of the answers Billy had been waiting for. 'Billy? Phone!' she yelled above the din. He snatched the handset from her with a grimace. Once he'd sorted this deal, she was next.

'Yep? Friday. Four dogs, two fights, you in? Good boy. Put it all on Killer in the second… 'Cause he's a Rottweiler! The other dogs a fuckin' Poodle, ain't it? It's a poof's dog, no chance. They'll be scraping it off the pavement with a shovel after two minutes.' His grotesque laugh was interrupted only by his billowing smoker's cough. 'Sweet!'

As he put down the receiver, he grabbed Tamara aggressively, pulling her forward by her delicate wrist. She struggled not to fall in her matching pink stilettos as Billy threw her into the back room and pinned her against the wall by her throat. 'Where's Michael?' he growled down at her.

Her pretty green eyes welled with tears from intimidation. Intoxicated by the smell of stale sweat, whiskey and cheap aftershave emanating from this small town thug, she struggled for words in Michael's defence.

'Erm... he's off sick. I'm covering his shift. You don't have to be so rough you know, Billy. You only had to ask.' A small black line of cheap mascara trickled down her pale cheek.

'Don't fuck me about, he lives upstairs! If he's sick, where is he?'

'He's gone to stay with a friend. He's got a migraine. It's very noisy upstairs Billy, you know it is. He will be here tomorrow. Anyway, I... err... I'd best get back to the bar.' She slowly and cautiously slid from under his giant frame and tiptoed quickly back out front, dabbing her blackened cheek with the back of her tiny hand. Billy was too distracted in thought to even notice.

'Staying at friends, eh? He ain't got no friends. He owes me big time. If he's pissing on my chips I'll rip his head off and piss on his fuckin' neck!' His hand left an indent in the plaster as it punched the wall.

CHAPTER FIVE

Michael's nerves were in shreds. The show had started with Connie's sluttish strip routine. He wore a naked female bodysuit under a see-through black mini baby-doll negligee. Bra and panties were held in place with Velcro strips. As the corny burlesque music pounded the speakers, he toyed with a phallic banana for a while, before removing his bra. A pair of pendulous fake comedy breasts dropped from the cups to swing at his waist. He then removed some jewellery, then his panties, and his rubber snatch dropped to swing at his knees. The whole performance was topped off with a couldn't-care-less gum-chewing attitude, as though this tarty character had done this routine a million times before. Unfortunately for Connie, on this particular night laden with heckling and jeering, it was clear the audience couldn't care less either.

In the dressing room, Chastity was holding a large white silk Gardenia flower to the side of Michael's wig. 'No, I think that'll be too much. I know it's drag, but you can over-do it. Connie's having a hard time tonight. Mind you, she did insist on that routine to open with. In her heart she's a drag queen, not a stripper. Though to half the men in London, she's more a hooker!'

Michael had been silent for some time now. Chastity sighed, 'Lulu love, you look terrified!'

'Of course I'm fucking terrified! I can't sing. I'm in a fucking dress. A fucking dress! Listen to them out there. Connie's an old hand. They're gonna kill me!'

'Think of it as a costume, not a dress. Like Boy George or Adam Ant. You're a drag queen, not a transvestite.'

'Is there a difference?'

'Absolutely. One's professional, the other's vocational. Now remember, one foot in front of the other, like you're walking the tightrope of death. Head and shoulders back. That's it, now when you tread on your left foot, let your left hip slip. Same the other side. That'll give you the Monroe wiggle, and don't smile till the songs over. That way they'll really believe you're a diva.'

Michael attempted the Monroe wiggle. That alone wasn't so hard. It was trying to doing everything at once in six inch heels he couldn't grasp. Every step threw him to one side, grabbing at whatever was nearby to avoid falling over.

'You'll get the balance after a while. Have you never been ice-skating before? Try to keep your ankles stiff. If only Viagra made tights! And women keep their elbows in to the waist, not sticking out like butch men on a building site.'

'OK. Monroe wiggle. Head up, shoulders back, elbows in. Am I supposed to bow or curtsey at the end?'

'Neither. Stay aloof and let them know who's in charge. I know you're in shock love, but that will probably make your performance better.'

'Why would Lettie do this to me?'

'In her great scheming wisdom, she probably thought we'd have a bit more time to prepare! But it's a lot to gain for just six weeks work, love. Could be worse... suppose you'd had to shag her?'

As Connie's song came to an end, Michael's heart was beating in his neck. So much to remember – keeping his balance, head, shoulders, elbows and... then it suddenly occurred to him that he also had to remember the words to the song. He'd heard Lettie sing it so many times, but had never sung it himself.

'OK. Connie's finished now, Lulu love, this is you. Are you ready?'

'No, basically! No I'm fucking not fucking ready!' Michael screamed desperately.

To lame applause, Connie came running into the dressing room from the stage, somewhat out of breath. 'The crowd's baying for blood. Good fuckin' luck! Now, smile as you enter and curtsey at the end. Don't bow. Show us your curtsey.'

'Don't complicate things now. He can hardly stand in those shoes, let alone dip! And put those piss flaps away you filthy whore, I've got fish fingers for tea!'

'And move about a bit,' Connie continued. 'Sparkle, Dolly! Sparkle! Think Brenda Lee.'

Suddenly came a drum roll over which a deep voiced lesbian from behind the bar announced Michael's debut.

'Madame Fifi is proud to present her new discovery. For the first time in London, please welcome to the stage Lulu L'Amore!'

Michael let out an involuntary cry of fear as his eyes welled up with tears. Chastity's heart sank. Despite twenty years treading the boards, he could remember this terror himself as though it were yesterday. Even hard-faced Connie felt for him. 'You'll be fine, it's only a song. Just a song, that's all. Chin up, Dolly! Don't cry or your mascara will run. You'll look like a racoon! Ooh, a singing racoon. That's a good idea for a sketch.'

'Shut up you! You're going to be fine, Lulu love. They will adore you. Now, on you go then.' Chastity handed him a radio microphone.

With a gulp and a deep breath, Michael took the first of two steps up onto the stage. But as he lifted his other foot, his heel hooked in the mass of netting under the skirt and he fell forward, landing with a loud thud on the back of the stage, in full view of the audience. Cruel laughter broke out. The microphone whistled feedback, filling the auditorium and abruptly ending the laughter to leave a void of painful silence.

'Shit! Shit! Fuck it!' Michael squirmed with embarrassment. There was no physical pain as his adrenaline was racing way too much for that. If only there was a hole to swallow him. A doorway to Hell and eternal damnation seemed an attractive alternative.

'Pick the front of the frock up, you dozy bitch,' Connie yelled from the dressing room, much to the delight of the audience. 'They're going to kill him!' he braced.

'It'll be a bloody massacre,' Chastity sighed.

Michael climbed back onto his daintily encased feet and turned to face the crowd. Two hundred expectant faces looked up at him, every pair of eyes burning into his soul, waiting to be entertained and impressed.

'Come on then, show us something!' shouted one unfeeling lout.

Seconds felt like hours, as Michael looked around the packed room. He could feel a wall of discontent and disapproval from the over-dressed audience, sweeping towards him like a glittery tsunami. He opened his mouth to sing the first word, but nothing came out. It was as though someone big and butch had a hold of his vocal chords, squeezing them dry of any sound. He noticed Madame Fifi standing by the bar. Coldly, she looked at her watch and folded her arms. There was no time left. This was it.

'*Here in the darkness, my eyes are drawn above. There in the brightness, there soars a snow-white dove,*' came his weak and wobbly first lines. The crowd had already lost interest and began chattering loudly amongst themselves.

His head raced, trying to remember a time when he'd had a higher mountain to climb than this. All those years, struggling to survive alone without support. Countless nights of sleeping in shop doorways in the cold and rain as a child. Stealing his meals from shops and hiding from other homeless kids who would pull the half-chewed food from his very mouth. Totally alone. But somehow this was different. This time he had Chastity and Connie behind him. The Sisterhood. He wasn't going to let them down.

He took a deep breath to continue. *'If I could fly, I'd lose the chains that bind me. I'd lift right up, to circle overhead. And from the sky, everything seems better. From above, nothing seems so bad.'*

As if by magic, a rush of sparkle and glow moved from his chest and spread across his whole body like a warm sedative. Slowly but surely, his notes became steadier and more pronounced.

'If I could fly, I'd see things much more clearly. All my problems wouldn't look so strong. And from the sky, each road would look much shorter. My journey wouldn't seem so long.'

Something had changed. A trigger somewhere in his body had moved everything up a gear. He was actually singing... and wow, could he sing!

'If I could fly, the wind would rush right through me. All my fears and doubts would blow away. And the sun would kiss me on the shoulder. Make me proud to face another day.'

A power and control took hold as his confidence grew. Michael knew that everything he had ever survived and experienced now rang from his vocal chords. The audience believed it too, as they stopped and stood open-mouthed in awe of this new diva, just arrived in Soho from somewhere on high. It was as though a light shone from their faces, feeding him and giving him strength, willing him to carry on.

'And up above the clouds, I'd shout my name out loud, and tell the world that I'd survived!'

As the song continued to build, it suddenly all made sense to him. He had never before been able to understand what drove people to perform. But the energy was electric, as though he could put out his hand and touch it. As addictive as any drug he had ever taken or imagined. This wasn't about dresses or wigs or stilettos. This was about being able to bare your soul and share your emotions, hopes and dreams with others. This was about family.

48

'If I could fly, I'd meet my guardian angel. He'd take me higher, everything would change. No longer burdened by the things that harm me. I'd be free, nothing would be the same.'

As the song reached its climax and the orchestral backing track swelled, the crowd rushed forward towards the front of the stage and began cheering their approval.

'*If I could fly. Fly. Fly!*' A high note somehow instinctively rang out from his whole body. On and on, as the crowd's cheer became stronger and louder. Finally, as quickly as it had begun, it was over.

Michael stood momentarily in disbelief at what had just happened. His voice was as much a revelation to him as to everyone else. Even Madame Fifi looked surprised. Michael noticed a glimmer of a smile across her face. She didn't have the sort of face that suited smiling. The words of the song rang true. Nothing would ever be the same.

CHAPTER SIX

Back in the dressing room, Connie and Chastity clung to each other and jumped up and down in a circle, screaming like two deranged lottery winners.

'My God, what just happened here?' said Chastity.

'Fuck's sake, my nipples have gone hard!'

'That's always a good sign.'

Michael ran back in from the stage. He was practically hyperventilating with excitement. 'Wow, what a rush!' he cried through a mixture of laughter and tears.

Chastity grabbed him by the arms and pulled him into a hug. 'Where the hell did that voice come from? I'm beginning to see what Lettie could see. Ooh, I feel like Googie Withers in Dead of Night!' Music started once again out on the stage.

Connie prised them apart. 'You're on, Tit.' Chastity ran for the stage. 'Well Dolly, that's some set of lungs you've got there! And you were so worried, poor little cunt. That's your only one for tonight, so you can take all that off now. We'll do the rest. At least you've woken the fucking crowd up, shouting at them like that. Sorry, did I say shouting? I meant singing!'

Michael's enthusiasm drained instantly away from him. Connie's bitter attitude had been unexpected, and after such a high was something of a shock. Surely it couldn't be jealousy? They were supposed to be part of the same team. Maybe this was really what families were about.

Before he'd had a chance to sing a note, the music to Chastity's first song of the evening was ground to a halt. Stopped dead centre stage, he shielded his eyes from the glaring lights and squinted, looking to find a reason for this abrupt end. As the audience parted like the Red Sea and began cheering, Madame Fifi walked through the corridor of people towards the steps at the front of the stage. Chastity turned and ran back to the dressing room.

'What's going on, Dolly?'

'It's Fifi. She's coming up onto the stage!' Chastity craned his neck from the doorway, trying to see what she was doing. As the crowd fell silent, Madame Fifi's blood red stilettos climbed the stairs and assiduously traversed the stage to a microphone on a stand at one side. She spun to face her audience, heels scraping varnish from the boards, and with hands on hips purred like Eartha Kitt. Her ruby red talons glistened as the spotlight spun to meet her. Standing with the poise and finesse of an old time movie star, she somehow glowed. The audience screamed with delight, and with a cackle she threw her head back and her arms into the air, like a sparkling trapeze act taking an encore.

'What's the sour old crab doing?' Connie couldn't see past Chastity's enormous wig in the doorway.

'Stealing Lulu's thunder, that's what. She can't bear to be upstaged.' Michael looked accusingly at Connie, who was clearly also feeling upstaged. Reading Michael's face, Connie grinned snottily back.

The moment was fleeting. Madame Fifi was now upstaging everybody.

'What do you think of my new discovery?' This was elemental to Fifi. 'I found her in the gutter the last time I visited gay Paris. I brought her back to London and trained her personally. Madame Fifi brings only the best to her gorgeous audience, does she not?' They roared their approval. Whether they had seen better or not was irrelevant now. At this magical moment in time, everything Fifi said was Gospel and they were her humble flock. 'You deserve her, enjoy! Now, ciao!' Then like a glamorous matriarchal mermaid, she descended back into the adoring sea of faces.

'Oh, no, no, no, no, no! I'm not fecking having this!' Chastity was angry now.

'What are you going to do?' asked Connie with glee.

'I'm going to teach that cow a lesson. I'm changing my next song. Get this CD out there to the lesbian. Tell her track eight. I'll get back on and do my intro. Quick! Quick!'

Connie checked himself in the mirror then snatched the disc from Chastity's hand before running out of the door to the customer area. Chastity took a deep breath and climbed the stairs back to the stage. He addressed his audience.

'Well, how marvellous was that? Make some noise everybody for the simply fabulous Madame Fifi!' The crowd reciprocated. 'What would we do without her? To demonstrate to you here tonight just how much we adore her, from the top of her cheap hair-piece to the tips of her tiny pinched toes, I'd like to dedicate this next song to our one and only...

Madame Fifi!' He certainly had their attention. 'Hit it dyke!' he shouted, pointing towards the PA rig. The backing track sprang to life through the giant speakers either side of the stage and Chastity sang.

'I have a vicious friend. She's bitter to the end. Her mouth is a disgrace. I ought to slap her face. Her evil never stops. Sequins and acid drops. She gets inside your head. Her words will cut you dead!'

His audience delighted in this bitchery, a twisted irreverence that had become expected of drag queens through thousands of songs over decades of performances.

'Somebody rescue me! Put strychnine in her tea. Smash her skull with a brick. Throw her off Vauxhall Bridge. Make her swim with a shark. Or drown her in the bath. Impale her on a spike. Cut the breaks on her bike.

'Poison snakes in her bed. Drop a fridge on her head. Re-wire her curling tongs. Play Justin Bieber songs. Sink a knife in her back. Tie her to a railway track. Garrotte her with a wire. Set both her tits on fire. Smear her with Winalot, then release all the dogs. Please just shoot her in a ditch. 'Cause she is such a...'

The audience didn't need prompting for the last line. Like a band of unruly fishwives, they screamed in unison, *'Bitch!'*

Two hours later the show was finally over. Even though Chastity had made the wise decision that Michael should only do one song, it wasn't until the building had emptied of customers that he finally felt he could breathe again.

Connie was of the same opinion. 'Thank fuck that's over. I don't think I've ever done a show as stressful as that. I'm sweating like Gemma Collins in a cake shop.'

'I wondered what that smell was,' Chastity quipped.

'No, that's my new washing powder. Do you like it?'

'Smells like urinal cubes!'

Michael's adrenalin was still pumping. 'Are all the shows like this? I need a drink.'

'You're going to be propping up the bar at AA meetings by the end of the six weeks,' Chastity warned.

Michael thought for a moment. With the trauma of having to survive his first ever performance, he had almost forgotten the cryptic terms of Lettie's strange eulogy. 'That's another thing. What the fuck occurs in six weeks time? And why the drag thing?' He'd got Chastity thinking now.

'That's a good point. Did Lettie know you owed this Billy ten thousand?'

'I don't know. My friend Tamara knew.'

'Tamara?' said Chastity. Connie could never resist a cue for a song from Annie.

'Tamara, Tamara, I'll love ya Tamara...'

To Michael's growing frustration, Chastity couldn't resist joining in. *'You're only a day away!'*

'She's my best friend. She works at Billy's Bar. She's a pet.'

Chastity was amused. 'What, like a dog?'

Connie was more concerned. 'They won't all come looking for you here with their concrete sling-backs will they?'

This hadn't yet really occurred to Michael. To fulfil the terms of Lettie's will and get the money and the Sugar Sugar shares, he would have to be a drag queen for six weeks. Even if he had gotten away with absconding from Billy's for one night by feigning illness, he'd never get away with as long as that. Believing he was owed ten thousand pounds, Billy would definitely hunt him down. Even though Michael would have the money to pay him off with interest, he knew that if Billy discovered he was gay, he would kill him, and the thought of Billy finding him in drag didn't bear thinking about.

'I'm up to me neck, ain't I?' There was no time to be solemn. He needed a plan, and he needed help. It was clear that Chastity and Connie didn't really want him there, but he also understood that without him they wouldn't get anywhere near Lettie's money. After all, from what he understood, it really should have been theirs anyway.

'Look, I don't really want to be here, but if I stay and do this you'll have to help me hide from Billy-no-nut and his henchmen.'

Chastity laughed, 'Billy-no-nut? Is that his name?'

'Fancies himself as a bit of a martial artist. Lost a bollock with a nunchuck.'

Connie was already way ahead of Michael. 'We'll hide you. But in six weeks time, give us the Sugar Sugar shares and you have the lolly, Dolly. Pay bollock-drop then fuck off somewhere else. What do you say?' It sounded as good a plan as any.

'Alright, it's a deal.' Michael hawked back and spat in his hand. 'Michael Small's word is his bond. Shake on it?'

Connie looked at him in disgust and then at the lump of spit in his outstretched hand. 'No, you're alright,' he said, screwing his face up.

Chastity was very excited by this agreement. Not only did it guarantee that Michael would stay around to find out what was really going on, but it would be the ultimate slap in the face for super-bitch Fifi, in a way he'd never imagined possible.

'That's a fabulous plan, Lulu. Ooh, it will be like Challenge Anneka! Imagine Fifi's face when she finds out we're partners? She'll be spitting acid. Lettie would be so proud.'

Suddenly they were silenced by a loud whistling feedback sound. 'What was that?' said Connie. Chastity knew this could only mean one thing. 'You did turn your radio mic off, didn't you Lu?'

'Radio mic?' Panic ensued.

'Bugger! That conversation will have gone all around the club. Is Fifi still here?' Chastity didn't have to wait long for an answer. The door flew open and a rather excited Madame Fifi rushed in, pushing Connie off balance into a box of stiletto shoes.

'Ah Fifi...' feigned Chastity with fake affection. 'Shut up, shut up!' she shouted, putting her hand on Chastity's face to push him out of her way. 'Michael, I can help you with your problem. I will buy your contract from this awful nutty... Bill... chucker person. Ten thousand, first thing in the morning. Just sign the practically worthless shares over to me tonight as a deposit, and then you can pay me back the difference when the cash arrives.'

Michael's eyes lit up. Perhaps this was the escape route he needed. Although it wasn't what Chastity had in mind.

'Ooh, you thieving gypsy whore!'

'Don't be fooled by these two performing monkeys. They will bleed you dry given the chance.'

'Speaks the Bride of Dracula,' shot back Connie, staggering to his feet while unhooking a stray stiletto heel from the back of his jumper.

'Come into my office. We can discuss this over that drink.'

Michael wasn't too sure what to do. He felt a certain loyalty to Connie and Chastity, and he had made a gentleman's agreement with them already... in a drag queen kind of way. However this offer from Madame Fifi could answer all his prayers in one swoop. If she could be trusted.

'Well, I can at least see what she has to say, can't I?' He was now unsure exactly who the anger in Connie and Chastity's faces was directed at. 'Free drink?'

'Ah, there's a good boy. Come, come!' She lifted Michael from his chair and directed him gently but firmly past Connie and Chastity and out of the door. She had at least for the moment beaten them both, though she couldn't resist underlining their defeat with one last twist of the knife. 'And Connie dearest? Chastity's for once right. You do smell like a toilet!' She turned on her heels and left, slamming the door behind her.

Connie fell back into the box of shoes with disbelief at the audacity of the woman. 'One day, I'm going smack her lips so hard, she'll swallow her own head!' he yelled, in the hope she may still be able to hear him.

Chastity's head was spinning. Only moments ago, all his efforts today had paid off with Michael's

58

agreement. Suddenly in an instant, it could all fall apart.

'Lulu's like a naive little fly caught in her big fat hairy web. She doesn't know how manipulative and cunning the rancid old crone is. Those shares must be worth shit loads. We owe it to Lettie to protect her.'

'Protect her? If Lulu jumps ship we get nothing. I'm looking after my own arse.'

'Most of the men in London have looked after your arse! The Sisterhood must prevail. Fasten your seatbelt, girl. This is war!'

CHAPTER SEVEN

Madame Fifi's office was a dimly lit small but plush room, if not a little dated and trashy. The magenta walls were covered in photographs of her posing in various designer outfits, many with famous celebrities from the world of television and film, some with people Michael didn't recognise. Across one corner was an oversized Headmaster's desk with a giant button-backed red leather chair behind. Fifi gestured to one of two smaller matching chairs.

'Michael darling, sit and make yourself at home. Whiskey?'

'Yes. Please.'

She crossed to a small, mirrored art deco drinks cabinet to one side, next to another door. Michael noticed two framed photos on her desk. One was Fifi with a very well dressed elderly man standing outside Sugar Sugar's main entrance, raising Champagne glasses to camera. The other he recognised as the old lady he had seen upon his arrival, mopping from the squeaky bucket. It seemed odd that a photograph of the cleaner would take pride of place. Not one image appeared reflective of a time earlier than Sugar Sugar. On the wall immediately to his left was a framed black and white photo of Fifi with Diana Ross. There was something odd about it that he couldn't quite put his finger on.

He knocked his drink back in one gulp. Fifi continued. 'Now. Let's expand on our delicious adventure. My gorgeous new star, at the most fantabulous club in the whole of swinging London. My club! I alone have made it what it is today and I intend it to stay that way. I will draw up a contract now and give you a cheque for ten thousand pounds.' She suddenly seemed aggressive, if not a little desperate.

Michael looked back at the Diana Ross photo. Eyes better adjusted to the light, he could now see that Fifi had been cut and pasted next to Miss Ross over someone else. The photo was a fake.

'Err... I'm not so sure.' He hadn't yet recovered from the rollercoaster of emotions of his stage debut. This was all happening way too fast.

'What do you mean?'

'I mean... yes, you can have them. I've got to pay off Billy. Probably. Oh, I don't know! I need time to think. Right now I feel like I've been kicked about, beaten up and had my head flushed down a toilet.'

Fifi looked puzzled. 'But Michael, every night men pay cash for that sort of thing in Soho.'

'Really?'

Her mood softened. 'Ahh, you are under so much pressure. My poor practically perfect precious pumpkin pip,' she spat. 'Let Madame Fifi help you.'

As the whiskey burned through his veins, Michael was awash with images of his head being flushed down a toilet for cash, first by Fifi and then by Chastity and Connie. He was tired and drained, and Fifi's instant change of tact hadn't made him any less intimidated or suspicious of her true intentions. And though the two drags had got him through the earlier horrors, he had only known them a day and didn't

62

have any real reason to trust them either. He needed time to think.

'Thanks but not right now,' he replied with alcohol-induced confidence. Fifi's face flushed with rage like a pressure boiler about to explode.

'As you wish! But think very carefully. This decision could be the best you will ever make. The wrong choice could be your last!'

Back in the dressing room, Chastity and Connie waited desperately for Michael's return. They were frantic to know what had just happened in Fifi's office, although the arrival of the squeaky-bucketed cleaning lady had calmed their tension, if only outwardly. Sitting on a chair just inside the entrance, the faded silk flowers on her favourite hat wobbled as her head bobbed slightly when she spoke.

'Horse piddle!' she said, plunging a petite ruddy hand into a brown paper bag and retrieving a grape. She popped it into her mouth before wiping her fingers down the front of her flowery wrap-around pinafore.

'Horse piddle?' Chastity was confused.

'Yeah, St. Thomas' Horse Piddle with his bleedin' liver.' She scratched at the back of her grey curls and pulled her wrinkled stocking up from her sensible brown shoe before going in for another grape.

'Oh, you mean "Hospital!"' Her East London accent was often as hard to interpret as her elderly train of thought.

'His liver's bleeding?' Connie was just as baffled.

'No, duck! He's been getting the nadgers and the doctor said he ought to get it looked at. You know my Bert's always had health problems. Poor bugger.'

'You must be very worried.'

'Well, you know.' Her crystal blue eyes sparkled mournfully.

The door opened and a very rattled looking Michael returned. Connie didn't make things easier for him.

'You was a long time, Dolly. Lipstick round your cock?'

'Shut up you!' scolded Chastity.

'I told her I'd think about it.'

'Aww. Bestest is what bestest does,' Edith offered. Chastity could see that Michael's feathers had been ruffled.

'I don't think you've met our favourite senile old lady yet, have you Lu? This is Edith.'

'Hello Edith, nice to meet you.'

'You too duck. I'm the woman what does.'

'Eh?'

'She means she's the cleaner.' Introductions over, Chastity was desperate to know what had happened. 'How did Fifi react?'

'Not too well. I think she threatened me.'

'You've got a lovely voice you know,' interrupted Edith. 'Our Lettie used to sing that song.' While she had Michael's attention, Chastity edged closer to Connie, whispering in his ear.

'Connie, we need a plan. We've got to think of a way to get Lulu on side before that conniving old troll persuades her to hand over our shares. Look at the way she's responding to Edith. What she needs is support. Think of something. Quickly!'

Connie broke into their friendly chatter. 'I think we should all go out for a drink. Wet our new sister's head.'

'What a fabulous idea!' agreed Chastity.

'Champagne all round!' continued Connie.

'Marvellous, hoorah!'

'Chastity's buying.'

'Steady now!'

For the first time since they had met him, Michael laughed. The plan seemed to be working. 'Great! You're coming with us aren't you Edith?'

'Well, I'd only be on me own tonight, what with Bert away. Alright, I will!' Her fluorescent white dentures glowed as she smiled. Edith coming with them hadn't really been part of Connie's plan. Michael had seemed to hit it off with her, so perhaps it wasn't such a bad idea, though it did make things a little more complicated.

'Well, as long as you keep off that Champagne, Dolly. D'you know what happened last time?'

'She punched a copper, Lu.'

'Really?'

'Well, he was gettin' on my wick!' Edith stood and winked warmly at Michael with a grin. It was going to be an interesting night. 'Right then, duck. I'll just pop to the boudoir for an Ivana Trump, then I'll get me coat.'

As they exited Sugar Sugar for their night out, Michael's head was a little dazed. He had just had whiskey but hadn't eaten all day. Stress had definitely got the better of him and the fresh air from the street just made it worse. Even the pavement seemed to be undulating.

'Oh Lulu, this is our doorman and security,' said Chastity. 'I know he looks like a giant Sumo wrestler that's been under the grill too long, but appearances can be deceiving. Lulu, meet Daisy.'

As Michael turned to say hello, he came face to face with Daisy's chest. Raising his eyes up and up and up, he finally met with Daisy's face about eighteen inches above his own. The man was a mountain! Tall, wide and black with the whitest natural teeth Michael had ever seen, he was dressed in a smart but massive dinner suit and a disproportionally small red bow tie. It was hard to accurately guess his age because of his bloated fat face, though he seemed quite young.

'Huh... Daisy? Bloody hell!' Yet as Daisy spoke, what had at first appeared to be a completely inappropriate name suddenly seemed perfect.

'Oh, hi! Ooh, you've got a strong voice. When you sang, the glass doors vibrated up my back. It was ever so nice!' Michael was gobsmacked. How could such a small, childlike, delicate female voice come from such a giant lump of man? He stood back in awe for a moment, trying to fit the whole of Daisy into view at the same time. 'What's the matter?' asked Daisy nervously.

'Take no notice Daisy, he's in shock,' Connie offered. 'We're going out clubbing. Are you coming?'

'No I'd better not. I've got Bingo with my mate Mandy tomorrow afternoon. It's the National Link Up, twenty nine thousand.'

'Ooh, Golly wars!' gasped Edith.

'I need a good night's sleep to keep me wits about me. Some of them geriatrics up there are fast as whippets. It's bad enough I have to put up with the smell of stale piss, let alone keep an eye on my numbers. I'll see you tomorrow night. Or if I win, I'll send you a postcard from Ibiza!' he gushed, performing a little victory dance in anticipation. Michael could feel the pavement beneath his feet vibrate.

'Alright Daisy, take care now,' said Chastity.

'I will girl. Terrah, then. Terrah! And for Gawd's sake, don't let Edith drink nothing!'

CHAPTER EIGHT

Michael's head was swimming. With the extraordinary stresses of the day, he'd forgotten to eat, and had spent the night as Guest of Honour on one of Connie's legendary South London Binge Tours. Downing measure after measure of alcohol at every gay pub in South London had taken its toll. Though not strictly a gay venue, Sugar Sugar had been a flagship homo-haunt in London's glittering West End for some time, and for this reason, Connie rarely had to pay for his own drinks out on the town. Everywhere he went there was either someone who was a fan of the show or someone he'd had sex with, so there was never a shortage of alcohol being bought for him and whomever he was with.

Michael was no stranger to pubs. He had spent most of his working life behind one bar or another, but the way Connie worked this circuit was something he had never imagined possible. Loud laughter, lots of bitching, the odd song or two. Connie seemed to know everyone. It didn't even matter whether a pub was open or not, his outrageous crew still got drinks. And what a crew it became! By the time they had decided to head home, there were fifteen people in their entourage. Connie was like the Pied Piper of inebriates.

Sitting at the bus stop later, Michael was trying to recall what had actually occurred. His most vivid memory was a kind of safe warm glow in the pit of his chest as though he was amongst family for the first time in his life. Something he had dreamed of many times but never actually experienced. As for what he had done after the first couple of drinks, it was all a bit vague. He remembered gyrating on a table with someone. Then lying on his back on the floor, being fed alcohol through some kind of funnel. He could recall his surprise at Edith tap dancing on the bar. Hadn't he also had to chase someone to retrieve Edith's teeth for her? Then there was something about Chastity rescuing him from some big hairy bloke's car. And trying not to laugh out loud with twenty or so other people while hiding from the police in a pub cellar. And of course, Connie slapping that fat woman.

He looked over at Chastity and Connie quietly chatting further along the bus stop bench. He could hear their voices echoing but not really make out what they were saying. A highly intoxicated Edith meanwhile was kneeling on her handbag on the floor attempting to coax a small traffic cone into taking a bite from her sausage roll. He then noticed how sweaty and hot he was himself. His t-shirt was on back to front and sticking to him, and he was wearing a watch he'd never seen before. His breath tasted of fags and vomit and he had something stuck in his hair. Above all, he noticed that for the first time in as long as he could recall, he was actually happy.

His train of thought was interrupted by Chastity taking his arm as an open backed red Routemaster bus pulled into the stop.

'This is us, Lu,' he said, lifting Michael from his seat. Edith pushed past and leapt onto the bus step with the traffic cone on her head. She ran at the stairs
70

but was met by the Asian bus conductor on his way down.

'Hurry up you, I wanna go upstairs and see the sights,' she snarled at him aggressively.

'I'm jam-packed full,' he advised.

'I don't care what your fuckin' name is, get out of me way!'

'Edith!   Come here this instant,' shouted Chastity, pulling her by the back of the coat to a long sideways seat just inside the lower deck.

'Ere, look at me witches hat.   I look like Witchypoo in H R Puff-n-Stuff.   Do you remember that duck? Do you?' she laughed.

'We don't want that traffic cone now, do we Edith love.' said Chastity, removing it from her head.

'Aww, spoil sport. That's my mate that is.'

'No Edith. This is the wrong bus for Mr Cone. He's got to wait for the number fifty-three.' As the bus pulled away, Chastity threw it back out to the bus stop.

'Oh, I see. Bye then little cone. Be lucky!'

'Bye, nice meeting you!' echoed Michael.

'Do you remember that then, Chastity?'

'Remember what?'

'H R Puff-n-Stuff?'

'Just how old are you woman?'

'I'm as old as the man I feel. D'ya get it?' She let out a long filthy laugh.

'You're going to get it if you don't behave.' Even Chastity and Connie had to smile. Michael meanwhile was hysterical with laughter.

'She's so funny!' he slurred, attempting to focus. 'I can't... it's Champagne... who... what?'

'Have you had a good time tonight, Lu?' asked Chastity.

'Fabulous, darling!'

'Well, what are you going to…'

'Aw, where's my shoe?' Michael looked down at his feet, one with nothing but a grubby sock.

'Bugger. You must have left it in the kebab shop when we got thrown out.'

'Kebab shop?'

'You had your foot on the table picking your toes?'

'That bit of your toenail went in that woman's chips,' laughed Connie.

'Anyway,' continued Chastity. 'What are you going to say to Fifi tomorrow about the shares?'

'What you lookin' at, ya stuck up cow?' screamed Edith.

'If Lulu's going to say that to her tomorrow, I want to be there!' said Connie.

'No her, the nosey Parker,' said Edith, pointing to a stout, well-dressed middle-aged woman glaring very disapprovingly from the bench opposite.

'Calm yourself, Edith,' warned Chastity.

'I suppose your shit smells of roses, little miss prim and proper?' The shocked woman looked for support as the conductor approached.

'Fares, please. Have your money ready.'

'Four to Trafalgar Square please,' Chastity sighed. 'We'll all have to stay at yours tonight Connie. I'm not going to get her home in this state.'

Edith now turned her attention to the conductor. 'Don't get all high and mighty with us, just 'cause they wouldn't give you a bleedin' council house!'

'Edith Pimm! Will you or will you not behave yourself?'

'You want to be keeping her under control mister or you'll be off my bus,' scowled the conductor in an East End accent. This tipped Edith over the edge. She lunged at him, grabbing him by the lapels and head butting his chest. He fell backwards and landed in the lap of the woman opposite, who cried out in shock. The rest of the passengers were now watching.

'And you can all fuck of an' all!' She sniped. Michael was crying with laughter as Connie and Chastity prised Edith off the conductor.

'Get her off of me! Get her off of me! I don't get paid nearly enough to put up with this. She's bloody mad!'

'It's not me, it's him!' screamed Edith, trying to struggle from her captors. 'He's cantangonising me!' she bumbled. 'I bet he's like this to everyone. Look, someone's already smacked him round the head.'

'That's not a bandage Edith, that's his turban.' Chastity attempted a smile of apology. 'You will have to excuse my Mother, she's on a lot of medication at the moment. Grab her other arm tightly Connie. And hold onto it so she can't get up again.' The unimpressed conductor brushed himself down and tucked his tie back into his jacket.

'Any more of this and you're all off, mister.'

'So you were saying Lu. About Fifi tomorrow? What you're going to tell her?'

'Was I? Chastatty, I really love you!' he slurred. 'No, but no… listen, right? Like, not in a jiggy-jiggy sort of way. But family, like.' In an instant he was tearful. 'I've never had a family before.' Edith was sympathetic.

'Ah, haven't you?'

'No. It was an orphanage. It's really sad.'

Edith turned her attention back to the woman opposite. 'Oi you, ya snotty cow? This bloke's me new daughter. He's got a lovely voice as a woman. Still, wouldn't expect you'd know culture if you sat on it with no drawers on!'

'Edith!' screamed Chastity. 'Well Lulu, I think you've made the right decision. We are your family now. You're part of the Sisterhood.'

'Family? I'm so happy!' said Michael, swallowing back a mouthful of stomach acid. 'I couldn't see it before, but under the affluence of incahol it all makes sense. I'm going to give all the shares to you. No, no... don't try and stop me.'

'We won't!' interrupted Connie.

Chastity sighed. With the hand that wasn't restraining Edith, he took a hanky from his pocket and wiped his brow. He then held it to her nose. 'Blow!' Putting the hanky back, he smiled across at Connie. 'Mission accomplished.' He wiped a little of Edith's remaining snot from his hand on his jeans and held it across to shake. Connie grimaced disapprovingly.

'Perhaps later, eh?'

The journey back to Connie's flat above Sugar Sugar had seemed to take forever. Edith, now semi-conscious, had to be carried up the steel fire steps from the back alley and propped up against the wall outside Connie's door, while Chastity had to run back down to stop Michael from climbing into a giant bin at the back of the neighbouring restaurant. However, the deal was done, Chastity was relieved and finally they were home.

CHAPTER NINE

Connie's lounge was a kaleidoscope of colour and mayhem. The room was dominated by a large, tatty crescent-shaped fake-leather sofa, scattered with a dozen luminous animal print cushions. In front of it was a big glass-topped coffee table, upon which sat a sewing machine and several newspapers. Shards of glittering fabric lay strewn in all directions. An old television set topped with a vase of dead flowers sat on a cardboard box in the opposite corner, next to a giant nineteen-fifties display cabinet with a dozen or so feathered and sequinned costumes on hangers hooked to the front. A towel was laid out next to a steam iron on a retro dining table to the back of the room, surrounded by untidy piles of wrinkled clothes.

On the floor up against the wall behind the table in dishevelled stacks were hundreds of fashion and porn magazines. What Connie couldn't achieve with style he made up for with bright orange and shocking-pink flocked wallpaper and a warehouse load of cheap and tacky ornaments and wall-mounted pictures.

Connie and Chastity dumped a now comatose Edith onto the end of the sofa. For Michael, entering Connie's lounge was a shock to his vision. He held his hand over his eyes for a second, dazzled by the sheer kitsch-ness of it all. Sight finally adjusted, he looked around.

'Oh my God, you've been burgled!' he cried in horror. Chastity found this very amusing.

'Ha ha! Did you hear that Connie? Burgled? No Lulu love, it always looks like this. She's such a messy cow.'

'This isn't just my lounge you know, it's my workroom. Where else am I supposed to make all the costumes?'

'Is that why you've got this flat above the bar? It's blinding isn't it?'

'That will be the wallpaper,' Chastity quipped. Connie wasn't impressed with humour at his expense.

'It's grace and favour, but I have to make all the stuff for the show. Props and all. I'm very good with clothes. So it's my workshop.'

'It's your knocking shop, you mean.'

'There has to be perks.'

'That's why Fifi said find somewhere else to live without her help.' Michael burst into fits of laughter. He wasn't really sure why he found this amusing, but he couldn't help himself. 'Why did she tell Chastity to find somewhere else to work without her help?'

'It was all a long time ago,' Chastity sighed, remembering like it was only yesterday.

It had been the late nineteen-nighties, though to look at the venue where his problems began, you'd think it was the eighties. He'd had so much trouble during the show. The microphone was constantly feeding back. Skinny Larry, the vicious queen on the mixing desk, was flying off his face on some pill or other and thought that his interference was somehow adding to the comedy of Chastity's show. While Chastity was singing, Skinny Larry was vary-speeding the backing tracks faster and then slower, making them impossible to follow. The audience began to lose interest and started heckling.

Upstairs in the dressing room after the show, Chastity had it out with the club's owner.

'How do you expect me to work under these conditions, Cyril?'

'You're a shit act in a shit frock with a shitty face. I won't be booking you again, dear,' he replied bitterly, pursing his thin lips and looking down his long bony nose.

'Cyril, I've been working here once a month for three years. It's Skinny Larry on the sound. I've told you before and I'll say it again, you've got to get rid of him. He will pull you under.'

'Oh, that old chestnut? A bad drag act always blames the sound. Well it's not good enough, dear. It simply won't do. I'm adamant.'

'You're delusional, you screaming old queen.'

'Don't mess with me lady, I'm running out of places to hide the bodies! Don't you know who you're dealing with? Ten minutes on that phone and Chastity Belt will never again dance the dance of the seven veils on the London stage.'

'Just get my money, bitch. I'm going,' growled Chastity throwing the last of his jewellery into his suitcase and zipping it shut.

'Money? Did you honestly think I was going to pay for that? You're more delusional than I am!' This was an insult too far. Chastity grabbed him by the throat and drew back his fist to punch.

'Argh! Not in the face, I'm an actress!' screamed Cyril, as Chastity thumped him squarely on the jaw. He flew backwards out of the door and head over heels down the long flight of stairs. He was still lying there groaning fifteen minutes later when Chastity climbed over him to leave.

Suddenly Chastity was awoken from his daydream by Edith screaming in her sleep, 'Shut up! Shut up!' momentarily waving her arms and legs in the air before falling once again unconscious.

'I told you not to let her drink, Lu. I think it's some sort of allergy. Anyway, Cyril sued me. She said I'd damaged her spine.'

'There was nothing wrong with her spine,' defended Connie. 'She wheeled herself around in that wheelchair like Blanche Hudson for three months. Then the day the court case paid out she was prancing on the bar like a psychotic wood nymph!'

'I went on trial. Ooh, I felt like Susan Hayward in I Want to Live. I had to sell my house. I lost everything and now no other venue that knows me will book me.'

'You're better off at Sugar Sugar anyway, Dolly. At least we've got a kicking sound system and a good budget. You're wasting your time at gay pubs with all those precious, complacent queens. Nobody should have to put up with that, even if their show is dated and unoriginal.'

'Thanks for your support!' said Chastity sarcastically. Michael was hysterical with laughter by this time.

'So Fifi's got you both trapped. That's so funny!' Connie and Chastity looked at each other amazed at Michael's reaction, drunk or otherwise.

'Hmm. Bit like you with this Billy, eh?' said Chastity. Instantly, Michael's laughter turned.

'I hate Billy! And I hate Fifi. Though I'm a very loving person, really.'

'When we get the shares we can annihilate Fifi,' said Connie. 'And Champagne Sharon here can pay off Billy when she gets her cash.'

'Yes, if we can keep her alive for the six weeks! Look Lulu love, you're going to have to hide out here at Connie's until we can figure things out. I know it's a push but we'll squirt some air freshener.'

Connie slammed his hand on the dining table. 'Oh no, she's not livin' here! I have to work here too, you know. Have her at your place.'

'She'll have to stay here.'

'She will not!'

'We're supposed to be hiding her. If she's back and forward to mine all the time she's more likely to be seen.'

'She'll cramp my style.'

'What style?' laughed Chastity, looking around the room.

'How am I supposed to audition potential ex-husbands with that closet bitch lolling around all day and night?'

'I don't see we've got any choice.'

'Alright she can stay,' sighed Connie resignedly, 'but don't let her use my Strawberry Sunset shampoo. I've only just bought it.'

'Go get some blankets for these two. I'll have to top and tail with you.' Connie spun on his heels and stormed into the hall. 'Now Lulu love, do you want to bring some of your stuff over?'

'But I live above Billy's Bar. He'll see me!' Panic surfaced as drunken laughter. 'No, no really it's not funny. I know, I'll call Tamara, she'll help me.'

'Won't she be asleep? It's past four in the morning.'

'No, Billy will have a lock in. He does it all the time.'

'Does he? What about the police?'

'It's the police he does it for!' Taking out his mobile, he realised that the battery was now flat. 'Shit! My phone don't work. Shhh! I think it's asleep.'

'Heaven spare us! Look Lulu, there's a land phone on the coffee table. Use that. It will be cheaper anyway. And it's awake!'

The drunken customers and pounding rock music at Billy's Bar were so loud that Tamara could hardly hear what Michael was saying.

'Oh Michael, I've been so worried about you, are you alright? You're drunk, aren't you? Yeah I told him you'd be back tomorrow... What? Another job where?' She was worried now, knowing the consequences if Billy found out that Michael had absconded. 'Oh Michael, be careful. You know he's got it in for you... You lost your shoe where?' She was doubtful he was thinking clearly, which just made things worse. 'Of course I'm going to help you. I'll sneak some bits out tomorrow. Meet me at Fenchurch Street station at about five. You won't forget, will you? Shall I bring Nigel too?'

Billy looked up from his card game and saw Tamara stressing on the phone. He swung out of his chair and stormed across the bar to her.

'Shit! It's Billy!' she panicked. 'Err, yes... left at the lights and it's by the Kurzal. Bye.' She slammed the phone down quickly just as he reached her. He grabbed her hand and she cried out in pain as he squeezed it tightly around the receiver.

'Is that your boyfriend Michael?'

'He's not my boyfriend. Billy, you're hurting me!'

'I'm warning you, you little slut.'

'It was just someone asking directions.'

'At half past four in the morning?' She tried to lean back as he moved his alcohol-drenched breath close to her face. 'I'm warning you!' he growled, looking down at her cleavage and fondling her breast. With a shriek she pulled away and ran to the other end of the bar sobbing.

He coughed and swallowed back a mouthful of smoker's spit. Lifting the receiver he dialled, one four seven one, and listened to the last caller number. Then he phoned the operator.

'What area is code four three four? Westminster? Soho? Sweet.' Putting down the receiver, he laughed to himself menacingly. 'Gotcha!'

The following afternoon, Michael's head was pounding. Chastity had still called a rehearsal while Sugar Sugar was closed to the public. If Michael was going to become a drag queen, he needed to work on his choreography and posture.

Chastity didn't feel much better himself. 'And to the left... and again... now cross your left leg with your right and turn. Now into the dip.' Michael was having trouble with the high shoes. Connie wasn't helping at all, sitting with his stilettos up on one of the tables, flicking through a gossip magazine wearing dark glasses and smoking a cigarette.

'It says here, "Serious addictions – cheese ruined my sex life." He wants to wash his dick more often.' Everyone ignored him. Strangely Edith, despite the previous night's carryings on, seemed totally unaffected. Or was she?

'Aw bugger! Where's my good duster? Now, I took it out the washing machine and put it in front of the fire.' She walked it through. 'It was in that bag when I went shopping. I got me polish, then got on the number twelve. So if my bag's over there...' Chastity's concentration was broken. 'What's the matter with her?'

'God alone knows,' sighed Connie. 'It's like watching Jessica Fletcher on smack!'

'What have you lost, Edith?'

'Reality?' Connie yawned.

'Someone's pinched me good duster.'

'It's by the kettle. Your memory's getting bad of late.' Chastity bit his bottom lip and shook his head despairingly as Edith waddled off in the direction of the trade kitchen.

'Don't worry. She'll have forgot about it in ten minutes,' said Connie.

'Anyway, where was I? Oh yes, now put that foot behind and turn,' Chastity continued. Michael tried to be elegant but just landed in a pile on the floor. 'I think those shoes are too big for you.'

'What with those fat ankles?'

'Shut up Connie! It's all in the balance, Lu. Have you never worn roller skates?' Michael shook his head. 'I said before, try keeping your ankles stiff. Perhaps we could try using a couple of splints down his socks.'

Michael was trying so hard to get this right. He was past the point of no return with Billy and, despite Connie's complacency, he did want to impress his new family.

'This is insane. Why do women wear these things?'

'The sex is in the heel,' Connie replied, flicking over the page of his magazine.

'If you get it right, it looks like you need shafting from behind,' advised Chastity.

'But if you don't, it just looks like you've shit yourself.'

'Put that bloody thing down and get your scrawny arse up here now.'

'I already know it... And I'm tired,' yawned Connie, pulling the collar of his jumper up around his ears protectively.

86

'I'm not surprised, after last night.'

'It's not that. I've not been sleeping too well lately.'

'Not that dream about the lesbian with the rubber hose again?' sighed Chastity. Connie nodded.

'I've been having nightmares too,' complained Michael.

'He dreamt he went camping,' said Connie.

'I said intense, not in tents!'

'Anyway, what are you reading?' Chastity craned his neck to see.

'Now Magazine. "Ten celebrities who have gone too far to lose weight."'

'Ridiculous! How can you go too far? People chew off their own limbs, for Christ's sake!' giggled Chastity.

'Oh and there's this... "Inside Victoria Beckham."'

Michael was desperate to join in. 'What, like… David Beckham's knob?' This took Chastity and Connie by surprise. They both laughed.

'Ha ha! We will make a drag queen of you yet,' praised Chastity.

'Alright then Dolly, what about this. A farmer's cultivated a field full of dildos. And you say?'

'Err... trouble with squatters?' Michael grinned, proudly.

'Ha ha! That's my girl!'

'Well done, Dolly.' Even Connie was impressed.

'Why do you call everyone Dolly?' asked Michael.

'Cause she's usually too drug-fucked to remember anyone's name.'

'True. Though funnily enough, I never forget a prick!'

Two men arrived at the bottom of the stairs. One was tall, slightly balding and forty something, dressed in faded blue denim. The other was shorter, broader and wearing a fluorescent green shell suit, which clashed hideously with his bright orange hair. Michael could see he was blind by his dark glasses and white stick. Arms linked, they walked together slowly across the dance floor to Connie's table.

'Talk of the devil, here comes one hell of a prick.'

'Now Connie,' Chastity quietly scolded. 'Hello boys. Lulu, the normal looking one is Slasher who writes and records all the songs for our show.'

'I've got the new song with me.'

'Slasher, this is our new sister Lulu.'

'Nice to meet you Lulu,' he said, shaking Michael's hand.

'Slasher? That sounds a bit fierce?'

'He's not fierce Lu, he's just got a weak bladder. And the blind one's Felix. He's a bit of a sadist, so watch him with that white stick.'

'Why has he got orange hair?' whispered Michael.

'Because he's a bastard,' Chastity chuckled. 'He thinks they dyed it black. Don't tell him, he doesn't know.' Michael stepped forward as best he could in six-inch heels and shook Felix's hand.

'Hello Felix, it's nice to meet you.'

'Can I feel you?' asked Felix.

'Eh? Oh you mean map out my features with your fingers? Sure, go ahead.' Michael closed his eyes and leaned his face towards Felix. Felix on the other hand, took a step forward and grabbed Michael's crotch tightly. He jumped back in shock, the only one in the room who didn't find this amusing.

'For feck's sake Slasher, control your friend,' said Chastity. 'Take him to the vet and get him spayed.'

'Our Lulu's pulled. And it's a blind man. How humiliating is that?' laughed Connie, spitefully.

'Lulu love, you look like you're going to cry. You've gone as red as a whore's chuff. I did warn you about him.'

'She's embarrassed, bless her. Anyone would think she'd not had a man grab her bollocks before!' There was a stony silence. Connie sat up in his chair. 'You are kidding, right? You've never had a man? Not ever?'

'Not where I'm from. You can't! It's too dangerous, someone might find out,' Michael squirmed.

'Look, erm... Why don't we try the new song with the choreography?' said Chastity, trying to distract from Michael's pain. 'Stick it in the machine would you, Slasher? We can do it in the show tonight. Ok, you've got those moves now, Lulu love, and you've learnt the words. Are you ready?' Michael was silent. Connie now had the giggles, which wasn't making matters easier. 'Shut up, Connie! Come on Lulu, it will take your mind off things.'

'I can't! I'll screw it up just like I always do.'

'Get a hold of yourself,' said Connie. 'Just because no man ever has!'

'Stop it, you! Now focus Lulu, focus.' The three drags jumped up onto the stage and stood in a line, facing front.

'I think Lulu may be a bit cack-handed. Swap over to this side Connie,' suggested Chastity.

'No, I always go this side. Like Ant and Dec. She's just going to have to make more of an effort.'

Michael was trying to avoid eye contact with Connie but it wasn't easy. He knew that he'd now be the butt of jokes whenever Connie was bored.

Slasher inserted the CD into the machine and pressed play. Chastity gave a count in for the first step, a rather complicated leg cross over followed by a spin. Then together, they began to sing.

'Some say that we're Venus, some say that we're toys. We're gentle and dainty, we like playing coy. We don't hang around with the rest of the boys, 'cause we're girls!'

So far so good... kind of. Chastity was watching Michael's every move. 'Head up Lu,' he shouted.

We've lipstick and makeup, and fabulous shoes. Big tits with pert nipples, and gorgeous hairdos. There's things in our wardrobes that never get used, 'cause we're girls! We like to play hard to get, and yet. If you buy me a diamond, I'll let you break my hymen!'

Then came the bit Michael had been dreading - the instrumental break. A series of interwoven spins and arm lifts. Panicking, he went completely the wrong way round and smacked Connie clean across the face with his elbow.

'Look out Dolly... Aargh! You did that on purpose, you bitch!' Connie pushed him in the back and he fell to the stage with a loud thud.

'Get up, get up! Keep going,' yelled Chastity.

'We can be sexy, or we can be sluts. We can be prudish, or we can be nuts. What you get more or less, is anyone's guess. You won't know what you've got, till you give us a shot. There's no turning back, once we're flat on our backs. 'Cause we're girls! Girls!'

Chastity ended the song with a deep baritone. *'Girls!'*

Felix and Slasher clapped. Connie wasn't so impressed.

'Well, a couple of dozen more rehearsals and you might just get it.'

'Sorry, I didn't hit you on purpose,' said Michael.

'Whatever!'

'Connie, why do you have to be such a bitch all the time?' scolded Chastity. 'Lulu's doing the best she can. Give her a break!'

'There's no need to take her sexual frustrations out on me though, is there?' Connie sniped back, stamping his foot.

'Don't listen to her Lulu love, you'll be fine.'

Michael was humiliated and upset. 'This isn't easy for me you know. It's alright for you, you're used to it. Don't you remember how hard it was for you when you first started?' The complacent look on Connie's face said it all.

'No,' he snapped, returning to his table and lighting a cigarette.

Edith walked back in. 'I still can't find that bloody duster!' Chastity scratched his head in frustration.

'Come on Edith, I'll help you find it.' Scowling at Connie as he passed, he warned, 'Be nice!'

However left alone to his own devices, Connie couldn't resist.

'Well. Our little Lulu's a virgin, eh?' He waggled his tongue making a cunnilingus sound.

Michael sat on the front of the stage with his head in his hands. It wasn't the first time he'd wanted the ground to swallow him up.

Just when things seemed they couldn't get any worse, Madame Fifi arrived.

'Ah, Michael. My little candy floss. Come into my office darling, come. Come!'

'Shit! I need this right now, don't I?' Michael reluctantly jumped from the stage and followed her.

Connie was disappointed that his muse had gone, just when he was getting warmed up.

'So... Felix? You ought to put a spike on the end of that white stick. Make yourself useful picking up litter as you walk around.' Felix swiped his stick in the direction of Connie's voice but missed him by a mile.

When Chastity returned from the kitchen a few moments later, he saw that Michael was missing. 'Where's Lulu? What have you done?'

'It isn't me! The child catcher's got her.'

'Oh, for feck's sake! You know what a state she's in! Why did you let that happen? You're about as much use as Sandy Shaw's shoes. We've probably lost everything now!'

Madame Fifi had left the office door open behind her for Michael. As he entered, she was pouring two drinks. She offered him one as he closed the door.

'Whiskey?'

'No thank you.'

'Oh. Anyway, I have the contract ready for you to sign. Here, use my pen. It's a diamond encrusted Rolex limited edition with twenty-four carat gold inlay. It has little birdies on it. Look at all the little birdies.' She feigned a smile as she handed him the papers, but he wasn't fooled by her light and fluffy demeanour. She did unnerve him, but his mind was made up to support family, despite Connie being such a bitch.

'Erm. I err... I've decided not to sell you the shares.' Fifi's attitude switched instantly to something considerably more sinister.

'What did you say?' Her eyes narrowed. Michael wanted to cry, but instead from the pit of his stomach came anger.

'I can't! Alright?'

'But darling, we had everything arranged.'

'I've changed my mind.'

'Changed it? Does the new one work any better?'

'I don't have to put up with this! You don't care about me, you just want my shares.'

'But Michael, we're practically family.'

'You're not my family, they are.' Fifi had no patience for this.

'Oh, that damned Sisterhood! You think they will save you from this Billy-nut-nut-chucker-nut person? Don't be silly Michael, darling. With just a squiggle of this pen you could be free from all this pain and torment.' This was pain and torment enough for Michael.

'I've made up my mind.'

'You stubborn fool. So be it! If I don't get my shares Michael, a catastrophe beyond your imagination will occur!'

Michael stood to his full height and lifted his chin, proudly. 'And it's not Michael, it's Lulu. I'm Lulu L'Amour!' He threw the contract in her face and stormed out of the office, slamming the door behind him.

Madame Fifi was incensed. With a scream of frustration, she threw his un-emptied glass smashing against the wall. Whiskey dripped down across the front of the Diana Ross photo. Knocking back her own drink, she slammed the glass on the desk.

'Just who is this boy and what exactly is he doing here? He doesn't act like a big star. I don't trust his fairy story.'

She picked up the phone and dialled. 'Hello? I want a detective. A woman... Soho... IMMEDIATELY!'

CHAPTER ELEVEN

In the dressing room later the same night, Chastity was beginning to panic. They'd managed to pull together several bits that Michael could do on stage, but since his meeting with Madame Fifi he was nowhere to be seen.

'I'm really getting worried now. We've got a full house out there. Where the feck is she?' Edith and Daisy looked as worried as Connie.

'Do you think she gave everything to Fifi after all?'

'After the way you treated her at rehearsal, nothing would surprise me. Anyway forget Fifi for a minute, it's Lulu I'm worried about. She's been through a hell of a lot the last forty-eight hours. She knows there's a show in a minute, she should be here by now.'

'Where is she then?' said Edith, screwing the front of her pinny in her hands.

'I don't know. She went to see the old crone then she just vanished into thin air. With this Billy after her, I do hope nothing bad has happened!'

It was all too much for Daisy. He began to sob.

'What's the matter with you, Dolly?'

'She's so lovely, but all these things keep happening to her. It's so unfair. Oh, I can't bear it, I can't bear it!'

Edith also began to cry. 'Oh don't start, you have me off now!'

Suddenly the door burst open. For a moment everyone paused what they were doing, thinking it may be Michael. But it was just Fifi - with a woman they hadn't seen before. A stranger in the dressing room was never a good sign, particularly if they were with Fifi.

'My, err, darling sisterhood! This is erm...'

'The name's Vera and I'm a manic depressive,' said the woman. Chastity and Connie looked at each other suspiciously.

Vera was tall and thin, wearing a grubby grey trench coat, a cheap short brown wig and too much makeup. And this was the worst attempt at a Welsh accent they had ever heard. Even Fifi was a bit taken aback with her new undercover detective.

'Huh?' she quizzed.   Vera leaned to whisper in her ear.

'I'm in character!'

'Oh, err... ah, yes! Depressive. She is very, very sad. Look at this choochy face.' Vera's already drawn features screwed up even more as Fifi took a hold of it to demonstrate. Releasing her grasp, she discreetly wiped the remnants of amateur dramatics character foundation that had come away on her hand onto the back of Vera's coat. 'I will leave you all to get acquainted. Now ciao.'

'Oi, what have you done with Lulu?' Chastity shouted after her aggressively. She ignored him and, with an acid glance at Vera, left the room. This just upset Daisy and Edith more as their snivelling escalated.

'Don't see the point of crying,' droned Vera. 'We're all surrounded by misery every day of our lives. Then something happens and sets you off.
96

That's when it all becomes too much to cope with. There's no point in crying about it. Better to just jump off a high rise and get it over with.' Daisy and Edith were now in a terrible state. Chastity and Connie couldn't believe what they were hearing.

'Oh, for feck's sake! Just who are you woman? What are you doing here?'

'I'm the new Coat Check.'

'I don't want her working upstairs with me!' Daisy sobbed, jumping away from her like she had the plague.

'Calm yourself Daisy!' scolded Chastity. 'But what are you doing in here? We're starting a show in a few minutes!'

'Well they're both in here, why can't I be?'

'Get her away from me! Get her away!' Daisy was very upset.

'Daisy!' scolded Chastity.

'So, which one of you is Lulu, then?' asked Vera, attempting to be discreet. The mention of Lulu's name tipped Edith and Daisy over the edge. They were now hysterical.

'Why are you asking?' shot back Connie.

'No reason, just curious.'

'Oh yes? See this one Tit?' said Connie, pointing into Vera's face. 'She's got that medical condition where she just can't mind her own fuckin' business!'

Just then the door burst open and in came Michael, struggling with several large overstuffed bags and a cat miaowing loudly from a wicker carrying-basket. 'What's going on? Why is everyone crying? Can someone help me with these bags?'

Daisy knocked the bags out of Michael's hands as he lunged and pulled him into tight a bear hug.

'Oh, Lulu, thank God you're safe! We thought you'd jumped off a building. Give me a hug.'

Michael was struggling for breath. Connie was angry.

'What time do you call this? And what's that cat doing here?' He let out an enormous sneeze. Then another and then another. 'I'm allergic. Atchoo! Tit, tell him I'm allergic. ATCHOO!'

'Lulu love, what happened? We've been so worried about you?' asked Chastity.

'So this is Lulu, is it? Hmm. Shifty looking.' squinted Vera.

'Shut your cake hole you. Daisy, for God's sake let her go, she can't breathe. Her ears are turning blue!'

Freed to draw breath, Michael was gasping and coughing. Daisy and Edith were bawling. Connie was sneezing and the cat was screeching hysterically from where his basket had landed when dropped. Chastity stared in bewilderment at the chaos.

'Jesus H Christ! That Fifi's like a tornado with lip gloss, leaving carnage in her wake.'

'You will have to sort this out. ATCHOO! I can't have that cat staying at my flat!'

'You will have to sort yourselves out, I'm busy. I've got to get this show underway, we're late enough as it is. Connie, help Lulu get ready as fast as you can, I'll create a distraction. Then get into your Swan Lake costume so you don't have to sing for a while, the sneezing will just make it funnier. Daisy, get upstairs on the door. And you, whatever you said your name was, go with her. Edith, take that blue CD out to the lesbian. Tell her I'm going to open with "The Show Is Over Now," that'll confuse the bastards. And tell her to turn it up loud so they can't hear that bloody cat.' Chastity plunged his hand into Connie's coat pocket and pulled out his door key, handing it to Edith. 'Then run upstairs and get Connie's antihistamine pills from her bathroom. Come on everyone, step on it!'

After the show, the dressing room was much quieter. Even the cat had settled down to sleep in his carrier. Chastity swallowed back a couple of aspirin.

'I'm sorry I got back so late,' Michael said. 'I was like a coiled spring, I just had to get out. So I went to meet Tamara at the station with all my stuff.'

'So what happened with Fifi?' asked Connie.

'I told her to stuff it. She wasn't happy. She said a disaster beyond my imagination would occur.'

Chastity scratched his head. 'Now where have I heard that line before?'

Connie wasn't so calm. 'Oh that's just fucking marvellous, ain't it? She's going to be spitting nails all week now, thanks to you!'

'But I'm giving the shares to you both, aren't I?' Michael shouted back.

'Yes... I know.' Connie backed down. 'Sorry, I'm just exhausted with all the sneezing. Thanks!'

'Phantom of the Opera! That's it,' said Chastity. 'Fifi saw it last week, that's where she got it from.'

'Oh that figures,' Connie nodded. 'She should try wearing a mask. Cover up that hideous face. Or perhaps a plastic bin bag, tied at the neck.'

'You're one to talk, covered in slag tags,' replied Chastity pointing at Connie's neck.

'I prefer to think of them as love bites.'

'Are they from that cute little bloke who looked like Sid Owen from Eastenders? What happened to him?'

'Got rid. Shame really. Shy, eager to please, hung like a pony... just my type. But every time we walked up the street together someone shouted, "Rickaaeey!"'

'We need to get rid of that new cloak-woman too. What's her name?'

'Happy Vera? Don't see the point in crying,' mocked Connie, in a drawn Welsh accent. 'She wants to piss off back over the Forth Bridge to Wales.'

'It's the Severn.'

'How many fuckin' bridges are there?'

'She's definitely not who she says she is. And she kept asking about you.' Chastity pointed at Michael. He was a little concerned.

'Me? Why?'

'I don't know. She hasn't got anything to do with that Billy-no-nut, has she?'

'I've never seen her before. Oh God, you don't suppose it's something to do with getting my stuff from above Billy's Bar do you?' Chastity looked to Connie for support, but he was distracted dropping a pill.

'What's that pill you're taking? Don't get off your face tonight, you've got to look out for Lulu!'

'Calm yourself, Dolly, it's just another antihistamine. I've got to go upstairs with that fuckin' cat, haven't I?'

'Oh yeah, I'm sorry about Nigel.'

'Nigel? Is that his name?' Connie laughed. 'That's a funny name for a cat!'

100

'He's not just any old cat, he's a guard cat.'

Chastity too thought the whole thing hilarious. 'Like them dogs that bark to let deaf people know when the phone's ringing?'

'My life, I've heard it all now!'

'He's very protective of his territory. He kept Billy away from all my stuff. He's like a little tiger.'

'Well good luck with that then Connie, ha ha! Anyway, I'm done. Let's get out of this dump.' With one last glance in the mirror, Chastity picked up his coat and bag and left the room, followed closely by Michael and Connie.

Daisy was still outside the entrance on the pavement as they left the building. Michael looked up and down the street nervously as he pushed through the glass doors. The past forty-eight hours had been a nightmare and he was very aware that it could all get considerably worse at any given moment, especially with this Vera snooping around.

Chastity took Daisy's arm. 'Goodnight then Daisy love. Have you calmed down now?'

'Yeah, I feel a bit better now misery-guts is gone. She didn't stay till the end. I had to keep helping people get their coats out and it's not even my job to do that!'

'That's a little odd, isn't it? With any luck she won't come back. Anyway, you go up with Connie, Lu, and I'll see you both tomorrow afternoon. More rehearsals, girls!'

'Coming up for coffee when you're done, Daisy?' asked Connie.

'No ta, I'm knackered. All that crying's worn me out. Terrah then. Terrah Lu. Terrah Connie.'

Connie helped Michael carry his bags, though he drew the line at Nigel's carrier. Chastity watched them walk a little way up the street and disappear around the corner to Connie's flat. He took out a cigarette and lit it, offering his packet to Daisy.

'Do you want a fag before I go, Daisy?'

'No, ta.'

'Stick one behind your ear for later?'

'My ears stick out too far. I can only do that with a bingo pen.'

'Alright love. Now keep an eye on that Vera, if she turns up again. Report back to me. If she's Welsh, I'm Shirley Bassey!'

'Perhaps she's not Welsh Wales Welsh?' offered Daisy.

'What other kind of Welsh is there?' Chastity was too tired to elaborate. 'Anyway watch her, OK? Night night, Daisy love.'

'Terrah!'

It was getting quite chilly by this late hour. Daisy looked at his watch. Just another ten minutes to see out the remaining staff and he could lock up and go home himself. He didn't notice the Daimler pulling into the opposite kerb a little way up the street. From the driver's side stepped a tall, stocky man with a shaved head and flat boxer's nose. Part of his left ear was missing from a fight years before. He looked around excitedly with a psychotic twitch.

'Is this Soho then, Billy?' he said. 'Cor, look at the tits on that billboard!' Billy stepped from the passenger door.

'Shut up, Knuckles. Yep, this is Soho. This is where he is. Somewhere in this square mile. I can smell him!' He laughed to himself, deeply and viciously, drawing his hands into fists. 'Hello again, Michael. Remember me? I'm Billy. And you're dead!'

CHAPTER TWELVE

In her office several days later, Madame Fifi was keen to hear her detective's progress.

'Well, what have you discovered about this Michael so far?'

Vera seemed very pleased with herself. 'Oh, he's a lovely looker, I won't lie to you. Big shoulders, like my Dada. I'd bonk him, that I would.' This wasn't what Fifi wanted to hear.

'Drop this ridiculous accent. Come on, come on! What else?'

'He's got a cat called Nigel.'

'Nigel?'

'Yeah, I know! Perhaps some kind of code or something. Oh yes, and you're going to love this... he's a drag queen!' She laughed out loud. 'I know, who'd have thought? Butch fellah like that!'

'This is preposterous! I'm paying you fifty pounds an hour for this? Call yourself a private eye? Up with this travesty I will not to put! I need to know where he's from, who he is and how he knew Lettie!'

'Early days, my love, early days! I've got to infiltrate his confidence. Get to know him. Perhaps go out with him, a little candle-lit supper for two...' This was too much for Fifi.

'He's gay, you fool!' she bellowed.

'Oh, bugger! The good looking one's are always poofs, aren't they?'

'You are trying my patience! Here. Take this key to the flat upstairs. That's where he's staying. The coast will be clear during the show tonight. I'm warning you Vera, this is your last chance.' Vera took the key and dropped it into her cleavage.

'No, Vera's my cover name. It's actually Florence. Like The Magic Roundabout?' Fifi clenched her fist ready to punch, but managed to hold back.

'Aargh! Get to work immediately, I want those shares. They're mine, mine, MINE!'

Two floors above, Connie was racing yards of black cotton fabric through the sewing machine. Michael was sitting at the dining table listening to an i-Pod, trying to learn the words to yet another song. Chastity let himself in with his personal key.

'Knock, knock. Are you decent?' he called from the hall before entering the room.

'Decent? The chance to be indecent would be a fine thing, with that-an'-a-cat sleeping on me sofa.'

'Hello, Lulu love. And you, you slag.'

'Come here and put your lips under this needle.'

'You're not getting anywhere near my lips, you lesbian! Anyway, what are you making? Looks a bit drab.'

'I'm a genius! Tell her what a genius I am,' beamed Connie with glee. 'Dolly's scared she's going to bump into this Billy. So I'm making her... a yashmak!' Chastity was impressed, for a change.

'Ha ha!'

Michael wasn't as confident. 'I'm really not sure this is a good idea.'

106

'Don't be silly!' replied Chastity gently, sensing Michael's fear. 'You can't drag up every time you have to go out. I think it's brilliant. Especially with this Vera sniffing around. The Welsh bitch. I'm sure she's putting on a show.'

'What like... Liza Llanelli?' Connie always laughed loudest at his own jokes. Chastity feigned a yawn.

'One of us needs to search Fifi's office and find out who she is. Let's take a vote.' Michael and Chastity both pointed at Connie.

'Why is it always me? Oh alright, I'll do it tonight while the show's on.' Connie snatched his cup of tea from the coffee table and turned his back on them, sulkily looking out of the window.

Meanwhile, Nigel had noticed Chastity's arrival and greeted him with a big miaow, rubbing up against his leg. His reputation as a guard cat was well founded. Big, muscular and confident, his short fur was mostly black and white with orange patches. He had a piece of his tail missing from one of many territorial scraps in his past, and a dark patch on his face gave the appearance of a permanent black eye. A real bruiser, he even walked with swagger.

'Oh hello, Nigel love, I forgot you were here,' said Chastity, bending to rub him behind the ear. 'What's occurring in the world of pussy?' Connie spat his tea up the curtains.

'Ergh! Do you have to say that? Anyway, just kick him. Little fucker pissed on my bed.' Michael didn't want to hear this, he was guilt ridden enough as it was.

'He's marking his territory.'

'That's my territory! This is his out here with you on that sofa. How am I supposed to find the man of my dreams if my bedroom smells like the Post Office queue on pension day? Oh and another thing, stop him parkin' his arse on my glass coffee table. It looks like it's covered in little kiss marks.' Chastity needed to diffuse the atmosphere.

'How are you getting along learning the new songs? You're going to need one for tonight.'

'Not too bad. Though I don't really understand some of the lyrics. Like this one... what's "fisting"?' Connie spat another mouthful of tea at the window.

'It's alright, I wasn't thirsty anyway!' he said, pulling forward the net curtain and shaking off the droplets.

'Are you going to tell him, or shall I?' laughed Chastity.

'You've seen Sooty, haven't you?'

Michael was gob-smacked. 'How? And more to the point, why?'

'Diabolical pleasure and divine pain!'

'And you've done this, Connie?' he asked. Chastity couldn't resist.

'Her arse flaps are so saggy, she's got a drawstring. Like a plimsoll bag! Before that, it was like a round of applause every time she ran for a bus! Personally, I've only ever managed the four fingers. It's the thumb I have trouble with. Would you try it, Lu?'

'She's got to find herself a man first. She's not even decided whether she's the train or the tunnel yet!'

108

Later that night, Michael stood on stage ready to perform the song he had spent all day memorising. It was a lot of words to remember and he still could not really understand most of the lyrics. He understood it was a prayer and that was why he was dressed as a nun, but most of the song still baffled him. Though he did trust Chastity's judgement, so was prepared to give it his all, regardless.

'I'd like to say a prayer tonight, to thank the Lord we're gay. If we were straight, at our age we'd do things a different way. With holidays at Butlin's or a B&B at Frinton. Spit social comment on such freaks as Barrymore and Clinton.'

The audience were tittering. So far so good.

'Spend Sundays in the garden 'cause the lawn is in a mess. Wear shoes with Velcro straps and comfy slacks from M and S. Each Friday watching telly with a jigsaw we've been doing, and changing channels every time that someone mentions screwing.

'We'd shop at Iceland 'cause it's cheap, and Woolie's is a must. For drawers with double-gussets and an orthopaedic truss. Shagging would be twice a year, safe-sex would be a kiss. We'd go to public toilets just because we need a piss.

'A rave would be the dog track, and coke would be a drink. If someone mentioned fisting there must be a fight, we'd think. Cruising would be caravans, the scene - a lovely view. And top or bottom - labels on the Tupperware we use.'

The crowd were laughing now. His confidence was building.

'Speed would mean go faster, special-k - a breakfast bite. And ecstasy would mean a weekend on the Isle of Wight. Drag would be a racing car, except

for TV shows. We love that Lily Savage, it's a man dressed up, you know! So as another year goes by, be grateful in your way. And say a prayer with me tonight, to thank the Lord we're gay.'

His turn ended to cheers of approval. He still didn't really get it, but at least it rhymed like a proper song, he thought. He took a deep curtsey and returned to the dressing room, where Connie was adding final adjustments to his enormous orange wig.

'You're next, Connie,' said Chastity, removing Michael's wimple for him and pinning it onto a polystyrene manikin head. Connie ran for the stage.

'Well, that wasn't so bad was it, Lulu love?'

'I still don't understand what they're all laughing at. I have Special K for breakfast. And what's wrong with The Isle of Wight?'

'It'll all come to you in time, dear. It's a world away from what you're used to so don't expect to understand it all in one go. Just trust me and follow my lead, I won't let you down. As Saint Lena Martell once said, "One day at a time sweet Jesus". You're doing very well considering. Was that old goat in the audience?'

'Fifi? Yes, she was giving me daggers. If she wasn't after the shares, I'm sure she wouldn't have me here.' Michael slumped into the chair, bowing his head. Chastity patted him on the shoulder.

'Don't under-estimate how well you're doing. You look simply gorgeous in drag, and you've got a voice to die for. It wouldn't be easy for Fifi to find another act like you.'

'But what about all the fuck-ups I keep making on stage?'

'People think it's part of the show... possibly. Look, I know you're vexed and you've still a lot to learn, but it's only another five weeks to cope with. Talking of which, here's your first week's pay packet as a drag queen.'

'Oh, thank God. I'm skint.' He opened the small brown envelope and looked at the large wad of cash. 'Wow! A Week? I wasn't expecting this much. I've only been on stage a few times.'

'Yes, but each show has all the stresses and pressure of an eight hour day crammed into just one hour. Then there's rehearsals and the time it takes to get ready. And we have to buy our own makeup. I'll take you shopping in Boots.'

'Well it'll make a nice change from these bloody drag shoes!' he said, pulling off a patent black sling back and rubbing his toes.

'You're lucky. I've hardly got anything in my pay packet this week.'

'Why?'

'Ages ago, I agreed to buy Fifi's old car off her. She's taken a big chunk of my wages towards it today. Still, I've already got the keys and it will save me a fortune in bus and cab fares getting home once it's paid for.'

'Well I've got far more than I expected. I can always give you something if you get caught out.'

'That's kind Lu, thank you. Though I'd only borrow it.'

'Should I offer some money to Connie for letting me and Nigel stay at her flat?'

'No, don't you dare! Just buy your fair share of the food and keep out of her way as much as you can. It's only a few weeks till we know what's happening.

Take no notice of the bitching, she'd be like that with you whether you were staying there or not. She's had a bypass.'

'Heart?'

'No, morality. She'll survive.'

Michael thought for a moment about Lettie's mysterious eulogy. Five weeks to go. A short rush of nerves gripped his stomach.

'These shares that Fifi's after. Why did Lettie leave them to me?' Chastity was as baffled as he was.

'I don't know. It's all a puzzle. Fifi got hers from Creighton Cross who owns the building. Well he did, he's dead now. A few weeks ago he fell out of his office window on the third floor. He bounced off the pavement, went through the plate glass window of his own club, then down three flights of stairs into the cellar.'

'Blimey, no wonder he's dead!'

No it wasn't the fall. It was when he got the invoice for the window the next day. Still, he was eighty-two. Fifi had an affair with him years ago and he gave her half the shares and Connie's flat on a lifetime lease. He adored Fifi.'

'What was he, deranged?' asked Michael sarcastically. 'Eighty-two? Just how old is Fifi then?'

'No one really knows, what with all that surgery. We did find out her birthday was April the twentieth though, the same day as Hitler. Lettie thought that was so funny. You know, I thought Fifi would get the lot when Creighton died. So how did Lettie get it all? There must have been a diabolical plan.'

'How do you mean?' said Michael, just as keen to unravel the intrigue. Chastity listened out for Connie's performance briefly. He had a little while

112

yet. Sitting on the chair next to Michael, he lowered his tone.

'Well, you said Lettie turned up at Billy's Bar asking for you. Why? And she hated Karaoke, yet she sang you the same song over and over again. Poor love, it must have been torture for you!'

'Perhaps so I'd know it for my debut song here?'

'My thoughts precisely, so she must have wanted you to be here. But why?' Michael thought for a moment.

'When she recorded her eulogy, she already knew she was going to be hit by a car. Maybe she thought I'd be a good replacement.'

'With no experience? Why not leave the shares to me and Connie?'

'Perhaps she knew I'd give them to you.'

'She must have tracked you down. Let's face it, she was a bit of a blood-hound. But why involve you at all? And apart from being dog-ugly, what did she do to make someone run her over?'

They pondered for a moment. Chastity could feel the beginnings of an idea on the tip of his tongue. But just at that moment, their train of thought was shattered as Vera entered.

Michael was frustrated. 'What do you want?'

'I've just brought you a cup of tea each. Four - you are all here, aren't you? Doing the show?'

'Yes, but there's only three of us. Why are you asking all these questions? Leave me alone,' Michael scolded.

'No reason. I'll have the fourth cup then. So, where's the other drag person thing?'

'On stage singing! Are you deaf?' Michael just wanted to get her out of the dressing room as quickly as possible but Chastity had suddenly had an idea.

'Have a look through that doorway into the wings over there, Vera dear,' he gestured calmly. Michael was confused.

'Dear? I thought you hated her?' he whispered, as Vera climbed a step to peer out behind Connie.

'Shut up, shut up!' Chastity whispered back, grabbing one of the teacups. 'Pass me Connie's antihistamine pills.'

'What are you doing?'

'Putting them in Vera's tea. It's not morphine, but it should put her out of action for a spell while Connie searches Fifi's office.' Chastity tipped a handful of pills into the drink and stirred it with an eyebrow pencil.

'My God, that's too many. It could kill her!'

'Don't worry about that, the prescription's in Connie's name.' He quickly returned the cup to the tray as Vera returned.

'Very nice. For a man in a bra. Anyway, I'll be off then.'

'Wait, wait! You nearly forgot your tea, dear. You can't have it out there, Fifi would be so angry. Best have it now. Drink up!' He passed Vera her cup.

'Oh, I don't want to piss her off again.' She drank the tea back in one, but it choked her into a cough. 'Ergh, that tastes really odd.'

'Does it dear? Perhaps the kettle needed fresh water.'

'I'm sure it had lumps in it!'

'Ah, yes. Now, err... that will be those cheap sugar cubes Edith keeps buying. We were just saying
114

the other day. Weren't we Lu, just saying the other day?' Chastity gave Michael a nudge to get his support.

'Eh? Oh, yes. Lumpy sugar... lumps. And I said, didn't I... I said, no more lumpy lumps Edith, I said...' Michael bumbled.

'Enough said, Lulu. Bye then Vera dear, yes bye then!'

'Well, best get back to my coat check I suppose.' Chastity manoeuvred her to the door then shoved her out, slamming it shut behind.

'Coat check, my arse! Daisy said she hasn't even been there.'

Connie rushed in from the stage. 'Right, super bitch is in the audience with her entourage. Keep an eye on her during your spot Tit and I'll go and search her office for info on this Vera woman. I don't know why it has to be me doing this,' he moaned.

'Why shouldn't it be you?'

'Well, it's a matter of ethics.'

'Ethics?'

'Yes. Someone might find out! Anyway, you stay here Lulu.' Grabbing a feather boa, Chastity ran for the stage while Connie left for Fifi's office.

As the next show song began, Michael sat alone staring at his colourful face in the mirror. How did he reach this point? 'Why did Lettie want me at Sugar Sugar? This is insane!' he said to himself. 'I'm sitting here dressed as a nun. I've got Billy after my neck, Vera spying on me, Fifi spitting nails at me. I'm singing... yes singing songs I don't understand, sleeping on a drag queen's sofa and to top it all, I've got to walk the streets in a yashmak. All because of Lettie. Could it get any worse?'

Suddenly, Edith came running into the room crying hysterically. As Michael jumped to his feet she ran at him, grasping him around the waist and burying her head in his chest. As he put his arms around her, he could feel her trembling.

'Edith? What on earth's wrong?'

'It's my old man Bert. He's only gone and died on me, ain't he?'

CHAPTER THIRTEEN

After twenty minutes or so back on the cloak desk, Vera was feeling a bit queasy. Her attention span was suffering, but she had made up her mind that tonight was the night to search Connie's flat for anything Michael-related. After a quick look in her bag to check she had the key and her camera, she left by the front doors. As the fresh air hit her lungs, she felt even worse.

'Where are you off to now?' snapped Daisy.

'I'm going for a walk. I feel a bit sick.'

'Not half as sick as I am, having to keep doing your job for you. How long are you going to be gone this time?'

'Never you mind, sonny. Just keep your eyes peeled for pick-pockets and bag thieves,' she winked, teetering off in the direction of Connie's.

'Where? Where?' gasped Daisy, clutching his chest and looking up and down the street with fright.

By the time Vera reached the bottom of the metal steps leading to Connie's front door, the handful of pills Chastity had put in her tea were really having an effect. The floor beneath her feet seemed to be swaying, as did the stairs in front of her. It took a few attempts to finally grasp hold of the undulating handrail.

'Come on Florence old girl, you're not beaten yet. This must be the place.' She conquered the rail, but when she put her foot on the bottom step, it bounced back off again. 'Oh, how fabulous, the stairs are made of jelly! Big black jelly stairs, wobble-wobble!' she laughed. To her amusement, the steps laughed back.

Lost in space and time, it was anybody's guess how long it took her to reach the front door, but reach it she finally did. 'Here we are then. Come on, little key. Now, three keyholes. Which one could it be?' The keyholes darted fervently around the door like naughty fireflies. Surely one of them must open the door, she thought. 'Eenie-meanie-mynie... lemon-squeezy, pig and a poke.' It was testing her nerve beyond the norm. 'Bloody bastard keyhole, keep still! KEEP STILL! Ah, there we are then.'

As she turned the key, the door clicked open. She pushed it further to a loud creek. Inside was darkness, but she could sense she wasn't alone. Eyes were watching her and she could hear a low, deep growl. As she stepped over the threshold, a giant wild tiger ran at her in slow motion from out of the abyss. She could hear a long drawn out scream echoing from her own lungs as the beast leapt at her shoulders and pushed her backwards onto the metal walkway at the top of the stairs. It tore at her relentlessly, ripping at her clothes through to the bare flesh beneath. Growling, biting and snarling like a demon from the very depths of Hell.

Managing to clamber shaking to her feet, she finally freed herself from the creature and bounced her way back down the jelly steps to safety.

Nigel calmly watched her from above as she ran frantically in the direction of light. With a quick lick of his bollocks, he turned proudly and trotted merrily back into the darkness of Connie's lounge.

Connie meanwhile, was doing some snooping of his own. He crept discreetly through the busy crowd towards Fifi's office. It wasn't easy, as every few yards one of the patrons grabbed him, asking to have a photo taken with him or offering to buy him a drink. It was unusual for Connie to turn down alcohol, but he didn't have much time to do what he had to do and get back to the dressing room unnoticed. As he approached the small corridor leading off the main area, he glanced up at the stage. Chastity was mid-flow, cruelly impersonating Katie Melua - though looking more like her grandmother. Strumming at a fake guitar he sang, *'There are nine million bicycles in Beijing... but fuck all else!'*

Connie looked to see where Madame Fifi was. He could just see the top of her head through the throng. Chastity nodded slowly from his clearer viewpoint, a signal that the coast was clear. Connie took a deep breath and darted into the corridor. He unhooked a barrier rope with the sign swung beneath, "No Entry – Private", and re-hooked it behind him before jumping swiftly into the office and closing the door.

The room was untidy. Paperwork was strewn everywhere, as were odd garments of clothing and junk jewellery.

'To think they called me a messy bitch!' he said under his breath. Glancing up at the clock to time himself, he thumbed quickly through the papers around the room looking for anything that may give a hint of Vera's true identity. Then he tried a three-tier filing cabinet, but it was locked. He hurried behind Fifi's desk and opened the drawer. Taking out a random stack of paperwork and placing it on the desktop, he began flicking through. Suddenly the door swung open and in walked Madame Fifi. She looked as shocked as he was. They both held their breath momentarily waiting to see what the other would do.

'What is the meaning of this?' Fifi finally snarled, slamming the door behind her.

'Ah! Fifi... I err...'

'This is an outrage! How dare you help yourself and fiddle about in my drawers? To invade my privacy in such a way. All my sacred secrets. You snooping weasel, I will have you shot!'

Connie's mind was racing. He was famous for being able to talk himself in or out of practically anything, but this was going to be something of a challenge.

But at that moment, Vera tore into the room. She was crying so profusely that she ran straight into the back of Fifi who flew across the room and stopped with a thud against the opposite wall, knocking the Diana Ross picture smashing to the floor.

Connie and Fifi both looked at her then each other in disbelief. Vera was in shreds. Her clothes were in pieces, hanging in shards from her shoulders. She had scratches that had drawn blood all over her face, arms and hands. She had patches of dirt everywhere and her hair looked like she had been dragged backwards through a garden hedge. She let out a long gargled, frantic scream.

Here, have your bloody key back!' she cried, throwing it across the room at Fifi. 'If you want to

120

know about this Michael, search his flat yourself because I've had enough!'

'What happened to your face?' Even Fifi was shocked.

'You didn't tell me he had a bloody tiger up there, did you?' Connie was now even more shocked than before. Vera was talking about his flat.

'Nigel?' he asked.

'I don't care what its bloody name is. I'm a private investigator, not Steve fucking Irwin! I'm off!' With one last scream of rage she spun on her heels and left, slamming the door behind her. Silence hung heavily in the air. It was now Connie who was outraged.

'Oh yes, it all becomes clear now. I'm the snooping weasel, but you've hired a detective to search my bloody flat! I may have the morals of an alcoholic shoplifting hooker, but you lady are something fuckin' else!' He didn't wait for a reply. Throwing his handful of paperwork into the air, he raged out of the office and back to the dressing room.

A week later Chastity, Michael, Connie and Daisy were about to accompany Edith to her husband's wake. Connie was getting very frustrated trying to lock his door.

'Is that a new double-lock?' asked Chastity.

'Yes, it's very tight. Just like my arse!' Suddenly with a loud snap, the lock turned. 'Ooh, that was hard. Just like the man who installed it!'

'Look, can you just get your mind off sex for five minutes,' scolded Chastity. 'We're on our way to a wake, for Christ's sake and you've already made us late with all your fiddling about!'

'Well I'm not leaving without double locking my door. I'm not having all and sundry wandering around my flat. Though Nigel is very good, isn't he?'

'I told you he was a great guard cat,' said Michael.

'You must be very proud of your pussy,' smirked Connie. 'I know I am of mine!'

'Jesus wept!' cursed Chastity, taking Edith's arm and heading down the stairs.

Finally they arrived at Edith's sister-in-law's posh suburban home. It wasn't a comfortable experience for Edith after the stony relationship they had shared for so many years. The wake was all a bit too calculated and civilised, with classical music, wine and Champagne, and a cornucopia of dainty fancies and vol au vents, most of which Daisy had already eaten in the first ten minutes. Despite being respectfully dressed in black, they stood out amidst the throng of smart, elegant mourners chattering politely. Chastity put his arm around Edith. She appeared very nervous, if not a little distracted.

'Who are all these people?' he asked her gently, trying to distract.

'I don't know. I doubt my Bert knew 'em neither. It's all show for her benefit. And this music's enough to make you wanna fuckin' cry, ain't it?' Chastity tightened his hug.

'Why are you having it at his sister's and not your own home?'

'It wasn't my idea, it was her'n. Taking control again 'cause she thinks I'm doo-lally-tat. She never wanted him to marry me in the first place.'

'It's a very posh house,' said Michael. 'She must have a few bob?'

'No, it's not Eileen's money, it's all Derek's. That's why she married him. Though he says it's all tied up in stocks.'

'Ooh, I wish I was!' Connie quipped. Chastity kicked him in the ankle.

'A Stock Broker?'

'That's the one. Trouble is she's forgot where she came from. Dyes her hair rustic turnip and thinks she's royalty.' Trying hard to not cry, Edith took a small bottle of pills from her pocket and popped one into her mouth.

'What are those pills you're taking?' asked Chastity, concerned.

'They're a tonic. I bought 'em in that new shop next to the betting office.'

'Edith dear, that's a pet shop. Let me see them, come on.' Chastity held out his hand to take the bottle. A look of shock came over his face as he read the label. 'Edith, these are Bob Martin's. They're supposed to be for dogs!'

'Oh!' Edith gasped. 'Do you suppose that's why I keep dreamin' about Lassie?'

'You can't take these,' said Chastity putting the bottle into his pocket.

'I've swallowed it now.'

'This is not good. Perhaps you should eat something. Connie, get her a sandwich.'

What do you want Edith – cheese, ham or Pedigree Chum?'

At that moment Eileen approached. 'Look out, here she comes,' said Michael.

Sensibly dressed in a brand new Marks and Spencer two-piece anthracite suit with sensible skirt and beaded jacket, Eileen glided towards them with an air of self-appointed aristocracy. Thatcher-esque hair swept on top with small but expensive pearl earrings, she walked with one hand held ahead and her wrinkled emotionless face tilted back slightly, just enough to enable her to look down her pinched nose at whoever she spoke to.

'Look at that choreography!' marvelled Chastity quietly, nudging Connie's arm.

'Who does she think she is, Bea Arthur?' Connie replied.

'Not drinking, are you Edith?' snapped Eileen. Her voice was hard with a guarded fake middle class accent. 'I don't want a scene. So who are all these people? Brought your friends have you. Safety in numbers?' Chastity and Connie delighted in this kitsch suburban caricature. Edith, on the other hand, had seen it all before.

'This is Chastity, Connie and Daisy, and this is me new daughter Lulu.' Eileen tilted her head back further.

'Very unusual, four men adopting women's names.'

'She calls us by our stage names.' Chastity stepped in supportively. 'We've no airs and graces when it comes to our Edith.'

'I'm sure she wouldn't notice if you had. Knew my brother Albert, did you?'

'No, we're here for Edith.' said Daisy, still chewing on the latest of several sausage rolls.

'And the buffet, evidently. Well, I'd like to say it was good to meet you all...' With that she turned and glided away. Michael was shocked.

'My God, how uncomfortable was that?'

'I'm sure that was a wig. Don't you think that looked like a wig?' said Daisy, starting on a crust-free ham sandwich. Chastity's fascination had turned to anger.

'Why do you let her speak to you like that? I'm surprised motor-mouth here didn't say something.'

'It's not my place. This is Edie's day.' said Connie. Edith was more rattled than before.

'That's why I don't have nothin' to do with her. Told you she was up her own arse, didn't I? Still, you can pick your arse, but you can't pick your family.'

Michael's focus had been on the subject of family considerably over the last couple of weeks. He'd felt he was beginning to understand its meaning. But this was a side of families he hadn't anticipated. Aside from their little group, Edith seemed isolated from everyone else in the room.

'So, are you alone now, Edith? Have you got children?'

'No duck, you're my daughters now. I fell when I was sixteen. Little boy. Marvin. But he died soon as he was born. Still, I was too young really. Bert had to get permission from me Dad to marry me at that age. But that's what I've got in common with Mrs F.'

'Fifi? How do you mean?' said Chastity, intrigued.

'Well, she lost a baby, didn't she?'

'She probably ate it!' Connie was still angry about Vera the detective.

'Oh, she's not that bad,' said Edith, patting Connie's arm. 'Gave us something in common. Reckon that's why we get on so. She puts up with all me foibles, you know. And then there's you, lost your Mum and Dad.'

Michael nodded. 'I often wondered who they were and how they died.'

'Didn't the orphanage tell you?' asked Chastity.

They said I'm probably better off not knowing, so I try not to think about it. Anyway, I've got enough problems right now as it is.' There was a short silence, interrupted only by the sounds of distant chatter and Daisy eating.

'Were you with Bert when he died?' asked Michael gently.

'Yeah, he started talkin' to himself about the olden days. You'd have thought I wasn't in the room. Going on about our first date together he was, under the railway arch on Tower Bridge Road, just across from the vinegar factory.' She smiled to herself, remembering. 'That was where I got hooked.'

'Ahh, hooked on romance?' Chastity mused.

'No, shaggin' outside. And then he went on about when he took me to see The Beverley Sisters at Streatham Ice Rink. Then all of a sudden he spat his teeth out. They shot right up in the air and landed on the sideboard. Made me jump it did. Then he just farted and he was gone.' She looked up at Michael poignantly. 'But the fart smelt funny.'

'How do you mean?' asked Michael.

'It smelt of death!' she cried, turning to sob into Chastity's chest.

'Oh Edith, darling. Come now, you said you wasn't going to cry.'

126

'Yes you're right, I did,' she said, pulling herself together and dabbing her eyes with a screwed-up lump of tissue. Connie looked mournfully at Chastity wiping a small tear away from his own eye. Attempting to lighten the mood, he grabbed a tiny sausage on a stick from the table and held it out to Edith.

'Here look, reminds me of someone I used to go out with!' he grinned comically. She smiled back.

'Yeah, and Bert. He only had an inch and a wrinkle.'

'That's better,' said Chastity. 'Don't let that bitch sister-in-law see you downtrodden.'

'Anyway, where's the loo, Edith?' asked Connie.

'Gawd alone knows. There's four apparently. Wander round long enough, you'll fall in one of 'em.'

'I'll come with you.' Chastity put his remembrance card down on Daisy's buffet table and followed Connie into the crowd. 'Let's try the hall,' he suggested.

'Or just piss on the bed like Nigel,' said Connie.

'Don't temp me!' This amusing picture in Chastity's head was interrupted by something far more sinister. 'Connie wait! Shh!' Pausing just feet away from Eileen speaking to a tall thin grey-haired man, they listened.

'And as if that's not bad enough, she's brought the whole bloody circus with her. Yes! There's even a big fat negro called Daisy. Have you ever heard such a thing, a man called Daisy? And black? I'll have to bleach the cups when they're gone. She'd have been better staying at home in that God awful council house. Netto crisps and peanuts around a plastic Lazy Susan! Doesn't bear thinking about, does it? I just hope they all leave before one of them uses the downstairs cloak.'

Chastity couldn't believe what he was hearing. He then saw the look of boiling point on Connie's face. He had seen this look before – when Connie lunged at Lettie's coffin in Lewisham. Restraint was needed.

'Don't! Just don't interfere,' he said holding Connie by both shoulders. 'Remember what you said, this is Edith's day. Family can be so cruel, betraying poor Edith like that.'

'Sound familiar?'

'You mean Lettie? I'm beginning to wonder. I think we'd better just leave.' Connie had a vengeful look in his eye.

'I need a dump first. I'll be back in a minute.'

Chastity re-joined Edith, Michael and Daisy.

'Find it, duck?'

'I think we've outstayed our welcome Edith. Come on love, we'll take you home before we head back where we belong. The Circus, apparently!'

'You what? Someone said we belong in a circus?' said Michael angrily, slamming his drink onto the table.

'Drag, Lulu love. There's a time and a place,' explained Chastity. 'And this isn't it. It's like that Billy. Don't expect the simple folk to understand.' Edith was used to being insulted by Eileen, but to think that the very people who were there to support her in her hour of need had been spoken of in such a way, was a step too far.

'It's her ain't it? Slaggin' off my daughters? I ain't having that!' Slamming both hands on the table,
128

she shouted loudly across the room in Eileen's direction. 'Oi! Face-ache? What you been saying about my family?' The crowd fell silent. Everyone looked at Edith, then at Eileen and then parted, creating a corridor between the two. Eileen spun to make eye contact with her.

'Edith dear, have some decorum. You're not at Bingo now.' She was outwardly calm, but Edith had been pushed too far to play these games any longer.

'Don't you "dear" me, you stuck up cow! Underneath all that la-di-da you're just as Saveloy and Pease Pudding as the rest of us.'

Eileen's eyes widened. 'How dare you say such things? And at my brother's wake.'

'I'll tell you how. 'Cause I don't forget. You didn't like Bert, and he didn't like you neither. 'Cause you're just an old lush who don't give a toss about anybody but yourself.'

Eileen was so outraged that she forgot herself, slipping back into her native Bermondsey accent. 'You can talk, you common little tart! He only married you 'cause you got yourself knocked up. And you even got that wrong, didn't you? You're a disgrace to the family, and to women. At least I made something of myself.' The crowd looked on aghast and open-mouthed, first at Edith then at Eileen, back and forth along the human corridor like spectators at a tennis match. This was a side of Eileen that her social circle had never seen in the twenty-five years she had lived in the Avenue.

She stormed towards Edith and stood nose-to-nose, eyes flaming like fire. Her husband pushed his way through the crowd to break up the row.

'Ladies, please! Darling, this is your brother's funeral.'

'She's no lady, Derek,' growled Eileen.

'Oh, you don't know the half of it, sunshine!' Edith put her hands on her hips. Eileen could sense that her well-choreographed, tidy little world was about to be shaken to the core.

'Edith, no!'

'Call me a common little tart? Haven't you ever wondered what she was doing in Blackpool just after you got married?' Derek looked confused. He didn't know Edith as well as Eileen did. He was beginning to see Eileen in a different light too.

'She was with her sick aunt.'

'Sick aunt? Is that what she told you? Was she fuck! She was up there gettin' shafted from all angles by that Curly Cartwright from the butchers up Jamaica Road!'

'Edith!' Eileen grasped at her pearls in horror.

'And she spent most of your engagement putting it about. By the day of your wedding, her ankles had forgot about each other. Wasn't so posh then, was ya?'

Eileen and Derek's teenage son had heard all of this. 'Mum? Dad?'

'He's not your father!' continued Edith. 'We never did fathom out which one that was, there were so many. She was like a ride at Alton Towers. Everyone had a go! Put a penny in the slot and she'd keep going for hours.'

'You vindictive little tramp!' screamed Eileen, grabbing hold of Edith's jacket. 'I ought to punch your fuckin' lights out. Spreading lies in my own house.'

130

'Lies, are they? Lies? At least I was faithful to my husband. And me daughters might be drag queens, but they're there for me, hell or high water. I've got no money and I live in a council house, but I've got me pride. And I've got me family!'

Connie returned. Ripping Eileen's hand from Edith's jacket, he pushed his way between them to face her off.

'She's right, you know, us circus folk stick together.'

'That's right!' Chastity stood at his side. Connie continued, 'Eileen, dahhhling! Thank you so much for having us freaks at your gorgeous little do. We would stay longer, but.. and I'll surprise you now... we have a life!'

Edith reached forward on impulse and ripped the wig from Eileen's head. She cried out in horror, trying to cover her nylon skullcap with both hands. The crowd gasped. Even Daisy stopped chewing. Edith poked out her tongue as a finale to her revenge.

Connie continued, 'But before we head back to our sparkly little caravan site off the A2, I just thought I'd help a little with your... what were we calling it... downstairs cloak?'

'My God, what have you done?' gasped Eileen, pushing through the crowd towards her loo. Connie and his entourage followed.

'A speciality of us circus folk. It's called "Le Petit Maison Marron". Shit on walls, sweetie. Everyone's doing it!'

To her absolute horror, Connie was true to his word. The toilet looked as though the drains had double-backed and redecorated every surface with several shades of effluence. Everyone stood for a moment silently aghast, as The James Last Orchestra played a soft light ditty from two small speakers in the toilet's ceiling. Eileen was annihilated. As her legs gave way beneath, her blood-curdling scream could be heard from several tree-lined avenues away.

Connie grabbed Edith's arm and linked it with his to escort her proudly out of the house. 'Come on girls. Our work here is done. Piped music in a loo?' he mocked. 'It was like having a shit in a lift!'

CHAPTER FOURTEEN

A few evenings later, Connie and Chastity were escorting Michael downstairs from Connie's to Sugar Sugar. He was for the first time wearing the yashmak that Connie had made for him. It was very hot and itchy and a little tight around the face, but it did make him feel safer in the street. The only alternative was for him to put his full face of makeup on before he left home, but for the sake of three minutes discomfort undercover, this was far simpler than carting half the contents of the dressing room upstairs.

'I don't know how you expect me to cope with this!' moaned Michael with a mouthful of fabric.

'What did she say?' said Chastity.

'It's that yashmak. I think I might have made it too tight around her mouth. I'll have to keep that pattern in case you ever need one.'

As they turned the corner onto Old Compton Street, they could see Daisy on the door up ahead, handing out promotional Sugar Sugar flyers to passers-by.

'Here's a good opportunity to see how well your disguise works,' whispered Chastity. Go up to Daisy and see if she recognises you.'

Michael was as keen as anyone to know if his new costume would protect him. As Chastity and Connie held back he marched on ahead, silently stopping right next to Daisy waiting for a reaction. But it wasn't the reaction he was expecting. As Daisy turned and saw the black-cloaked figure with expectant eyes staring back at him, he screamed and jumped backwards against the glass doors, throwing the flyers up into the air. The door flew open behind him and with a loud thud he landed on his back in the lobby, a bumbling quivering wreck.

'Daisy! It's me, Lulu. This is my new disguise.'

Daisy was in floods of tears. 'Oh, don't creep up on me dressed like that. You look like the grim reaper. I've been watching Buffy the Vampire Slayer on UK Gold all afternoon!'

'Don't be silly, Daisy! I think you're over-reacting a little,' scoffed Michael.

He managed to get Daisy to his feet as Connie and Chastity arrived at the door. But as Michael turned to face them, instead he found himself face to face with his own personal grim reaper. It was Billy.

Michael froze. He couldn't move, he couldn't even breathe. And he couldn't take his eye off Billy.

'Excuse me gents… and lady,' he said, looking at Michael.

The shock was too much. Michael's brain had disengaged and his mouth was working on instinct. 'Shit! Fuck!'

Billy looked at him a little oddly, but continued. 'Have you seen this bloke? His name's Michael. Michael Small,' he said, showing a photograph. Connie and Chastity looked at each other open-mouthed. They all new instantly who this was and what they were dealing with. Daisy wanted to cry in shock, but managed to restrain it to a small sharp fart.

'Jesus! Fuck!' shouted Michael.

134

'What's the matter with her?' said Billy. Chastity knew he had to keep the situation calm or this could be extremely dangerous, not just for Michael but for all of them. 'Oh, err... you'll have to excuse our friend... Shakira Shakira. She's, erm...'

'Got Tourette's Syndrome,' Connie assisted.

'Shit! Shit! Bastard!'

'You ought to get her seen to.'

'Yes, perhaps. If we can just get her inside.'

'Wanker!'

Billy shook his head and returned to the matter in hand. 'If you see this Michael, here's my card. Give me a bell. There's a reward.'

'How much?' asked Connie.

Michael couldn't believe the betrayal. 'Bitch!'

'Shut up, both of you!' Chastity stepped in. 'Why do you want this... Michael, did you say his name was?'

'Let's just say we've got some unfinished business. Call me.' Billy handed Chastity his card and walked away.

'Tosser!' Michael sniped after him.

Two massive shocks in a row were too much for Daisy to bear. He started bawling, but his feelings did not compare to Michael's at that moment. He was still rooted to the spot like a statue. Unintelligible rambling was coming from under his head-dress and his eyes had glazed over.

'What's he saying?' said Chastity, concerned.

I don't know. I think he's speaking in tongues.' replied Connie.

'Look, can we just get Lulu inside? Stop crying, Daisy! Come on Lulu, love.'

'I... I can't move. I...' they tried to guide Michael, taking an arm each. But he was glued to the pavement.

'She's got that epileptic shock. It must be like death creeping up on you, poor cow,' said Connie, looking at Michael's eyes darting about randomly.

'Now you know how I felt!'

'Shut up, Daisy, pull yourself together. Help us carry him inside. This could be worse than we thought. If Billy finds out that was Lulu in the yashmak, and that we've been hiding her, we'll all be swimming with concrete flippers!'

It took quite some time to get Michael to the dressing room. Connie likened it to trying to carry a dead body after rigor mortis had set in. The problem escalated further when they couldn't bend him in the middle to sit him down.

'Jesus, Mary and Joseph, that was all a bit too close for comfort. Daisy, go get Lulu a brandy from the optic. A double! And get yourself one while you're at it.'

'And me!' Connie called after Daisy as he left for the bar. 'Lulu? Lulu, can you hear me in there? It's your sister, Connie. The pretty one?'

'Get that thing off her face so she can breathe,' said Chastity, tugging at the back of the hood. Michael made a choking sound.

'Not like that you silly bitch, you'll strangle her!' Connie lifted the hood off from under his chin. He gasped for air. He was bright red and dripping with sweat. 'Are you with us, Dolly?'

'She's gone a very odd colour, you don't suppose she's having a heart attack?'

136

'It's us, Dolly. The Sisterhood. Your family.'

Michael had caught his breath. 'Fine family you turned out to be! You'd take the reward and hand me over to Billy.'

'Now you're just being silly.' said Chastity.

'Yes, silly girl. The shares are worth much more!'

'Just go away, leave me alone!'

'You're making things worse, Connie.'

'She's hysterical. Shall I...'

'No! Don't slap her again, just give her a minute to calm down.' Daisy returned with a drink for everyone.

'Here you are, Lu. Get this down you. Put hairs on your chest. Mind you, you'd only have to shave them off again.'

'Daisy love, go upstairs and keep guard. Make sure that Billy's not snooping around up there.'

'What, on me own?' he gasped.

'You're supposed to be the doorman! Just do it.' Still snivelling, Daisy grabbed a nearby platform shoe as a weapon and left for the front entrance.

Michael was broken. 'God, so much stress! This is insane! I can't do this anymore. I just can't! Why is this happening to me?'

How had he allowed himself to reach this point? Just a couple of weeks ago his life was unhappy but at least it was stable. He knew who he was and where he stood. He was suppressed under Billy's thumb, but at least it was in a world he understood. Now he was sitting in one of the campest venues in London wearing a yashmak and expecting to be hidden by two drag queens. Why did he believe Chastity and Connie would be able to protect him? Or even really want to? He began to cry. Chastity could feel his pain.

'Doesn't it just break your heart? It's like her whole world's falling apart and there's nothing we can do but try our best to hold it all together. Ooh, I feel like Greer Garson in Mrs Miniver!'

'What about tonight's show?'

'She's in no fit state to do a show. We'll have to cover for her. You can do her song.'

'What again? Stick a mop up my arse and I'll do the floors at the same time!' Despite her catty remarks, even Connie was sad for him.

The atmosphere in the dressing room that night was very heavy and depressing. Even though he wasn't in the show, they kept Michael with them, if only to make sure he didn't do any damage to himself. He just sat in the corner staring at his hands resting in his lap. After a few slapstick attempts to joke and lighten the mood, Connie and Chastity admitted defeat. Nobody really spoke for the rest of the performance. Edith popped in now and again with a fresh cup of tea, though Michael never touched a drop. She even sat stroking his hair and holding his hands, humming to him like a baby.

Finally it was time for the closing song. While Chastity sat silently removing his makeup in the mirror next to Michael, Connie checked his brow beaten cowgirl costume in the mirror.

'Do I look like a country star?' he asked, flicking back his long blonde pigtails and adding another freckle with an eyebrow pencil.

'You're half-way there!' Chastity bitched.

With a fake basket full of washing under his arm, Connie put the evening's events to the back of his mind and climbed the steps to the stage to perform his best huckleberry ballad.

'When times are hard, and life seems at an end. 'Cause your old man's been sent to jail again. The kids are being bastards and the baby wants your tit. The toilet's blocked, you're touching cloth and need to have a shit!'

To demonstrate, he squatted and blew a raspberry.

'The money's tight, you've got no food to eat. The rent man's knocking and you'll be on the street. And after having five kids, you can't get another guy. 'Cause unlike cash, you're not so tight, his dick won't touch the sides!

'It takes a woman to keep it all held in. When we can't face the stinking world we're in. It takes a woman to have to turn to gin.'

He pulled a bottle from amongst his washing and took a swig, spraying a mouthful of fake gin out across the audience.

'It takes a woman!'

Towards the end of the show, Michael had come to his senses a little, though he still felt ill. Chastity had been watching his reflection in the mirror and noticed him smile a little at Connie's song echoing in from the stage. Being confronted by Billy had been such a horrifying shock, but after some thought he realised that he would have to find the strength from somewhere to continue, if only because it was not possible to turn back.

Edith was still cradling him as Connie removed his makeup.

'Alright then, Duck?' she asked, giving his hand a squeeze.

'I'm sorry. I did fall to pieces a bit, didn't I?'

'Mummy's poor little Orphan Annie.'

'The girl they invented child-bashing for,' added Connie.

'Do you feel a bit better now, Lu?'

'Actually, I feel like shit. I feel like I can't breathe. Like Shelley Winters on that boat.'

'The Good Ship Lollipop?' offered Edith.

'No you daft old bat, that was Shirley Temple! He means Shelley Winters. Poseidon,' said Chastity.

'Shelley Winter? Is that her off The High Chaparral, with the lace curtains?'

'Edith may be here, but she's not all there!' smiled Connie, wiping the last of his lipstick off with a hand towel.

'Let's be serious for a moment,' said Chastity. 'I think we need to get Lulu away from Soho. Hiding away upstairs all the time will just make things worse.'

'What do you suggest, Dolly?'

'Well, I wasn't going to say anything, what with everything else. But we've been offered a Ladies Night on our day off and I think we should just jump in my new car and go do it.'

'Fifi will go absolutely ape-shit if she finds out we're working somewhere else.'

'Fifi's not going to know. And it'll be good experience for Lulu. She's got some new songs to try and she needs to escape for a bit and have a change of scenery. Somewhere we can keep an eye on her.'

140

Connie could see the sense in what Chastity was suggesting. 'Where is it?'

'Basildon, in Essex.'

Michael jumped to his feet with horror. 'Oh no, no! I'm not going to Basildon. It's too near Billy!'

'But Billy's here in Soho looking for you. The last place he'd expect to find you is closer to home.'

'Tit has got a point, Lu,' said Connie, trying to be supportive. Well, as supportive as he could be with a more exciting personal plan on his mind. 'Anyway, that's nearly a week away yet. But tonight, we're having... a séance!' Michael sighed. He wasn't shocked at Connie putting himself before everyone else, he was growing used to it.

Connie continued. 'For my anniversary... You've forgotten, haven't you?' But Chastity hadn't forgotten.

'Here you are.' He reached into his coat pocket and pulled out a greeting card. 'To commemorate the passing beyond the veil of your idol – Her Royal Highness, Miss Dusty of Springfield.'

'A card? For me? What have I done to deserve this?'

What have I? What have I? What have I done to deserve this?' sang Chastity and Connie.

Michael thought for a moment. He had never been to a séance before. Maybe this could be his chance to get some real advice about his situation. 'I'd quite like to see if my Mum and Dad would talk to me. What about you, Edith?'

'What Bert? No! He hardly spoke to me for the last twenty years. I don't see no reason why he'd wanna bloody start now!'

'Well I've got a few things I'd like to say to Lettie!' said Chastity. 'She's planned and schemed, manipulated and toyed with all of us. She's turned our world upside-down and set us all against each other. Oh yes, I've got things to say, alright! I'm angry and I want answers. And if she wants a fight from beyond the grave, so be it!'

CHAPTER FIFTEEN

Later that night in Connie's lounge, they prepared for the séance. Michael was still a little shaky from bumping into Billy, but he was determined to see if he could make contact with his parents, or at least find out if they were alive or dead.

'Right, let me move my sewing machine and we can use that coffee table,' said Connie, kicking aside a pile of newspapers from under the window to make room. Switching on a table lamp, he closed the curtains.

'You ought to clear up this mess you dirty bitch. There's bits of costume and shit everywhere. It's like a bomb went off in Carmen Miranda's head-dress!' said Chastity.

'It's not all my mess! Everything on that sofa's hers. Now, for a séance we need lots of bits of paper with letters of the alphabet around the outside.'

Connie took a pad of paper and a marker pen from the top drawer of his cabinet. He pulled several pages out and then tore them into smaller pieces.

'How big do they have to be?' asked Michael.

'Each one has to be about as big as a Turkish Delight.'

Sitting at the table, Connie wrote one letter of the alphabet on each piece and spread them around the outer edge alphabetically and facing into the centre. 'Then we all put our fingers on an upturned glass in the middle and the spirits spell out what they want to say by moving the glass around the letters.' He took a whiskey glass from the cabinet, blew off the dust and placed it rim down in the centre of the table.

'Suppose you get one that can't spell?' asked Chastity.

'They're not all backward like you!' Connie smirked, rummaging through a pile of fabric remnants by the side of the sofa. He selected a dark purple flowery silk and laid it over the shade of the lamp to dull the light. Then he went into the bedroom.

'So what are you going to say to Lettie?' Michael asked. Chastity wrinkled his brow.

'If I could just get to the bottom of how she died, we might have a clearer picture of what's going on. And why she wanted you at Sugar Sugar.'

'And why she left the shares and all that money to me?'

'Precisely. Oh by the way, I didn't tell you did I? I looked it up in my diary and six weeks exactly to the day from the wake it'll be Halloween.'

'Does that mean anything?' Michael fidgeted in his seat as a cold shiver ran down his spine.

'Where Lettie's concerned, who can say?'

Connie returned with half a dozen candles. He placed them onto the table and handed Chastity a cigarette lighter. He lit them one by one, handing them to Connie to place around the room.

'If she knew she was going to be hit by a car before it happened, then it can't have been an accident. So who murdered Lettie?'

Still downstairs in the bar, Edith was frantically running her mop over the tatty floor across the front of the cabaret area.

144

'Edith, darling? Please try to leave some of the pattern on the floor if you can. I need it for tomorrow,' said Madame Fifi, emerging from the office corridor.

'Sorry Mrs F. I'm in a bit of a rush. We're doing a séance tonight up Connie's on one of them squidgy boards,' she answered excitedly. Fifi shook her head.

'But whatever for? When you are gone, you are gone. Is it so good to contact your husband so soon? You should have taken the evening off as I suggested.'

'I'd rather be busy. Anyway duck, it's not for me. Chastity wants to talk to Lettie.'

Fifi was suddenly suspicious. She still wasn't sure who Michael was, but she did know that this whole thing had started after Lettie's wake. If they were to find out any information before she did, she would lose her advantage.

'Talk to Lettie? Why?'

'Something to do with her accident. And Connie wants to talk to Dusty Springfield, said he'd have liked to have met her. Did you ever meet her?'

'Meet her? I slept with her. We all slept with her! What time is this séance?'

'Midnight. The witchin' hour! That's why I'm rushing. Are you comin'?'

'No, dear. Someone might tie me to a stake and set fire to my pigtails again. I'll just be there... in spirit.'

Back in Connie's lounge, they were still debating Lettie's untimely death.

'What I don't understand is, if this was murder, why aren't the police investigating it?' said Michael, puzzled.

'They think it was a hit and run,' said Chastity. 'They can't find the car, so they've closed the case.'

'But Lettie said about the accident in her eulogy. Don't you think someone should report it?'

'No one's going to believe a load of dippy drag queens, are they?'

Chastity was probably right. Michael sat on the sofa staring at the Ouija board. Perhaps if spirits did visit they would all get some answers. Then a chill ran down his back as he realised that this whole séance was about to take place next to his bed!

'Here, these ghosts won't all hang around when we've finished, will they? I've got to sleep here tonight. It will give me the willies.'

'Someone needs to!' Connie quipped. 'Anyway, if it's a ghost in a blonde beehive, then it's probably Dusty Springfield. The worst she's going to do is sing at you!'

'So, she actually died on this day, did she?'

'Yes. On this very day in nineteen-ninety-nine she collected her sparkly little angel wings and rose through the clouds to that spectacular, glittering hair salon on high.'

'And her being only twenty-four hours from Tulsa!' laughed Chastity.

'So you're a bit of a fan then?'

'Bit? Bit?' growled Connie comically. 'I was her GREATEST fan!'

Chastity shook his head and sighed. 'You see Lu, I get this every year. Last year was worse.'

'Why, what happened?' Chastity moved around the sofa closer to Michael.

'I get this phone call at four in the morning telling me she can't cope and wants to drown herself. Five o'clock I get to Trafalgar Square and there she is, sitting in the fountain wearing my Dusty frock. Heavy mascara streaks down her face like a badger, with a bottle of vodka in her hand singing "I Just Don't Know What To Do With Myself".' Chastity thought for a moment. 'Where is that frock, Connie? It's not in the dressing room. In fact, I haven't seen it for ages.'

'Well, I haven't got it.'

Michael was intrigued. Though he had never done fancy dress in his old life, costumes were now part of his job.

'What was it like?'

'Well, fabulous of course! It was a pale blue French sequin Empire Line, in at the waist with those really pointed tits they had in the sixties, you know? It was lined in silver with matching sequins across the bust. Split up the thigh with a train to die for.' He drew a diagram on his own body as he talked Michael through.

'Sounds fantastic!'

'And matching five-inch shoes. Although I was going to go for the six-inch, you know to get that tall thin look she had. But the colour wasn't right, so I settled for the fives and glued some bits up the back of the heel just so I could do that dramatic turn at the end, do you know what I mean?'

Michael nodded enthusiastically. 'I'd love to try it on. So where is it now?'

Connie was finding this all highly amusing. 'Listen to Mister Michael here, getting all excited about sequins. Steady Dolly, you're starting to sound like a drag queen!'

Chastity continued. 'Anyway, there's these two coppers by the fountain. Luckily they were Dusty fans, so we got away with it. She shagged one of them. It was useful at the time - got me off a parking fine.'

'Oh yes! Marcus, with the enormous truncheon,' Connie smiled to himself. 'I've still got his hand cuffs. If you really want information about Lettie's hit and run, you should talk to him. Get him to look it up on their database. I wonder where he's stationed now?'

Edith and Daisy finally arrived somewhat out of breath.

'Don't panic, we're here!' said Daisy, throwing his hands up and air-kissing everyone.

'I got your bit of shopping,' said Edith, walking a carrier bag through to the kitchen. 'I went local. I didn't go up that twenty-four hour supermarket, 'cause I don't know what time it shuts.' Chastity and Connie looked at each other, confused. Unaware, Edith continued, 'They didn't have any donuts Daisy, so I got you a tin of salmon. And there weren't any double cream Connie, so I got you two singles.' Chastity shook his head despairingly.

'Perhaps we should put her back on the Bob Martin's,' Connie shrugged.

'My mate Mandy from bingo did one of these séances once,' said Daisy, taking off his jacket. 'She contacted a woman who died on the Titanic.'

148

'The Titanic? Ooh, golly wars!' cooed Edith, joining them at the table.

'Really? What happened?' asked Michael.

'The spirit said she couldn't understand where all this water was coming from.'

'You're taking the piss!' Connie laughed.

'No straight up, on my mother's eyes. Then she said she'd been on a diet. But if she'd known they were going to hit an iceberg, she wouldn't have bothered skipping her pudding.'

'Have you done this before, Edith?' Chastity was concerned for how she would react, so soon after her husband's death.

'Ooh yes! It was all the rage in the blackouts. Used to pass the time, you know. My Uncle Ernie would fill the glass with whisky. Then they'd all have a sip to wet the spirit's head. 'Course, I was only a child. But if nothin' happened, he'd fill it up again.'

'Did you make contact?'

'Ooh no. By the time we got warmed up they were always too pissed!'

'Right, is everyone ready?' said Connie, keen to begin. 'Daisy, grab two chairs so we can sit all the way around. And switch off the main light.' Daisy did as he was asked, positioning a chair for Edith.

'I'll need a pillow,' she said. 'My piles are playing me up something awful. All just hanging there they are, like a set of ruched blinds.'

'Have you got a drawstring to pull them all up in the morning?' Michael laughed, fetching her cushion.

'Ooh, isn't it creepy with just the candles?' whispered Daisy.

'It's gotta be dark like this,' said Edith, sitting. 'If it's too bright and they don't like the look of ya, they won't say nothing.'

'Now, all put one finger on it.' Connie leaned forward and gently touched the bottom of the upturned glass. They all watched expectantly then followed his lead. 'Is there anybody there?'

A few moment's silence was broken by an enormous fart from Daisy. Everyone moaned, though it did make them all laugh.

'I'm so sorry, that'll be my kebab.'

'Kebab? It smells like a rotting corpse!' cried Chastity, covering his mouth with his hand. Connie stood up from the sofa and coughed.

'Daisy! I can taste that.'

'I can't help it if I'm always hungry. I'd have a gastric band if someone offered me one.'

'Yeah, and a donut!' bitched Connie.

'I'm full of gas. Do you think it weighs anything? If I had two stone of gas then it'd mean I was really two stone lighter than it says on my scales.'

'Unless it's Helium lifting you up. Then you could be four stone heavier!'

'Come on, let's be serious now, you two,' snapped Chastity. Everyone settled back into solemn silence. Chastity took as deep a breath as he could manage with the kebab fumes, tipped his head back and closed his eyes. 'Is there anybody there? Lettie? Are you here? Tell us about your murder.'

'Are you there, Dusty?'

Everybody screamed with shock as the phone rang. Connie picked it up. 'Hello? Oh hi! Sorry Dolly, not tonight I'm in a séance. Yes! It's all healed up now. Ooh, I know!' He laughed dirtily. 'I know!' he squealed, laughing even dirtier. Chastity was losing patience.

'Oh, for feck's sake!'

'Got to go. No you hang up! No, you hang… Oh, he has!'

'Who was that?'

'One of me boys. Wanted a shag tonight. See how Dolly here on my sofa's cramping my style?' Michael looked down, embarrassed. Chastity elbowed him a nudge of support.

'What's all healed up? Can't be your arse?'

'My lip. I caught it in the zip of his crotch. Couldn't get his attention, nearly choked to death. It could have been me you was contacting here tonight. Imagine… death by penis!'

'Can we be serious?'

'It was serious. I had lips like Jackie Stallone for a week.'

'We need to contact Lettie! Settle down, this is important.' Calm returned as everyone once again placed their fingers on the glass. 'Is there anybody there?'

The room was silent other than the sound of breathing and the faint din of London traffic in the distance. They waited nervously for something to happen.

Suddenly, Nigel sat bolt upright in his basket. Facing the door to the hall, he arched his back and hissed. Fingers on the glass began to shake. A loud click came from the hall followed by the creak of the front door opening. Daisy began to quietly panic.

'Oh my God, oh my God! They're coming, they're coming!' Daisy warbled.

'Shh!' said Chastity, himself a little shaken. 'Is there anybody there?'

Still touching the glass, they all stared intently at the door, waiting to see what would arrive from the hall. As the candlelight flickered, the door appeared to wobble slightly, making it all the more creepy. Nigel let out a long, deep growl. The door swung slowly open, and to everyone's horror, there stood a figure. It was a glowing woman. Her dress seemed to have a life of its own, sparkling and glistening in shades of blue, white and yellow, reflecting shards of shimmering light around the whole room. In the dimness and blinded by the sparkles, they could just make out a blonde beehive piled high upon the figure's head.

Their breathing quickened as they all took their fingers from the glass and sat silently back. Rooted to the spot with fear, none of them could tear their eyes away from this eerie apparition as it took a step into the room. Even Nigel seemed glued to his basket.

'Dusty?' asked Connie nervously, choking back tears.

'Jesus H Christ, it's her! It's really Dusty!' whispered Edith under her breath. The ghoul took another step forward, put its hands on its hips and spoke.

'Boo!'

Pandemonium broke out in Connie's lounge. Screaming hysterically, everyone jumped to their feet and ran in every direction possible away from the ghost. The coffee table and whiskey glass flew into the air, as did every letter of the alphabet, zig-zagging slowly back to the ground like tic-a-tack. With a screech Nigel ran at the ghoul, Michael into the kitchen and Connie into his bedroom. Edith pulled her jumper over her head while Daisy did his best to fit in the gap between the television and the cabinet, knocking several tacky ornaments and lit candles from the shelves in the process. Chastity meanwhile managed to reach the overhead light switch. Flooded with light, Dusty Springfield's ghost took on a new identity.

'Wait, wait! That's not Dusty. It's Fifi! What are you doing up here snooping about?' Chastity was angry now. So was everyone else as they returned to the centre of the room.

Fifi stood her ground in the face off as best she could with a giant beehive balanced on her head. Poised with hands on hips and her nose in the air, the front of the costume suddenly felt heavier than usual. She looked down to see Nigel staring back up at her - back legs swinging freely, with a front claw hooked into the tip of each of her ample breasts. She shimmied her torso and he fell free to sit at her feet snarling. She was suddenly a little uneasy.

'Have you made contact with my darling Lettie?'

'Darling Lettie? You hated her! Why do you care?' Chastity yelled, throwing his arms into the air. But then he stopped and looked her up and down, eyes now better adjusted to the brighter light. 'Hold on a minute... you thieving chavy toad! That's my feckin' Dusty frock!'

'You've just let yourself into my flat!' screamed Connie. 'I'm getting sick of this. I should have changed the Yale lock too.'

'I was worried about you all,' said Fifi. 'It's not safe to dabble in all this hocus-pocus. My darling Sisterhood, I wanted to protect you.'

'Protect us?' Chastity was having none of it. 'You were snooping, you lying cow!'

Fifi had been caught out. Too proud to admit defeat, she became bitter.

'You have nothing that I do not already know! Do you think you can outwit the great Madame Fifi? How dare you?'

'Aw shut up, you rancid old corpse!' spat Connie. 'And give him back that frock. It's not one of Sugar Sugar's costumes, Tit had that one before she came here.' Fifi's eyes narrowed.

'Have your damn frock! It's way too big for me anyway, I had to pinch it up the back with bulldog clips.' Michael grabbed Chastity as he lunged towards her, fists flying. Undaunted, Madame Fifi spun on her heels and left.

CHAPTER SIXTEEN

They arrived in the dressing room the next night to find Chastity's Dusty frock and wig in a heap in the middle of the floor.

'Sloppy bitch couldn't even be bothered to hang it up,' moaned Connie, yanking a hanger from one of the rails.

'Leave it on that chair, I'm going to open the show with it. I promised I'd do a tribute for you and that I will,' Chastity said, winking at Michael.

'You're right, it is a lovely frock,' he said, holding it up in the light.

'You wait till you see it on!'

An hour later to the delight of a packed house, Sugar Sugar was transported back to the mid-sixties as Chastity's Atlantic Soul backing track spun into play. Dressed head to toe as Dusty reincarnated, he stormed powerfully to the microphone centre stage and threw his arms dramatically into the air.

'*Hey there, I'm Dusty, and I am addicted to hairspray,*' he sang, in a commanding but wispy voice. Madame Fifi looked up from her conversation at the bar and grimaced. As she turned and walked briskly out to her office, Chastity poked out his tongue.

'*My voice is husky 'cause I breath in far too much hairspray. Most of the time I'm off my face, because I'm always breathing fumes. That's why I wave my arms around, to keep my balance in these shoes.'* He demonstrated the famous Dusty windmill hands, flipping his head to one side.

'*And there ain't nothing I can do about it! Woah, woah.'* His audience squealed and applauded with delight.

'*It's such a problem. I keep needing more and more hairspray. My head's like a soufflé, and I can't get through the door. Hairspray.'* He grasped either side of the huge blonde do, gurning at the front row.

'*I never sleep – I can't lay down, because my head just bounces back. I have to carry hairspray round, so I can keep myself awake.'*

Pulling a can of hairspray from within the back of his enormous wig, he feigned a long spray up his nostril. Then with a drunken stagger, he slurred into the microphone, '*And there ain't nothing I can do about it!'*

A couple of days later, Sugar Sugar was closed for its monthly deep clean and maintenance overhaul. Usually this was a good time to dress rehearse some of the more complicated new bits for the show and to give the dressing room a tidy. But sitting at the mirror putting the finishing touches to a full face of makeup, Chastity had other plans.

'Well, tonight's the night Lu, your first Ladies Night. Are you excited?'

'No! Can't you go and do it without me?'

'The main reason we've taken the booking is to get you out of Soho for the day.'

'Some people are so ungrateful!' Connie bitched, flicking through costumes on one of the rails.

'Well, I think that's about all of them in those two cases. I've put all the wigs in this laundrette bag.'

'Great. And I've got the makeup here for touch ups,' Chastity confirmed.

'And I've packed her yashmak, 'cause she won't have makeup on when we come home.'

'And Sally from the newsagent's let me borrow her parking permit, so my car's just around the corner in Soho Square. Everyone ready?' Connie's nod was quite excited compared to Michael's. Chastity continued, 'Now, Fifi was here but she went out shopping. Let me just double-check so we can get these costumes out unnoticed.'

Chastity left the dressing room for a scout. There were several men in white overalls, steam cleaning every nook and cranny of the bar, but no sign of Fifi. He returned to the dressing room and grabbed a case.

'Come on, let's do it!' They all headed out.

Upstairs at the entrance, Chastity put his shoulder to the huge glass door and stepped outside, holding it open for the others. As Michael stepped into the sunlight, he walked smack bang into Fifi.

'Err...''What are you doing?' she stabbed suspiciously. 'What have you got in those bags?'

'Ahh,' Chastity bumbled. 'Lots of alterations to do. For the new bits in the show.'

'And why are you wearing makeup?' Fifi's eyes narrowed. Chastity looked to Connie for support.

'Testing a new brand. What do you think?'

'I think I'm being taken for a kipper that's giddy.'

'Hmm. I thought I could smell fish,' Connie bitched. Chastity glared at him.

'Come on then, lots to do. Bye then Fifi, missing you already!'

Michael and Connie followed Chastity up the street and around the corner towards the flat.

As he walked, Michael glanced across the road. There was a figure on the opposite corner, though he couldn't tell from a distance if it was a man or a woman. It wore a long black coat and sunglasses and a hat over a heavily bandaged face. It seemed to be watching him. A shiver ran down his spine as he quickened his step.

They ducked around the corner and stopped. Chastity peeped his head back around. Fifi had gone inside.

'All clear, come on,' he said, leading the way back out to Soho Square. Michael sheepishly looked back to the corner where he had seen the figure. It had vanished.

An hour and a half later, they were on the road. Chastity stared intently ahead as he drove. Connie sat next to him clutching an atlas with an addressed piece of paper inserted as a bookmark. Michael was sitting in the back trying not to throw up.

'Are you sure we've come the right way? This looks like a council estate,' asked Chastity.

'I know where I am. My sister's shacked up with some long-distance truck driver around here somewhere,' said Connie.

'I didn't know your sister lived in Basildon.'

'This is Vange. Rhymes with flange. Chucks off a bit like one too,' said Connie, winding his window shut. 'You know, I think Ladies Nights are my favourite.'

'It's because of the male strippers, Lu. She's only coming with us for the cock.'

'And for the cash. I do have some morals.'

'This woman could ride for England. She's had so many men, it's hard to keep up with them all. Shagging that must be like throwing a saveloy up Rotherhithe Tunnel.'

'There are times in my life when it all gets too much. I climb off, limp over to the mirror and say to myself, "Connie, why do you allow so many men to use your nubile, naked self in this way?" Then in a flash, it comes to me. I'm a woman of substance performing a public service.'

'To the masses!'

Connie smiled back and nodded in agreement, crossing his legs. 'Sometimes I swallow so much juice, people think my nose is running!'

'Ooh, you filthy whore!' said Chastity, slapping him on the leg.

'I use mouthwash!'

'It's your flange that needs bleaching. Scraping along on the lino every time you take your drawers off, it's unhygienic. Lulu's feeling sick enough as it is.'

'Hark who's talking? At least I don't have to kick my arse back like a train on a dress every time I turn a corner!'

Chastity ignored him. 'How're you getting on, Lulu love?' he asked caringly, glancing at Michael in his rear-view mirror.

'I can't handle this! Basildon's too close to Billy's Bar. What if someone recognises me? Can't I just stay in the car?'

'No one will recognise you,' said Chastity. 'That's why we all put our makeup on before we came out. If you still feel sick, just stick your head out of the window.'

'Like a Rottweiler!' smirked Connie.

'Shut up, you! I just thought it would do you good to get away from Soho for the night. Feeling like you're constantly being watched.'

Michael recalled the creepy figure. He hadn't intended to say anything, but since they were talking about being watched.

'When we left the club tonight, there was someone watching me from across the road.'

Chastity was concerned. 'Who? Not Billy?'

'No. Their head was all bandaged up.'

Connie laughed. 'Aw my Gawd, she's seeing things now! That's stress that is. I saw a programme about it on telly. When people get anxious they can hallucinate. She's lost her marbles! They've probably fell out of her ear-hole. She has got big ears.'

'Shut up! SHUT UP!' Michael shouted. He knew what he had seen, but just the slightest possibility that he may be losing his mind was enough to make him want to give up.

'Yes, shut up!' agreed Chastity. 'God, Connie! Sometimes it amazes me just how venomous you can be!'

Suddenly with a huge jolt, the car ground to a halt.

'What you stopping for?' said Connie.

160

'It isn't me, it's the car! Oh, Feck, feck, feck! What are we going to do now? It's curtain up in an hour!' Thick black smoke began billowing from under the bonnet. 'Do you know anything about cars, Lulu?'

Connie was angry now, too. 'I don't know why you bought this heap of shit from Fifi. I told you it was a death trap when you got it.'

'Have you run out of petrol?' Michael was beginning to panic. In a broken down car in full makeup in the middle of a rough Essex council estate, he felt trapped like an animal in a cage. As if it couldn't get any worse, through the fog blowing over the roof from the bonnet, he could see blue flashing lights approaching from behind.

'Oh Jesus, it's the filth. They're pulling over,' said Chastity, panicking.

'It's only a dog unit,' observed Michael.

'Same police, just uglier!' shrugged Connie.

Chastity wound his window down as an officer approached. Glancing around inside the car, he raised his eyebrows and coughed.

'Good afternoon, sir. And what have we come as today?' he said sarcastically, taking a notebook and pencil from his top pocket.

'We're on our way to work officer. We're drag queens. We've a show to do.'

'Your car is it, sir?'

'Yes. I bought it a short while ago.'

'Would you step from the vehicle please sir, and let me see what's in your boot?'

'It's just my foot. And there's one in my other boot too!' Chastity chuckled in a vague attempt to lighten the moment. The policeman wasn't amused.

'We haven't got time for this!' he cursed under his breath. 'You stay here, Lulu. Connie, come with me. Keep the other officer busy, speed things along a bit,' he said, climbing from his seat.

The policeman walked to the front of the car and inspected it, rubbing his hand suspiciously across the rim of the bonnet. Chastity opened the boot while Connie approached the second officer on the pavement. Then the policeman re-joined Chastity at the rear as he unzipped one of the cases.

'So, just dresses and wigs then?' he said, making a note in his book.

'Yes, that's it. Like I said, we're on our way to a show.' The officer scratched his head.

'Course, my brother-in-law used to dress in women's clothes.' Chastity was in way too much of a hurry for this.

'You don't say?'

'My sister's, in fact. She didn't like it. Said it stretched all her seems out of shape. Saw him once... strangely erotic.'

'Yes, wonders never cease. Look, we are in rather a rush. Can you suggest how we might fix this and get under way?'

The policeman shook his head. 'Sorry sir, but you won't be taking this car anywhere?'

'Is it that bad?'

'I'm afraid we will have to tow it back to the pound. It matches a car on our list. Hit and run in South London several weeks ago, I believe. It was the drag thing that reminded me. The victim had something to do with drag queens. You can see that the whole front has been replaced from the wing mirror. And it's had a re-spray, the colour underneath
162

is different.' Chastity followed him back to the front of the car. 'Look, here. Not a very good job, which is probably why there's smoke billowing profusely from under your bonnet.'

Chastity didn't know what to say. A shiver ran down his spine. Surely this couldn't be the very car that killed Lettie?

CHAPTER SEVENTEEN

The policeman paused from making notes and looked up at Chastity. 'You seem very quiet under the circumstances, sir?' he said, with a suspicious tone.

'Oh... I just... just had an epiphany.'

'Is that an alcoholic drink, sir?'

'No, I mean... I've just realised that we're going to be late for work unless we can get a lift. I don't suppose there's a chance...'

'Sorry sir. You'll have to make your own way. You've got about twenty minutes to remove anything you need from the car before the tow truck arrives. Now, if you could just confirm your name and address?'

Chastity's mind was racing. If this was the hit-and-run car, then it must have been Fifi that murdered Lettie. But why? Surely, just not liking someone isn't motive enough for murder?

'Yeah, six-three. We need a tow truck to Vange, repeat Vange,' the copper said into his radio, as he walked back to the squad car. Michael and Connie joined Chastity as he lifted the cases from the boot.

'They're towing the car,' he said. Michael was horrified.

'What? We're on an Essex housing estate wearing makeup. They can't just leave us here, can they? Oh God!'

'Marcus was just telling me.' said Connie.

'Who's Marcus?' Chastity asked.

'Marcus with the big truncheon. Trafalgar Square fountain? That's him, he's been posted to Vange. Small world, ain't it? We was only talking about him the other day. He's coming round mine tonight after the show. He's got a new piercing he wants to show me, said it will knock the crowns off me teeth!' Chastity put his head in his hands. 'No, listen, Tit. I'll ask him to look up Lettie's accident. You see? I'm performing a public service!'

'It's Fifi!' said Chastity.

'How are we going to get to this show then?' said Connie, looking up and down the street. He could see curtains twitching and as self-confident as he was, he knew they wouldn't be safe there for too long once the police had left.

'Shut up, shut up! You're not listening,' interrupted Chastity. 'Fifi killed Lettie!'

'Eh?'

'They think this car was used in a hit-and-run a few weeks ago. I bought it from Fifi a week after Lettie died. That copper said it's been re-sprayed and everything. That's why they've arranged for it to be towed away for forensic investigation,' said Chastity, frowning. Michael was momentarily distracted from his fear.

'But why would Fifi do that?'

'I don't know,' sighed Chastity. 'I'm not sure what to do about it. If she did kill Lettie, there must have been a very good reason.'

'The haggard old trout hated Lettie, that's why,' said Connie. 'And the feeling was mutual. Don't you remember? Lettie said that if she'd had the affair with Creighton Cross instead of clack features, she would have done everything better?'

166

'Perhaps that's how it happened,' added Michael. 'By shagging this Creighton Cross she got the shares and the half a million.'

'Ergh, he was eighty-odd. It would be like sucking on a stale prune with no pip!' Connie cringed.

'But Lettie liked older men, and for that amount of money?' It was beginning to make sense, Chastity thought. But would it be enough to make Fifi want to kill her? It all seemed so dastardly. 'Ooh, I feel like Jean Peters in Blueprint For Murder!'

'NOBBY!' Connie shouted suddenly into the distance.

'What?' said Michael.

'It's my sister's boy, Nobby. Look, over there! That's his ice cream van, I know it is. It's his new job, selling cornets and ice-lollies to all the feral Essex brats. He can drive us to the show!' As the police car pulled away, Chastity and Michael watched in amazement as Connie's skinny legs carried him off, waving and shouting towards an ice-cream van parked against a kerb further up the street. 'Nobby! Nobby!'

Chastity put his head in his hands again. 'Oh for feck's sake no! Not spotty Nobby Banister? Surely he can't have a driving license? That can't be right in a sane world.'

'Why? What's wrong with him?' asked Michael nervously.

'Oh he's harmless enough. It's just hard to believe the sperm that created him beat twenty million others!'

A little out of breath, Connie finally reached the van. A small group of children had formed a queue at the hatch. Connie pushed in front.

'Nobby. It's an emergency,' he said to the tall, skinny teenager within.

'Hello, Uncle Connie!' he answered, scratching at his facial acne.

'Uncle Connie?' questioned the mother of one of the children, sarcastically. Connie ignored her.

'The car's broken and we've got to get somewhere.'

With a goofy cigarette-stained grin, Nobby climbed out of the serving hatch. As he dropped from the counter to the pavement, the back of his red and white striped uniform caught on the ridge of the Perspex sliding door, pulling his shirt inside-out up to his armpits.

'What are you doing, you nonce? Get back in, we need to use the van!' Connie scolded. But this was easier said than done. Arms trapped above his head and face covered, Nobby flapped around like a fish in a net for a while, banging the back of his painfully thin rib cage against the side of the van until Connie unhooked his garment and pulled it back down. He stood for a moment, matching cardboard hat hanging upside-down in front of his face, held in place only by the mass of cheap gel spiked into his mousy blonde fringe. Connie pushed it back into place and repositioned his bow tie from his mouth to its original position around his scrawny neck.

'Oi! There's a queue here, mate!' complained the mother.

'Oh piss off!' Connie spat back. 'Nobby we need your help. You're going to drive us.'

'Come away from the disgusting pervy old man, Beyonce,' said the mother, pulling her child from Connie in his outlandish drag makeup.

168

'Did you say old? How dare you!' Connie scolded back.

'People like you ought to be put away,' cursed the mother.

'That's what I told your old man, the last time he fucked my arse!' As the woman yanked all of the children away from the van with disgust, Connie turned back to Nobby.

'Is it an emergency, Uncle Connie? Like International Rescue?' Connie knew his nephew wasn't the brightest sparkler at bonfire night, but he had wheels and they had a show to get to. Nobby wiped his nose on the back of his arm and turned to face the waiting children. 'Sorry kids, no more ice-cream,' he shouted after the now crying children. 'Thunderbirds are go!'

Five minutes later the van was pulled up behind Chastity's car. He lifted the last bag from the boot and slammed it shut. 'What am I supposed to do with my car keys? Do I have to wait for the tow truck?'

'Let them figure it out when they get here,' Michael stressed. 'Let's just hurry up and get out of here!'

'I've got a really bad feeling about this,' said Chastity, passing one of the cases up to Nobby inside the hatch. Connie was more enthusiastic.

'What's the chances of Nobby and his ice-cream van being gobbing distance away when we need a lift? I tell you, its fate!'

'Speaks Miss Serendipity Nineteen-Fifty-Four!' bitched Chastity as they all climbed into the van.

'How sweet of you to remember,' cooed Connie, fluttering his enormous eye lashes.

'You don't even know what that means, do you?'

'No. Now Nobby, this is International Rescue and it's your job to save the day and get us to The Guild Hall in Basildon as quickly as possible.'

'Jesus wept!' Chastity shook his head in despair. 'Let me drive, for feck's sake!'

'I've found it on the map,' said Michael, joining Connie in the back.

'Lulu's Jeff Tracey, Chastity's Gordon and I'm Lady Penelope.'

'OK. Who am I Uncle Connie?'

'You're... Spencer... Tracey, in Thunderbird... the rocket thing!' Connie jumped into the front seat as Chastity climbed aboard.

'No, this is wrong! I should be Lady Penelope and you should be the baddy for sending us all to an early grave in this contraption!'

'I don't mind being Gordon,' said Michael, just grateful they were no longer marooned in this dangerous neighbourhood. Chastity glanced at his watch impatiently.

'Look, in the name of all that's holy, just DRIVE!'

With an air of determined authority, Nobby crunched the van into gear, spun the steering wheel and stamped the accelerator to the floor. Everyone screamed with shock as the van leapt forward ten feet into oncoming traffic, barely missing the back of Chastity's car. It bounced onto the grass bank beyond, roof scraping through the branches of a tree. Chastity plunged to the floor beneath the dashboard, as did Connie, landing on top of him. Michael, who had been standing behind, somersaulted to the back of the van and launched up onto the counter, banging his head on the rear window.

For Nobby this was a big adventure. Laughing hysterically, he spun the wheel back in the opposite direction, driving around the tree and back into the oncoming traffic. Just as Connie managed to pull himself back into his seat, Nobby turned right and mounted the pavement to avoid an oncoming lorry.

'He's insane! Make him stop, make him stop!' Chastity pleaded, sliding along the floor and knocking the passenger door open. Head hanging out, he gasped with horror as he realised his face was only a foot away from the fast moving pavement beneath.

'LAMP POST! LAMP POST!' shouted Connie, grabbing Chastity's feet and pulling him back in. Nobby slammed on the brakes as the lamp post battered the door shut, narrowly missing Chastity's head. Michael catapulted from the back counter and landed on the floor with a loud thud. He dragged the length of the van on his shoulders, finishing in a heap on top of the suitcases behind the front seats, as a torrent of cornet cones emptied on him from the shelf above.

Putting the van back into gear, Nobby rocketed along the pavement, hitting every object in his path before swerving back out across the oncoming lane of traffic and over to the left. Michael was rolled at high speed back to the rear of the van on hundreds of small round multi-coloured bubble gums, which rained on him from all directions. Chastity meanwhile lunged back towards the driver pedals, jamming his foot under the brake.

'Red light! Red light! RED LIGHT!' Connie ducked his head into his lap. Nobby tried to stop, but with Chastity's foot in the way, nothing happened. Instead, he leaned forward to switch on the van's chimes. They sped across a traffic junction as cars spun to a halt, frantically sounding their horns.

'Missed!' Nobby shouted from his window with glee.

'Your foot's under the brake! Get your fat piggy trotter out from under the brake!' warned Connie, grabbing at Chastity's trouser leg to pull it out. With a jolt, he freed it from the brake, but got it caught through the steering wheel. Michael clung desperately to the wobbly shelving as the bubble gums turned his shoes into roller skates.

'Bloody Hell Nobby, get off the main road!' Connie demanded. Nobby attempted to take a left turn, but with Chastity's leg through the middle of the steering wheel, the best he could manage was to miss the turning altogether and mount the left hand pavement. The chimes, which were now straining at double speed, gave little warning to the scattering pedestrians.

Two hundred yards and several smashed wheelie bins later, the van ricocheted off a tree and came to a dead stop, trapped under the awning across the front entrance of a nineteen-sixties community hall. A loud metallic scraping sound accompanied that of broken springs, as the speeding chimes finally sang their last. Chastity and Connie once more disappeared under the dashboard, followed momentarily after by the launderette bag full of wigs and Michael, still clinging onto the now detached shelf. There was a moment's stunned silence.

'Well that didn't go too badly considering,' said Connie.

'Are we dead?' asked Chastity, a little muffled from under the pile of bodies. Michael was a jabbering wreck. Shaking like jelly, he pulled himself up and over the seats, back into the rear of the van. Connie pushed himself up and looked around outside. The sign on the front of the building read "Guild Hall".

'No, we're here!' he announced, kicking open the battered passenger door and jumping out. Michael clambered out of the van as quickly as he could, considering his nervous disposition. He sat on the pavement with his head between his knees attempting to get his breath back. His heart was pounding through his back as he tried to comprehend what had just happened. Chastity crawled out from the van floor and joined him on the pavement.

'Don't worry, not all away games are as stressful to get to,' he said, apologetically. Connie brushed himself down, checking his makeup and hair in what was left of the van's wing mirror.

'Nobby, park this roller-coaster in the kerb like normal people and get the bags,' he said calmly, before turning and walking gracefully into the hall.

CHAPTER EIGHTEEN

Fifteen minutes later, the Ladies Night had begun. Connie and Michael were in the dressing room preparing for their first spot while Chastity was on stage getting the show underway. The main body of the hall was a very large room about the size of an indoor tennis court. The Guild Hall may have seemed a glamorous name some forty years ago when it was first built, though now it was rather tatty. At dozens of tables sat a few hundred loud and rowdy women, pouring gallons of alcohol down their throats in anticipation of the obligatory male strippers they'd seen on the posters outside.

Standing with a radio microphone on a large podium at the front, Chastity began his warm-up routine.

'Well here we are in this fashionable... pig sty,' he said, looking around disapprovingly. 'Downtown Basildon. Any local girls here this evening?' An approving cheer came from his attentive audience. 'You know, I've always liked Basildon. It's very central. Five minutes in any direction and you can be somewhere feckin' interesting!'

Back in the dressing room, Connie was holding an empty crisp bag over Michael's mouth to stop him hyperventilating. As if the nightmare journey in Nobby's ice-cream van hadn't been enough, he was now about to perform on stage in Essex, way too close for comfort to Billy's social circle. And Connie's nephew fidgeting about wasn't helping.

'Nobby sit still! And stop picking your scabs and eating them!' scolded Connie.

They'd been put in the hall's sports locker room. Dozens of testosterone-soaked wooden rails with coat hooks were now strewn with glittering costumes and wigs. A row of grey metal lockers were grouped together in one corner. Bright orange plastic corporation chairs with black metal legs surrounded the walls, and two dark-wood tables had been pushed up against a large wall-mounted mirror, by way of a dressing table. They had already emptied their collective array of makeup in front of the mirror next to a stack of cans of Pepsi supplied by the venue, some of which sat atop ice in a steel bucket. At Connie's request, they'd also given Michael a brandy.

Now, deep breaths, Dolly. It's not as bad as it seems. You can do this. Remember, it was like this your first night at Sugar Sugar and you got through alright.'

'It's not the same! I know some of the women out there from Billy's bar. They're going to recognise me, I know they are!'

'What, fully made up in a long red wig and white trouser suit? They've all been knocking back alcopops for three hours, they probably don't even recognise each other!' They could hear Chastity's run of one-liners interrupted by a loud scream from the audience. 'That'll be the first stripper arriving. Just chill, you'll be fine. I'm sorry I called you a Rottweiler,' said Connie in an attempt to calm him down.

'That's OK. I wouldn't mind if I could lick me own bollocks.' The door flew hastily open and in ran a male stripper.

'I bet he can!' came back Connie, licking his lips.

Michael looked around and couldn't believe what he was seeing. The man was over six feet tall with short-cropped black hair, wearing a leather jacket and tight 501 Levis tucked into metal-studded biker boots. His bright-green eyes sparkled as he removed his crash helmet, and his whiter-than-white perfect teeth glistened into a big smile as he looked back. Michael felt his heart flutter. He'd never seen a man so good looking this close-up before.

'I bet he can what?' responded the stripper.

'Lick your own bollocks. Alright, handsome?' Connie said, tip-toeing to kiss him on the cheek.

'Connie! I didn't know you were going to be here tonight. You still up Fifi's gaff?' he said, putting down his sports bag and removing his jacket. Michael could see the outline of his muscular shoulders and big chest stretching the fabric of his crisp white shirt.'

'Yeah - same old shit, different day. This is our new sister Lulu L'Amore,' said Connie, putting a finger under Michael's chin and snapping shut his awe-struck open mouth.

The stripper smiled at Michael and winked. 'Hello gorgeous!' he said, leaning forward to kiss him on the forehead. Michael was agog yet at the same time a little intimidated by this man's openness and utter gorgeousness.

'Oh, er... hello.'

'She's single, a virgin and looking for a man just like you!' Connie continued.

'I'm Stud Muffin. And sorry, Lulu darling, you're very beautiful but I'm straight. I drink from the furry cup.'

'Arrgh! I'm gonna be sick, blarrgh!' retched Connie, pretending to throw up in the ice bucket. Stud Muffin glanced at his watch.

'How long have I got?' he asked. Connie batted his huge eyelashes.

'If I recall, about ten thick and juicy inches!' Stud Muffin laughed. Michael laughed too, though it sounded more like a nervous guinea pig squeaking. He turned his head away squirming, only to realise that he now had a full frontal view in the mirror of the stripper tearing open the popper studs on his shirt and unbuttoning his fly.

'No, about twenty minutes, Dolly. You'd better start getting ready now. What costume you doing tonight?'

'Copper.'

'Huh, the irony!' laughed Connie, enjoying seeing Michael gush with embarrassment. 'Now drink up that brandy Lu and try to relax a bit. You'll be fine once you get on stage. I can't do the next song without you, can I?'

Michael beckoned Connie to move closer and whispered, 'What's Stud Muffin doing?'

'Getting ready for costume,' Connie giggled, mischievously.

Michael was trying very hard not to look, but it was impossible. Wearing nothing but tight white Aussie Bum underpants, this tanned and sculpted, tattooed god checked himself in the mirror. Michael took another discreet look over the rim of his brandy glass while taking another sip, glass rattling against

178

his teeth as his hand shook. The stripper saw him, and with a broad smile and a cheeky teasing wink, swiftly dropped his underpants to the floor. Michael coughed and spat his drink up the mirror. Devoid of reaction, Connie handed him a tissue.

'What was it you said that first day?' he whispered in Michael's ear. 'Where d'ya put yer willy? I bet you've already thought of a dozen places you'd like him to put that monster!'

'Who the fuck is that?' interrupted Stud Muffin, nodding towards Nobby sitting in the corner biting the nail on his big toe.

'Oh sorry, that's my nephew,' said Connie, walking across and slapping Nobby up the back of the head. 'He's not been fed since we let him out of his cage.'

Michael's eyes watered as brandy burnt into the lining of his nasal cavity. He'd never seen a flaccid penis so large, not even on the internet. Stud Muffin grabbed a Razzle magazine from his bag, sat down and began masturbating.

'Now is that or is that not just the kind of stud you'd like to muff?' teased Connie.

'But he's naked! And... and he's reading porn!' Michael put his hand to his brow trying desperately not to watch, but even without looking he could still hear it. And as if that wasn't distracting enough, the hunk wanted to chat.

'So Lulu, how long have you been working with Connie and Chastity?'

'Oh, err... just over a wank... WEEK!' He stuttered, in disbelief at his own reply.

'Are you enjoying it?'

'Oh, yes! Oh, sorry you mean Sugar Sugar? Well, I erm... It was hard... I mean difficult, at first. I didn't think I'd pull it off. The job... I mean. I thought they'd suck me... SACK ME!' This was even more painful than his ride in the ice-cream van. Connie on the other hand, was in his element.

'Building up a lovely shine on that, Mr Stud Muffin!'

Meanwhile, Chastity was on stage whipping the women into a frenzy with filthy jokes.

'His dick was huge! It was like a baby pig. Don't get me wrong, I like a big one as much as the next girl, but I'd rather find a guy with a fourteen-inch tongue who can breathe through his ears!' The women screamed with delight at this bawdy language. 'So... blow jobs, girls? The trouble is, you don't know if it's going to taste of Dairylea till it's in your mouth and too feckin' late! And if you swallow, it all goes down in one lump like a raw egg!'

At the back of the hall through the darkness, Chastity could make out what appeared to be two men. 'Oi you, get out! This is supposed to be women only.' Jumping excitedly from their table, a group of women pushed the men out through the door and pulled it shut behind them.

'Good girls! I hate it when men interrupt me, don't you? If they can't manage the job in the first place they should just roll over, go to sleep and let us get on with it properly!' The girls cheered and applauded their approval. 'Anyway, where was I up to? Oh yes! So we're in his car and he's climbed on top of me, pumping away. And my legs were flapping up and down. He said, "Why are your legs doing

180

that?" and I said, "Give us a chance to take me feckin' tights off!" Then caught in a wave of unbridled passion I shouted, "Hurt me! Hurt me!" So he shut my left tit in the car ashtray!'

Back in the dressing room, Connie was now dressed in the same white satin suit as Michael but with a long blonde wig. Stud Muffin was doing up the buttons on his police costume.

'OK, Dolly. Me and Lulu are just going to do one song and then it's you. Is that alright?'

'Sure,' said the stripper putting on his hat. 'Can't keep my knob tied up too long now it's hard or it will go blue. And I've got another one in Billericay after this. What about him?' he said, pointing to Nobby.

'Eh? Nobby! Put yer willy away!' screamed Connie at his hapless brother.

'But he was doing it.'

'Yes but he's working! Now Lulu, deep breaths. You can do this. This is us, are you ready?'

'Oh, God!'

Chastity's applause was rapturous. 'Well, we've got a special treat for you now. They've just flown into Basildon from the Stockholm Archipelago this evening especially to entertain you. And if you believe that, you really are pissed! Put your glasses down and your hands together, welcome to the stage... ABBA!'

Leaving the locker room for the stage, Connie walked straight into the back of Michael, who was grabbing the doorframe with fear. Prising open his white knuckles, he shoved him hard in the back, throwing him precariously out into the auditorium. The women thought this was all part of the show and screamed with approval. Chastity handed the radio mic to Michael as he flew past, before walking off into the darkness to one side.

'Oi!' Connie shouted at Michael from the stage. The crowd roared as he sheepishly ran to join him. Then as the backing track began, with a deep breath Michael sang in his rehearsed Swedish accent.

'*My name is Frida. This is Agnetha. I know she looks the type you'd shag if you could get her. But she's impossible, she's unbelievable. And given any opportunity I'd smack her!*'

In true ABBA style, Michael span to face Connie, staring into his ear. Connie played it dumb, pretending his character couldn't understand a word Frida was singing.

'*Look what we're wearing. She thinks it's funky. She got the dress sense of a schizophrenic junkie. Remember she's a blonde, so don't expect a lot. That's why she married someone who looks like a monkey!*'

Michael turned to the front and ducked as Connie threw both hands out, missing his head by inches.

'*We may be dancing queens, but I am the talented one!*'

Michael raised a clenched fist as though about to strike an oblivious Agnetha. Then with their backs turned on each other, they bobbed up and down alternately like two figures on a barrel organ, mocking the song Super Trouper.

'*Pa pa pa, pa pa pa! Pa pa pa pa, pa pa pa!*'

Michael had been as nervous about this performance as he was his very first at Sugar Sugar, not just because he was afraid he may be recognised by one of Billy's Essex circle. Having to sing with an accent, in costume and with complicated choreography all at the same time had also been a terrifying prospect. But the adoration from the audience fuelled him to continue.

'She thinks she's special. So super-dooper. But she's as special as a super-pooper-scooper. She'd send an SOS, but I could not care less. Oh mamma mia, how I wish that I could lose her!'

Grabbing Connie by the waist from behind, they marched in unison across to one side of the stage and then reversed back again.

'Her head is empty. She's kind of hazy. And if you take a chance on her you must be crazy! If for the music you should thank her, then you must really be some kind of tone deaf wanker!'

Facing front they swayed from side to side.

'We may be dancing queens, but I am the talented one! My name is Frida. This is Agnetha. She's a cun...'

'Michael, is that you?' interrupted a petite woman standing directly in front of them. In the adrenalin rush of this complicated routine, he hadn't notice Tamara edging her way towards the stage. He was mortified.

'Tamara?'

'Michael!'

'Shit!' said Connie, as every woman in the hall jumped to her feet and cheered the end of the song. To one side of the stage in the dark, Chastity had been so engrossed in their new routine that he too hadn't notice Tamara in her sparkling black cocktail dress with matching high-heeled shoes.

'Bugger!' he said running over to Connie. 'Quick, quick! Get them both into the dressing room. I'll get the stripper on. What's his name?'

'Stud Muffin.' As Connie ushered an equally stunned Tamara and Michael into the locker room, Chastity snatched the mic and turned back to the women.

'Ok ladies, it's Willy Time! Put your glasses down, your hands together and welcome to the stage, Stud Muffin!' As the heavy beat of the stripper's music filled the hall, Chastity switched off the radio mic and ran after them.

Michael was in a blind panic. Of all the things he had predicted could go horribly wrong, this wasn't one of them.

'What the fuck are you doing?' said Tamara, throwing her arms into the air.

'Oh God, no! Tamara... I'm so, so sorry. Really I am,' Michael cried. 'You're my best friend. I'd never lie to you or do anything to hurt you, never!'

'But you're... a drag queen? I don't understand!'

'It was Lettie,' Chastity jumped in nervously.

'Who the fuck's Lettie?'

'*If I could fly,*' sang Michael.

'Oh, not that karaoke wanker!'

'But the wanker landed in a swimming pool and the eulogy said it was half a million!' Chastity bumbled.

'And I don't like tap dancers, so I punched the corpse and it jammed in the wall!' flapped Connie.

184

'And there was just two hours or we'd all be sacked, but he hadn't sung in a frock!'

'Because it was like ice-skating in the stilettos, but I had to get the Sugar Sugar shares instead of concrete shoes off the pier!' Michael was desperate.

'So they put pills in the detective's tea and Nigel ate her, but Billy saw Lulu in the yashmak!' said Connie.

'Who's Lulu?' Tamara was understandably confused.

'I am, but the car had a re-spray, because Fifi killed her! So we had to come in an ice-cream van!'

'And Fifi was dressed as Dusty Springfield at the séance...'

'Stop! STOP! I don't get any of this Michael, but I do hope you know what you're doing. I'm really worried about you.' She rubbed Michael's arm. As she looked up at him supportively and smiled, something else distracted her line of vision. 'Who's that? And what the fuck's he doing?'

Nobby was lying across the top of the lockers wearing nothing but his Power Rangers underpants. Connie strode across and grabbed him by the hair, pulling him crashing to the floor. 'Get dressed you dirty little bugger!' he shouted, slapping him across the face.

Removing his wig and placing it on the counter, Michael took Tamara by both hands and looked her in the eye. 'Tamara. I've got something to tell you. Huh, I don't really know how to say this. Err... I'm, err... I'm gay.'

'Tell me something I don't know!' she laughed. 'Oh, come here you silly poof and give me a hug! I've really missed you. But why didn't you tell me you wanted to be a girl? You could have borrowed some of my clothes.'

'Tamara love, it's just a job. Nothing more. I'm Chastity,' he said shaking her hand. 'And the skinny bitch who keeps slapping everyone is Connie. You see, it's a condition of Lettie's will. Your Michael's getting shares in the drag club where we work and half a million quid if he does this for six weeks. He wants to be a drag queen about as much as I want to be Joan Rivers' tampon.'

'But it's a lot of money!' said Connie. 'In the meantime, we've got to hide him from Billy-no-nut until he gets the cash. Then he can pay him off and find himself a man to give him a good shafting. Sort his fucking head out!'

Tamara stepped back in shock. 'Shit, I forgot about Billy. He's here! He drove us all up in the van.' This was absolutely the last thing Michael needed to hear.

'What? Oh God, no! He's going to find me and he's going to kill me! He's going to kill me!'

'Calm down, Dolly! You may be in drag but you're more of a man than he'll ever be. He's only got one bollock, remember? You'd come away from that still hungry!'

'We'll figure something out,' said Chastity. 'Was that Billy at the back of the hall earlier?' Tamara nodded. 'Where is he now?'

'He's probably in The Rose and Crown next door. Or he might be in the van in the car park. Shall I go and have a look?'

'Not just now, it'll look odd. Go back to your seat till the end of the show. But try to be inconspicuous.'

186

'Eh? What does that mean?'

'Don't look suspicious.'

'But the girls might already wonder where I've been.'

'Tell them you couldn't find the loo. Do your best, love, there's a good girl.'

'Thanks, Tamara. I owe you,' said Michael smiling sheepishly.

'You still owe me for last time, you tart! When you're rich and Billy's off your back, you can buy me a drink at that club of yours and we'll have a good laugh about all this. Right then – incon... spunkulous, was it?'

'That'll do, dear' said Chastity.

'Wish me luck.' Checking her appearance in the mirror, she tiptoed out the door.

'You know I like her, I really like her,' said Connie. 'Common as a shit in the kerb, but classy with it!'

Michael put his head in his hands and groaned. Connie and Chastity looked at each other unsure what to do to help. On impulse, Connie swapped his long blonde wig for Michael's red one, and throwing the cans of Pepsi out of the ice bucket, held it against his chest.

'Look, Lu... "Jack! This is where we first met!"' he said, doing his best Kate Winslet impersonation. Michael glanced through his fingers. 'You know... Titanic? Ice?' Though Chastity admired Connie's efforts to lighten the mood, it clearly wasn't working.

'Right, we need a plan, girls. When the show's finished, we've got to get Lulu back to the ice-cream van without Billy recognising her.'

Suddenly without warning, the door flew open and in walked Billy. Michael gasped with horror and jumped back, quickly grabbing Connie's blonde wig and throwing it on to disguise own his hair. Connie stepped protectively in front.

'What do you want? It's supposed to be ladies only here tonight. Get out!'

'What was that common little tart doing in here just now?' Billy snarled.

'What's it got to do with you?' Chastity growled back.

'She works for me.'

'If you must know, she thought this was the toilet. Why?'

'I want you to wind her up for me. It's her birthday today and I want you to lay into her. Go on, here's fifty quid.' He held the crisp pink note out to Connie who snatched it, shoving it into his cleavage. 'She's a lying little bitch and needs to be brought down a peg or two in front of all her mates. I want you to be really nasty. Anything you like.' Michael panted with anger ready to lunge at Billy, but Connie held him back. 'What's the matter with that faggot?'

'He's allergic to half portions of spunk!' snapped Connie. Chastity stepped in, pulling the money from between Connie's tits.

'Yes thank you, I'll take that. Leave it with us. Off you go then. We've got to get changed, and you don't want to see that now, do you?' He turned Billy by the shoulder and pushed him back out the door. Michael was alight with rage.

'Did you hear what he called her? I'll kill him! Oh God, I forgot her birthday. After everything she's doing for me.' Chastity handed him the cash.

188

'Here, take this. Buy her a present with it.'

'It's blood money!'

'Think of it as revenge. Don't worry. We're going to find a way to get rid of this Billy once and for all. He's going to pay for this. I'll make sure of it!'

CHAPTER NINETEEN

Later that night, Chastity and Michael sat in Connie's lounge with a cup of tea. It was impossible to ignore the sound from the bedroom of Connie having very loud sex with Marcus.

'How long's she going to be shagging that copper in there? I'm exhausted after that Ladies Night. I need to get some sleep!'

'Where Connie's concerned, it's anyone's guess. Oh, I'm so worried. Suppose it WAS my car that hit Lettie? They might think it was me that killed her!'

Michael put his hand on Chastity's. 'If Fifi did plough into her and she finds out you know, she might kill you too!'

'Ooh, I feel like Veronica Lake in This Gun's For Hire.'

Connie came out of his bedroom wearing a pink satin dressing gown trimmed with matching marabou feathers. Dropping himself in the armchair, he lit up a cigarette. Chastity was desperate for information.

'Did you ask him? What did he say?'

'You're in the clear, Tit. They've found no evidence on your car so you can go and get it back tomorrow,' he said, rolling his tongue around in his mouth. Picking up the ashtray from the coffee table in front of him, he spat. 'Oh, I think that was one of my fillings. He said he'd knock me crowns out! So what about Fifi? Are you going to challenge her about murdering Lettie?'

'Ssh! Keep your voice down!' warned Chastity. 'Remember there's a pig in there. Well he was grunting like one, anyway! Is he going now?'

'No he's rolling a joint. He got some from a raid they did last week. And anyway, we're doing the Karma Sutra. We're only on page seventeen.' This was the last thing Michael wanted to hear.

'Oh God, I'm never gonna get any sleep!'

'You've been at it for two hours. Hasn't your clack had enough for one night?' added Chastity.

'My clack is on a voyage of discovery! The Karma Sutra says there are three types of vagina: The Lotus, The Lily…'

'And The Bucket?' added Michael sarcastically. Connie shot him one of his acid looks then smiled bitterly.

'Ahh! Frustrated are we, Dolly? After watching that stripper tonight fiddling with his truncheon?'

'No, just fuckin' tired!'

'Hasn't Nigel coughed up any more fur-balls on my carpet you can use as earplugs?'

'Stop it, you two! This is serious. I still believe Fifi killed Lettie. And I believe Lettie got all the shares and money by shagging Creighton Cross.'

'Which is probably the real reason why the deranged gargoyle run her down in that car,' said Connie drawing back on his cigarette.

'Perhaps. But it still doesn't answer the biggest question of all. Lulu love, why did Lettie want you here?'

The following night in the dressing room, Connie and Michael sat at opposite ends of the dressing table. The mood was icy. Connie broke the long silence.

192

'Oh well, another day, another dollar. I think I'll do the same songs as last time. I just can't be arsed this evening.'

'That's 'cause you was arsed so much last night,' said Michael. 'It makes a change to see ya sitting upright!' Connie was just ready to fire back when Chastity arrived.

'Hello girls!' Michael was relieved to see a friendly face.

'Hi, Tit. How did you get on?'

'I got the car to the garage. They said it's something to do with the radiator. Eighty pounds. I could have bought a new diamante necklace for that. Or six pairs of stilettos in Shoe Save. Talking of which, I found this.' He held up a tiny cube of black plastic.

'What is it?'

'It looks like the sole off a stiletto heel,' said Connie.

'It is. It was jammed inside a tiny tear in the carpet under the car pedals.'

'Didn't the forensic team see it?' asked Michael.

'Yes, but they assumed it belongs to me because I'm a drag queen. But I know it's not mine, I've never worn heels driving. Fifi must have rammed her foot so hard on the accelerator that it tore the carpet and came off.'

'Ooh, creepy. That could be from the very moment she killed Lettie!'

Connie was suddenly distracted from his chain of thought. Glancing up to the corner of the room, he noticed something that hadn't been there the last time he was in the dressing room. Across the corner was a small metal cage behind which was a closed-circuit camera. And it was pointing straight at him. 'Hold on a minute... what the fuck is that up there?' he shouted. Chastity and Michael followed his gaze. They were horrified.

'It's a camera!' cried Michael. 'Fifi's installed a camera to spy on us. And it's got a microphone underneath it. Oh God!'

'Oh for Feck's sake! It must have been put in by the maintenance team when we were in Vange.' Chastity slammed his bag down on the floor. 'Oh, no no no no no, I'm not having this! That's coming down for a start. Pass me those mules, the pink fluffy ones with the six-inch heel, give me a bit of height. Now, give me a leg up.' Slipping on the heels, Chastity held onto Michael's shoulder as he stepped on a chair and climbed onto the dressing table.

Connie was spitting acid. 'That cunning, evil, spying, cheating, vicious, conniving, venomous, warped little goblin! How dare she spy on us? And in our own dressing room, can you believe it?'

'It's bolted to the wall behind a grill. I can't get to it,' said Chastity poking his finger through the wire mesh. 'What are we going to do now?'

'I'll deal with this! Give me that hairspray.' Grabbing his cigarette lighter from the counter, Connie climbed up to join Chastity. 'Right, stand back girls!' He sprayed the hairspray through the grill at the camera then ignited it. A massive jet of flame shot forward. There was a loud hissing followed by a strong noxious smell of burning plastic. 'Burn baby, burn!'

'Bloody hell, Connie! Let me get down off the table first. You've singed my feckin' eyebrows!' Heavy black toxic smoke instantly hit the back of everyone's throat. The heat from the flames knocked Connie and Chastity back off the counter. Coughing, spluttering and blinded they ran from the dressing room into the empty customer area.

'Leave the door open for a while, let some of the fumes out,' choked Chastity.

After a few minutes catching their breath, they walked cautiously back in to see the damage. What had been a camera and microphone was now a black plastic lump hanging inside the cage from a strand of bare wire. 'There must be a CCTV monitor in her office,' said Chastity. 'I'm going to go have a look, make sure the job's done.'

'Take the stiletto stub with you,' suggested Connie. 'See if it matches any of her cloven hooves.'

'Keep an eye out in case Fifi turns up. And if she does, stall her.'

As Chastity tiptoed cautiously off into the darkness, Connie looked at himself in the mirror. The front of his gelled fringe was edged with black singe marks. Michael watched as he trimmed them with a pair of pink glittery nail clippers.

'Take more than a pair of scissors to repair that hideous face!' he bitched. Connie chose to ignore him.

There were six CCTV screens in Fifi's office. 'That must have been the dressing room one,' Chastity whispered to himself, looking at a blank screen. Another showed the pavement outside the front entrance, and one was facing the stage. One looked into the safe room, the other side of the second door in Fifi's office just a few feet away from where he was standing. He jumped with shock... Fifi was in there!

His immediate reaction was to run, but something in the back of his mind urged him to watch. She was removing her clothing. He could see the evening dress she had laid out to change into draped across a large wooden table in the middle of the room. She removed her bra and then her knickers. He was just about to leave when she suddenly turned towards the camera. His whole body shuddered cold with shock at what he saw.

'Mary, mother of the blessed drag queen, would you be looking at that!' he whispered in amazement. 'Gawd blimey, it's horrible!'

Back in the dressing room, Edith stared up at the black mess in the corner. 'Is it broke?' she said, nudging the chargrilled cage with the end of her mop. The door flying open nearly knocked it out of her hand.

'Oh my God! Oh my God! I feel sick!' shouted Chastity, running into the room with his hand over his mouth.

'That's a nice welcome for me, I must say!' said Edith. 'What's the matter duck? You look like you've seen the creature from the black lagoon.'

'I have!' He threw himself panting into a chair as Edith, Connie and Michael gathered around him. 'I found the monitor and saw Fifi in the safe room getting dressed for tonight. And brace yourself for this... she's got a penis!'

'Eh? So she's a... man?' Michael was gobsmacked. There was a moment's silence as it all sank in, before Connie screamed with laughter.

'She can't be, duck!' Edith was as shocked as everyone else. 'She lost a baby. And I use to buy all her muff pads before she dried up.'

196

'I swear on my life, I saw it! Hanging there, covered in veins like a pensioner's leg.'

'Well I never did!' Edith screwed up her face. Connie was hysterical with laughter by this time.

'Perhaps she's got both bits,' suggested Michael. 'You know - a willy and a snatch? Let's face it, she ain't normal, is she?'

Edith nodded. 'You mean one of them ham-afro-bites?'

'Hermaphrodite?' corrected Chastity. 'That would explain why she's such a bitch, all that testosterone. And using a car to murder Lettie is such a masculine thing to do. She could have just hit her with a house brick in a handbag.'

They watched Connie fall to the floor laughing, crying and gasping for breath. Michael didn't get the joke. To him this was serious. He turned back to Chastity.

'What you going to do?'

'There's no time now, we've got a show to do,' said Chastity, pulling his chair into the dressing table. 'We need time to think before anyone says anything. And tomorrow my friend Frenchie's meeting us at Connie's to talk about this wedding. Lulu love. You're going to be a bridesmaid!'

'What?' Michael leapt to his feet.

'Don't worry about it now, just get ready for the show. We're running late. And you, get up off the floor, ya silly bitch!' he said, kicking Connie.

An hour later and Michael still couldn't get what Chastity had said out of his head. As big a shock as it was that Madame Fifi may be a hermaphrodite, it didn't hold the same horror as the thought that he would once again have to venture outside the relatively safe confines of Sugar Sugar once more in drag. But as much as he questioned him, Chastity would not elaborate. "Concentrate on the show," was all he would say. And Connie's noisy marathon shagging session meant he hadn't had nearly enough sleep to think it all through clearly, let alone perform on stage. What with Connie bitching all day and Chastity refusing to speak, as he stepped onto the stage for his first song, he felt quite lonely.

'I'm jealous of my sister. She's found herself a mister. And every time I see her, she rubs it in my face. I'm tired of being lonely. I need a one and only. Someone who's gonna love me, and knock her into space.

'I need to find a man, and I need to find him now. I ask her for advice, but she never tells me how. I'm always on my own, and he's always by her side. Don't wanna be a bridesmaid. I wanna be a bride.'

He could see Fifi in the audience dealing pills. Every now and then she glanced up at him suspiciously. He knew she didn't trust him, otherwise why else would she hire a detective and install a camera in the dressing room? And she could be Lettie's murderer. He felt empty inside.

'I don't want to live forever. I don't want to rule the world. I am not expecting Heaven. I just want someone to love.'

He remembered Connie accusing him of being jealous of Marcus. He often dreamed of sex with a man, but seeing couples in the audience giving each other undivided attention made the thought of someone special far more attractive right now. That one individual who would be there for him and him

198

alone. To prioritise him and put him before anyone and anything else. Someone truly on his side.

'I see what I am missing, each time I see them kissing. I try to make her listen, but I'm not getting through. I wish that she would help me. Inside I'm going crazy. But she's says I'm not ready. What am I gonna do?

'I could be a woman that could make a man believe. I'd give him everything, my heart is on my sleeve. I need to find a lover 'cause I'm burning up inside. Don't wanna be a bridesmaid, I wanna be a bride.

'I don't want to live forever. I don't want to rule the world. I am not expecting Heaven. I just want someone to love.'

CHAPTER TWENTY

Michael hadn't really made up with Connie. They just hadn't discussed Marcus further. Now Michael had had a decent night's sleep he thought it better that way. Perhaps after all, this is how real families were. And at least they now knew that Chastity wouldn't get blamed for Lettie's murder, though it was all still a bit of a mystery. They were sitting in Connie's lounge watching telly when Chastity arrived.

'Alright you two?' he said, putting his coat over the back of a dining chair. 'No sign of Frenchie yet, then?'

'She wants to hurry up,' moaned Connie. 'I'm not waiting in all day for her, fat cow.'

'What are you watching?'

'It's a repeat of the Richard and Judy Show,' said Michael. 'You'd think with a new series she would have taken the opportunity to have a face-lift - update her hairstyle, tidy herself up a bit.'

'You're not wrong, Lu,' replied Connie. 'But then, look at the state of Judy!'

The doorbell rang. 'That'll be Frenchie now,' said Chastity. 'I'll get it.' As he ran for the door, Michael turned to Connie. They hadn't spoken for some time, this could be an opportunity to break the ice.

'What's she like, this Frenchic? Does Chastity see a lot of her?'

'You can't help but see a lot of her, she's twenty-three stone! Think Elizabeth Taylor, post-Flinstones. She's not the brightest crayon in the tin. And you could park a double-decker bus in the shade of her arse. But she is quite funny and one of Tit's best friends, so...'

Then Michael remembered why she was coming. 'Oh, God! A fucking bridesmaid? I can't do that, it's insane!'

'You'll have to do it Dolly, 'cause I'm not going. I hate weddings. You don't want to let Chastity down, do you?'

'What about you letting her down?' complained Michael. Connie switched off the television as they entered.

'Frenchie, this is Lulu,' said Chastity. 'And Lulu, this is my dear friend Frenchie.'

She was indeed a big girl. Her orange Lycra blouse and matching leatherette mini skirt seemed several sizes too small for her considerable bulk. Her huge tits looked as though they could spring free and knock over the furniture at any given moment. Long lanky bleached-blonde hair hung half way down her back and she had more gold necklaces on than it was possible to count just by looking. But she did seem very bubbly.

'Hi Frenchie, nice to meet you,' said Michael enthusiastically, holding out a hand to shake. He figured the friendlier he was, the more likely she would be to understand him not wanting to be a bridesmaid.

'Hello handsome,' she said, looking him up and down. 'He'll look gorgeous as a bridesmaid, won't he?'

202

'Well, I'm...'

'Don't you dent my sofa, lard-arse,' interrupted Connie, determined to be the first to pull out of the wedding.

'You're lucky I'm not sitting on your face, you poof! Here you are then, see what you can do with these frocks. Luckily Oxfam had three the same,' she said, tossing a drab carrier bag at Connie. He opened the bag and looked inside. His grimace said it all. He lifted out a shiny peach sheath with huge puff sleeves edged with small yellow and white daisies.

'Bloody hell, Dolly! Who designed these, Helen Keller?'

Frenchie had a filthy, raucous laugh. 'Fuck right off, babe! Bit of a fiddle they'll be fantastic.'

'Bit of a fiddle? Box of fuckin' matches! What am I supposed to do with these?'

'Whatever kind of look you were aiming at Frenchie, I think you missed it,' Chastity laughed. 'When I said something with a label, I didn't mean "clearance". But then, you are my favourite fag-hag so...'

As Frenchie sat with Chastity on the sofa, Nigel came up to greet her with a big miaow.

'Aah! Look at the little cat. Hello little cat! Connie's got a pussy as well as a cock.'

'I'm not the only one! Anyway, it's not my cat, it's Lulu's. Frenchie, meet Nigel.'

'Nigel? Aah, bless!' she laughed.

'I, err...' Michael's attempt to mention not being a bridesmaid was once again thwarted by Connie seizing the moment.

'Look, I'll sort out the frocks for you Frenchie but I'm sorry, I'm not going. No offence, but you know I'm allergic to weddings. And I'll need the fabric from the third frock to make the other two any good anyway.' Upstaged, Michael looked at him with daggers. Connie continued, 'Anyway, why are your mates not being bridesmaids?'

'They will be at me hen night. But the next day, all the girls are off on their Eighteen to Thirty Holiday. Us four will be the only shaggable birds there. So I'm relying on you, you slut. You've got to come.' Chastity already had this all thought through.

'I knew this would happen. But you'll want to go when you hear this. Frenchie's fiancé is a twenty-four year old kickboxing champion. His name is Shaun and he looks like something from a wet dream.' Chastity had his attention.

'I'm listening.'

'Well, Shaun's whole team will be there, minus girlfriends. They're going to do a kickboxing display at the reception. In lycra micro shorts. But of course, if you can't go...'

'Hold on a minute, I didn't say I couldn't go. How many of them are there?'

'Eight,' said Frenchie, lighting a cigarette. 'And every one of them looks like a young Jean Claude Van Damme.' Connie thought for a moment. How bad could it be? More to the point, how good could it be - surrounded by fit men with no female competition?

'Well... I'll... I will have to do something with these hideous frocks. And what about this hen night?'

'Try and stop me babe. It's going to be fucking ace! The only problem is Shaun's Mum Maureen wants to go.'

'What's wrong with that?' said Chastity.

'It's a pub crawl! I'm not going to get a man from each pub to shaft me in the toilets if the groom's mother's there, am I?' Michael was surprised. Connie was convinced.

'Huh, call me a slut? I think you're fabulous!'

'I know you like me really, I can see your tail wagging!' giggled Frenchie.

'Aw, weddings are so romantic,' Chastity gushed. 'Do you take this woman...?'

'You'd need a forklift to take her!' grinned Connie. 'Are you going to carry on stripping at that club after the wedding, Frenchie love?'

'No, he was taking the piss. He kept turning the heating up to make my nipple patches fall off. I told him, I want an extra fifty quid a night to show me filter tips!'

While Connie was busy laughing, Michael finally saw a good opportunity to mention his concerns.

'I... erm... I don't think I can do this. The bridesmaid thing, I mean. Connie and Chastity will be there. Can't I just go as a normal guest?'

'No, you're being a bridesmaid with us!' Chastity was determined. 'It will be good experience for you. And it gets you away from Soho for the day. And you will be in disguise. You can't spend all day in a yashmak, can you?'

'No, but I could just not go and stay indoors here with Nigel instead.'

'We're not leaving you here all miserable and on your own with this nutcase snooping around after you. You're coming and that's that!'

'What's a yashmak?' questioned Frenchie. 'And who's snooping after him?'

'It's a long story Frenchie, I'll fill you in later,' said Chastity.

'But all those straight men there. It's not going to be safe. Suppose they don't like drag queens? What if they're queer bashers? They're trained fighters!' Frenchie couldn't understand why Michael was over-reacting.

'Eh? What you so worried about? I thought it was any excuse to dress up for you drag queens? Anyway the blokes will think you're women, not poofs in frocks! Come on, it'll be a laugh.'

'But what if... '

'So this Shaun. Is it love, Frenchie?' Connie interrupted. If he had to go, then Michael would have to suffer it too.

'He's six-foot two with a dick like a punch-bag. He can touch the back of his head with the sole of his foot and his tongue's so long he can lick his own scrotum. And his best man's a drug dealer. Sorry, what was the question, babe?' laughed Frenchie.

'Point taken!'

'I still don't feel comfortable about this!' Michael put his head in his hands close to tears. But Frenchie was confident.

'We're sorted! It'll be fine. You three as bridesmaids. My Brother Kevin's giving me away, 'cause we still can't find my Dad. He's paid for everything too - my dress and all the men's suits, the cars, the buffet and the hall for the reception. I don't know where he got the money from, he don't get paid very much. Still, ask no questions. Oh, and my Uncle Ernie's putting a hundred and fifty quid behind the bar at the reception. What could possibly go wrong?'

A week later, Michael still hadn't convinced Chastity to let him stay at home. And he hadn't seen Frenchie since that first meeting. As he pulled on jeans and ironed a shirt for her hen party that night, he decided he was going to have one last attempt at talking her into having just two bridesmaids - Chastity and Connie.

Dance music thumped relentlessly at the disco she had chosen for her do. Some of North London's best looking men danced and flirted with scantily clad women everywhere Michael looked. He was used to straight clubs and pubs where he could act straight and conceal his true feelings. But he had never before had to cope with Connie's extrovert campness or Chastity and Frenchie's openness to everything gay. Just being part of a group of drunken women was enough to make them stand out in the crowd. Feeling unsafe, he decided to stick to what he knew and not to make eye contact with any straight guy, no matter how gorgeous he may be. But Connie, Chastity and Frenchie were determined to make the most of the night.

'That's the old goat over there,' Frenchie slobbered at Chastity, pointing to a very uncomfortable looking middle aged woman close to the exit. Everyone looked across at Maureen - tan leather gloves tightly grasping her matching handbag against the jacket of her tweed two-piece, her dark sunken eyes darted fervently around the room. Her sullen wrinkled frown deepened when two young men looked at her and laughed as they walked by. Padding at the side of her salon-prepared greying curls, she marched sternly towards the group.

'Twin set and pearls in here? I see what you mean,' laughed Chastity. 'She's got about as much charisma as a Woolworth's knitting pattern! She's coming over. Connie, we need a plan.'

'Get her some pork scratchings,' giggled Frenchie. 'She's allergic. Her neck'll swell up like a bullfrog.'

'I've got a better idea. Leave this to me,' said Connie as Maureen approached. 'You ever been to one of these do's, Maureen?'

'Certainly not!' she clipped, eyes glancing about defensively. 'It's vulgar beyond belief. Most of these girls hardly have any clothes on. And they're allowing these debauched young men to grind up against them willy-nilly.'

'I agree, it's disgusting. Animals they are Maureen, animals,' he said with a wink to the others.

'And look at that young man over there. They call this fashion? His trousers are hanging so low from his waist that you can see the back of his underpants, revealing everything.'

'Yes, I can see,' said Connie, licking his lips. 'I don't know where to put my face!'

'And the music's so loud. We should all go somewhere else. Somewhere nice.'

'Frenchie was just saying the same thing. But there's a problem. You see that security guard over there? Look! He's told us to stay inside, just for ten minutes. There's a fight outside. Then we can go to somewhere a bit more... Christian.' As Maureen looked back to the exit, Connie dropped some white powder into her drink.

'Yes, good idea,' she said, believing she had found an ally. Connie was trying hard not to laugh at her naivety.

'Go sit yourself down over there, Maureen love and finish up your sherry, and I will go tell Frenchie to drink up her fizzy pop.'

'Yes dear, I think I will.' She smiled kindly at him and walked to a small dimly lit alcove. Sliding in behind the table, she raised her glass to Connie and drank it down. Chastity was quite drunk and very excitable.

'What did you put in her drink?'

'Only a bit of powdered ecstasy.'

Michael was shocked. 'Oh my God, isn't that dangerous?'

'No, she'll be fine,' said Connie, knocking back a shot of Vodka. 'In a couple of days. You know what her trouble is? She's got delusions of blandeur!'

Frenchie thought it was all very funny. 'At least it'll stop her being such a pain in the arse tomorrow at the wedding. And I'll get me shag tonight! YES!!'

'Spoken like a true Essex girl.' Chastity raised his glass to her. But it was warning bells not wedding bells that rang in Michael's head.

'Essex girl? Err... where are you from?'

'Billericay, babe.'

'Oh God! Your wedding's not in Essex is it?'

'Lulu's got some personal problems at the moment,' slurred Chastity, patting the front of Michael's face. 'She's a bit touchy. Calm yourself, Lulu love, it's here in North London. You're not going to get in any trouble. We'll protect ya, me and my friend Frenchie, here.' Michael could see there was no point in trying to persuade Frenchie to let him off being a bridesmaid. She was so drunk she could hardly stand, let alone listen. And he didn't want to let Chastity down after all the support he'd given him over the past few weeks. At least it wouldn't be in Essex. Resigning himself, he knocked back another shot of Sambuca.

'So, you got Shaun a wedding present, Frenchie?' asked Connie.

'I got him leather chaps, a back-street hood, a whip and some handcuffs. Tomorrow night I'm going to tie him to the bed and ride him till his spine snaps!'

'Ooh! Into a bit of S and M is he?' questioned Connie.

'Well, you know he's a mechanic? The night I met him, he winched me up in his garage at work.'

'Well let's face it, it would have to be a car winch now wouldn't it, Frenchie love?' said Chastity dryly. Frenchie laughed.

'Fuck right off, babe! And he bought me a rabbit.' Under the influence of a third Sambuca, this seemed like an odd wedding present to Michael.

'What, in a hutch?'

'No you silly cow. It's a vibrator!'

'Why is it called a rabbit?'

'Cause when you stick it up, it's got two long ears to tickle your love mound.' Connie spat his drink back into his glass.

'Errgh! Love mound? I'm going to be sick!'

'You know, your little man in a boat.' Frenchie waggled her little finger.

'Sorry, means nothing to me!' said Chastity to a stranger next to him at the bar. The equally inebriated man nodded his approval. Michael was baffled.

'A boat? With a little man and a rabbit in it?'

At that moment, Maureen came over again. She did appear to have loosened up a bit.

'Oh, look out. Here comes Lady Ga Ga!' said Connie, laughing. 'That was quick, look at her bopping!' She twirled the last yard of her approach, landing with a bump nose to nose with Connie.

'You know, I like you,' she slurred with a hic-up. 'You brought me into your world and I like it.'

Connie spun her around to face the busy dance floor, then resting his wrist on her shoulder, he whispered in her ear, 'Maureen, every man in this gorgeous, sparkly little club has just realised what a celebrity you are and they all want to get it on with you,' he advised. 'So ask yourself this: Do you want everyone to see the real you? Or do you want them to like you?' Maureen looked around and sniffed.

'Well, my tubes might be a bit rusty now, but I will do the best I can. I am adamant that I will not let you down!'

'Maureen love, I can hardly contain my indifference!' said Connie, shoving her out into the middle of the dance floor. Frenchie laughed and gave Connie the thumbs up.

'Right, that's her sorted. Now, let's go find a tongue for my crack!'

CHAPTER TWENTY ONE

Though Michael hadn't drunk very much alcohol the night before, he felt sick. Standing with fellow bridesmaids Chastity and Connie in the porch of the church was taking its toll on his nerves, making it hard to stop himself from shivering, despite the hot weather. Considering what he'd had to begin with, Connie had made a marvellous job of the three dresses. He had completely removed the dated puff sleeves and recut the neckline into a v-shaped plunge which, with the help of perfectly placed falsies and pre-positioned Gaffa tape across the pectorals, gave the perfect pert cleavage. He had also reshaped the waist and detached the sheaf low on the hip before re-positioning it with dye-matched lace darts and netting behind, to create a gentle modern flare out to the floor. He had even created matching neckbands to assist in disguising any sign of an Adam's apple. But Michael still hadn't completely got his head around being a drag queen, let alone having to pretend to be a real girl.

'She's nearly twenty minutes late,' said Chastity, glancing at his watch. He looked out through the huge gothic arch of the porch for any sign of a wedding car.

'I hope she doesn't turn up. Then I can take this dress off and go home,' said Michael, kicking the floor like a spoilt child. Connie was more preoccupied with the groom.

'Look at Shaun!' he gushed, staring at the gathering of fit hunks at the top end of the aisle. 'He's so fucking cute. And look at his team mates! Bugger, I'm horny. I need a cigarette. Ponse us a fag, Tit?' He held out his hand expectantly.

'You can't smoke in a church. Anyway, I haven't got any. Why didn't you bring your own?'

'I forgot.'

'Oh you, you'd forget your own bollocks if they weren't in a bag!'

'Why are all his team mates looking at us like that?' said Michael. 'They know we're blokes!'

'No, it's tradition at weddings. They're deciding who's going to shag which bridesmaid.' Chastity wasn't making things easier for him.

'Oh God, no! I can't do this, they're going to kill us!' Chastity grabbed his arm as he turned to leave.

'They're all drunk and they think we're women. There's not going to be any trouble. Trust me, I'm a drag queen!'

'Somebody in this God forsaken fucking church must have a bastard fag!' moaned Connie, wringing his hands.

'Don't speak like that in here, or the baby Jesus will strike you down with herpes. It happened to someone in Woman's Own.' They could hear Frenchie's future mother-in-law laughing from within.

'Maureen's still having a lovely time,' observed Chastity. 'You'd think she would have come down off that ecstacy by now, sitting there flirting with all the boys.' Connie was way too interested in all the boys to be distracted by Maureen's drug-induced frivolity.

'I can picture them all at the gym, building up a sweat in those tiny, tiny white shorts with the jock showing through,' he said with a deep sigh, licking his lips. 'Little beads of sweat trickling down tattooed muscle. Then in the showers, flicking each other's arses with towels, bragging about the tart they shagged in Billericay bus station the night before.' It was all too much. 'No, sorry! I can't do this without nicotine. She'll have to start without me, I'm off!' As Chastity grabbed Connie's arm, the wedding car pulled into the kerb at the end of the path through the ancient graveyard.

'No, you can't! Here she is. Here's the car.'

Rather than wait for the chauffeur, Frenchie opened her own door and attempted to climb out. But the huge wedding dress was making it difficult.

'Ahh, would you look at that? Doesn't she look... big? My, that's a lot of fabric in just one dress. It's like two white satin king-size quilts strung together!' mused Chastity.

Her brother Kevin lolled casually round from the other side of the car. Placing his silver-grey top hat on the car's roof, he grabbed her by both arms and yanked her onto the pavement. She clung onto the broad shoulders of his matching tailcoat in an attempt to keep her balance. Regaining her composure, she readjusted the long white veil, attached to the top of her head with a bunch of pretty silk snowdrops. Staggering a little himself, Kevin retrieved his hat and lit a cigarette, kicking her door shut and banging twice on the roof of the car. As it gently pulled away so did Frenchie's veil, the back of which was still trapped in the car door. Head yanked backwards, she screamed and grabbed hold of it as it pulled her running up the street behind the car.

'He's shut her frock in the car, silly bastard!' giggled Chastity. Even Michael had to smile.

'Kevin's pissed!' laughed Connie. 'And he's got a cigarette, oh thank fuck. I can ponse one off him.'

Frenchie screamed a stream of abuse at the chauffeur as he released her from the door's clutches. Returning to the top of the path, she fluffed her hair and slapped the veil back into position. Grabbing her dress either side of her huge bosom, she pulled it up and shook it to allow everything to fall back into its rightful place. After grabbing Kevin's burgundy cravat and giving him one almighty slap around the back of his head, she took his arm and headed up through the graveyard.

'You will have to have a fag after, there's no time now,' warned Chastity. Connie scowled and stamped his foot on the flag stone floor. As they slowly got closer to the porch, Kevin lifted his head and looked at the three bridesmaids. To Michael's horror he realised for the first time that he'd seen him before. He could feel his heart beating in his neck as his eyes widened and welled with tears.

'Oh, no! No! NO! It's Knuckles!' he gasped desperately, grabbing Chastity's arm. 'Oh, God, get me out of here! Get me out of here!'

'Ssh! What are you talking about? Calm yourself, love!' His grasp was hurting Chastity's arm. 'That's Kevin her brother. Who's Knuckles? You're getting paranoid now with your...'

'It's Knuckles. Billy's henchman! Oh, this is it now. This is it. I'm done for!' Chastity grabbed him as he backed away panting for air.

'Billy's henchman? Are you sure?' said Connie, squinting his eyes out through the arch for a clearer view.

'That's him, I tell ya! I would recognise him anywhere. It's his fault I'm in this mess. He's the one who stole the ten grand and told Billy it was me! Oh, this is insane. I can't do it. I can't do it!'

'Bloody hell!' Chastity froze.

'Erm... relax, Dolly, just relax!' Connie was thinking on his feet. 'He's pissed and you're in drag. Don't look suspicious, you're a girl remember? You'll just have to cope. Just keep telling yourself, you're a girl.'

'I'm a girl. I'm a girl. Oh, God!'

As Frenchie reached the porch, she could sense something was wrong. 'What's up? He has fucking turned up, ain't he?' she growled, looking up the altar to check the groom was waiting. Connie nudged Chastity back to life.

'Err, yes love. Don't worry he's here. We were... erm, just a little overcome. You know, girls and weddings!' Frenchie lifted Michael's chin with her finger.

'Don't cry Lulu, it could be you next!' Although he had his back to Knuckles, he could feel his eyes burning into his back. He must recognise him! This would be the confrontation he'd been dreading. While Chastity and Connie put on a brave front for him, Frenchie was still blissfully unaware.

'You did a good job on those dresses, Connie. You look like The Three Degrees.'

'And that's a lovely maternity smock, Frenchie,' returned Connie. 'No time to get your roots done then?'

'Fuck right off, babe!'

'And your tits pushed up round your neck. Looks like you've got a couple of skinhead page boys stuffed down there!' Chastity added.

'Wouldn't be the first time!' giggled Frenchie. Chastity glanced at Michael, head down and breathing deep and slow. He silently willed him to keep his composure under what he knew was intense fear and pressure. As he lifted his eyes to glance back, Chastity gave a small wink of support before turning back to Frenchie.

'Are you nervous, love?'

'Shitting a brick, babe.'

'Well, if there's any advance on that let us know. Remember we'll be walking behind you!'

'This is my brother Kevin. These are my three girlfriends Chastity, Connie and Lulu.' Chastity grasped Connie's hand as they held their breath and waited. As Knuckles moved in close behind and grasped his waist, Michael stopped breathing. He could feel the heat from lager-soaked breath on the side of his face. The world around him slowed down and stopped, and the only sound he could hear was his own heartbeat. The moment seemed to last an eternity. Then Knuckles spoke.

'Well, hello Lulu, you're fucking gorgeous. You look very nervous sweetheart. Don't worry baby, uncle Kevin will look after you later!' The sound of Knuckles' gentle kiss on his ear was deafening. Michael slowly closed his eyes, a tear of relief running

218

down his face as the world came back into focus. He hadn't been recognised.

Chastity and Connie began to breathe again too.

'Can I ponse a fag, Kev?' said Connie breaking the silence.

'Sorry darling, I just got that off the driver,' he replied, releasing Michael. Chastity looked towards the aisle. An elderly vicar was slowly waddling towards them from the altar. Connie and Frenchie had noticed him too and they couldn't help but laugh. After what seemed about ten minutes, he finally reached them.

'Ready?' He gasped raucously into Frenchie's cleavage. Frenchie nodded. He turned and laboriously began making his way back.

'Did you see the way he looked at my tits? Dirty old bugger.'

'Is it any wonder? Racked up like that, you could see them from the NASA Space Station!'

Michael was fully focussed again now, though he couldn't bring himself to join the laughter. After an age, the vicar reached the altar once more and signalled to the organist to begin playing. The bride and her brother headed up the aisle, followed by Connie. As Michael turned to follow, Chastity touched his arm.

'I'm so sorry Lulu, I really didn't know.' Michael nodded with a half-smile. Though ultimately it was Chastity's fault he was here, he believed him. 'He didn't know it was you. Just stay calm and before you know it, it will all be over. Let's face it, things couldn't get any worse than that now, could they?'

The ceremony itself went without too much of a hitch. Other than Connie walking back afterwards from the altar ahead of the bride and groom trying without success to find someone who would give him a cigarette. He stood with Chastity and Michael in the porch waiting for Frenchie to stop nattering with her guests.

'There you see Lulu, we've been here an hour and nobody knows we're drag queens,' whispered Chastity. Michael nodded. He had calmed down a little, though he was still a bit concerned their cover would be broken. 'There's just the reception and then it will all be over.'

'I want to go home. Can't we all just go now? It's only tempting fate if I go to the reception!'

'It will look suspicious if we don't go. Besides, we've promised Frenchie we will do that song with her. We can't let her down now. Connie's made the costumes and everything. This isn't Frenchie's fault, she didn't know. And it's her wedding day. We've got to do this.'

'But Connie's in a state too! She can't cope with all these straight men either. She's as horny as fuck.' They both looked over at him, pacing up and down wringing his hands.

'She just needs a couple of cigarettes. She'll be fine after that. I just need you to help me keep her hormones under control until then.'

'That's not going to be easy. Look!' As Michael glanced out through the door to the graveyard, he could see all of the groom's teammates. They had lined either side of the path to create a kickboxing arch for the bride to walk under, one foot on the ground and one held high, leaning at the top

220

against the foot of the athlete opposite. 'They must be fit to get their legs up that high.'

'What? Oh God in Heaven above! She's not going to make it through that arch with all them crotches pointing in at her! It's like a running buffet.'

'Well, I'm having to cope. She'll just have to cope too. Remember you're a girl,' he quoted sarcastically. Chastity took Connie's arm.

'Err, Connie love, there's a bit of problem.'

'Don't stress me now! Bastard non-smokers. Sixty guests and not one of them has got...' As Chastity took his shoulders and turned him to face Shaun's team, he let out a blood-curdling scream. This was too much for even hard-faced Connie to cope with without a cigarette. 'I can't walk through that! No, don't make me do it, I need nicotine! I need nicotine!'

'Come on love, you can do this!' encouraged Chastity. 'It's only a few yards.'

'Ooh, at least,' teased Michael. 'That one at the end must have a good foot-and-a-half on his own!'

'You're not helping, Lulu!' scolded Chastity.

'Sorry, I was just thinking about those white lycra shorts at the gym.'

Connie was resisting and close to tears by this time. 'Don't make me do this! I need a cigarette!'

'Come on, we'll do it together,' said Chastity, taking his arm and leading him forward. 'Now, brace yourself. And in the name of all that's holy, for feck's sake don't touch anything!'

CHAPTER TWENTY TWO

Michael felt a little ashamed of himself for antagonising Connie at the church. At the time, it had seemed a good way of loading his own stress onto someone else, but now they'd arrived at Frenchie's wedding reception and Connie had had a few cigarettes, he recognised that he was once again the only one in fear. It made him feel a little isolated, if not worried that Connie would take revenge for the things he'd said, but he need not have worried. Connie's nicotine deprival had been such a distraction at the time, he hadn't even noticed.

Chastity was well aware that he needed to get Michael home as soon as possible, or at least away from any risk of being found out as a man, or perhaps worse, being recognised by Knuckles. Just a week before, Frenchie had begged them on quite a large bended knee that they would join her on stage to do a sexy Pussycat Dolls routine as a tribute to Shaun and his team mates. Reluctantly they had agreed, and Connie had made her a costume and headdress to match the three feathered showgirl outfits they already had. Michael was the least happy about this agreement, but knowing it would signal the end of their commitment to being bridesmaids was helping him to cope.

The reception hall was quite tatty, though someone had made a bit of an effort with a few brightly coloured balloons and streamers here and there. There was a bar to one end and a DJ had set up his tacky, dated equipment on a table to one side. The entire kickboxing team had an inkling of what was to come and had gathered around the front of a large stage to one end. Standing in the wings, now all dressed in pure burlesque corsetry and frilly knickers, Chastity had reassured Michael that it was only a short while before they could leave. This didn't stop his teeth chattering and his knees shaking with fear.

The DJ stopped his music to make an announcement. 'Gentlemen prepare. Brace yourselves. Here comes the Pussycat Go Go Girls!' He pressed play on his CD player and a carefully selected rock-n-roll vamp song from the nineteen-sixties blasted from rope-light draped speakers at either end of his table. Connie ran across the stage into a slutty pose to one side.

'*I'm Connie, hi!*' He sang blowing a kiss to the delight of the men. The others followed.

'*I'm Chastity, hello!*'

'*I'm Lulu, bonjour!*'

'*And I'm Frenchie, let's go!*'

Rubbing their hands across their breasts and crotches, they all shouted together, '*Wow! Miaow! Wooh!*'

Gyrating their hips while spinning around on one heel, they each threw their feather boa out to the baying crowd. Shaun and his mates were whooping and whistling up a storm at the filthy routine. Connie ran his hands up and down Michael's body in a straight man's lesbian fantasy as Michael theatrically turned to face the audience with shock. Chastity grabbed hold of Frenchie's tits and rubbed his face in them, blowing a raspberry as she squealed with

224

delight. It all seemed to be going quite well, considering they'd only rehearsed it twice in Connie's lounge the week before. It was certainly achieving the desired effect.

'*Pussycat, pussycat, where have you been?*' Chastity shouted.

I've been to London, it's quite obscene!' gushed Connie.

'*Pussycat, pussycat, what did you try?*' Lulu sang, turning to Frenchie.

'*The entire home guard, until they were dry!*' She winked at her new husband and licked her lips.

'I love you, baby!' he shouted at her, grabbing his substantial crotch.

'*Wooh! Wow! Miaow! Wooh!*' they all screamed.

Michael suddenly noticed that Knuckles wasn't on the floor jumping up and down with the other men. A cold shiver ran through him. If he couldn't see him, he couldn't keep an eye on him. He didn't want to be crept up on like he had been earlier. He was relieved to see him coming out of the toilet and walking across to the bar.

His attention returned to his choreography when Chastity slapped him playfully on his arse. He returned the favour by bumping Chastity with his hip. Connie on the other hand gave one almighty slap to Frenchie's buttock. With her enormous hip she bumped him clean off the stage and into the wings. There was a loud crash as he landed head first into a pile of electrical equipment and drum kit.

Their routine ended to rapturous applause and whistling from the entire hall. They all stepped down from the stage. Frenchie ran into the open arms of her new husband and Chastity linked his arm with Michael's and walked him over to a small round table at the side of the DJ stand. As they sat, Agadoo began blaring from the speakers and a dozen or so people took to the dance floor.

'There now, our responsibilities for the day are done. We'll just hang around long enough to be polite and then we'll go,' said Chastity, patting Michael's hand.

'Thank God it's over, I feel a bit stupid sitting here dressed like a French tart,' said Michael re-adjusting his corset. Chastity looked down at Michael sitting like a geezer. He put a hand on each of his knees and pushed his legs shut.

'Remember you're a girl, not a drag queen. Besides which, I can't lip read!'

'I just want to get out of here now. Where's Connie?'

'I don't know,' said Chastity, looking around the room. Connie was nowhere to be seen, though Frenchie's new mother-in-law was up and dancing. 'My God, would you be looking at Maureen? I've seen people dance better when they're on fire!'

Frenchie skipped to their table and pulled on Chastity's arm. 'Come dance with me, Tit?'

'I can't love. I have had these shoes on all day and they're pinching. Who's that over there?' he said, pointing to an elderly bald man dancing with Maureen.

'That's me Uncle Ernie who paid for the drinks.'

'The one you said was a Portrait Artist?'

'No, I said piss artist! It's a shame really. He spent all morning washing and combing his hair then forgot to bring it with him!' Michael was more concerned about being able to leave.

'Do you know where Connie is?'

'In the toilet. On her knees in the end cubicle, servicing the kickboxing team.' Michael put his head in his hand. Chastity was angry.

'Tell me you're feckin' joking?'

'Doing what she does best - Community Service. She's alright now she's had a fag. And they're all so pissed, they haven't realised they're having a fag too!' She danced away laughing.

'God, I need another drink! We'll go as soon as we've had another drink.' It was Michael now patting Chastity's hand. Although he was Frenchie's best friend, it had still been an exhausting day. Michael looked around at all the revellers laughing and dancing, joking and drinking. It occurred to him that this wedding was probably being paid for with the money Knuckles had stolen, the very money that Michael himself was being blamed for and the reason for him having to hide from Billy. Despite making him feel sick to his stomach, he decided not to mention it. Chastity already seemed racked with guilt at forcing him to be there and now the day was nearly over, he saw no point in adding to that distress.

'It's quite odd this whole wedding thing,' he mused solemnly.

'How do you mean?'

'It's seems so forced. You know, two families forced together all in one place at the same time.' He sighed. 'Perhaps I'm just being bitter because I haven't got one.' Chastity patted his hand.

'You know Lu, it's not all a bed of roses. I don't really have that much to do with my lot. I call my mother once in a blue moon but then she's in Ireland, it's not that easy to just pop in. Still, she doesn't have to explain me to anyone anymore, so she's happy.' Michael was surprised at this revelation.

'What do you mean, the whole drag thing?'

'God no, I wouldn't even know where to begin explaining that one, although she does know I'm in show business.' He twisted his chair in closer. 'No, I told my mother I was gay when I turned eighteen. Of course, nobody in Kilmacanoge knew what the feck I was talking about. Do you know what she said to me?' Michael shook his head. 'She said, "Would you be talking like him out of the Carry On films, the little fellah with the glasses?"'

'Charles Hawtrey?'

'That's it.'

'What did you say?'

'I said yes. It was easy at the time. It's funny you know, some years later when my father died I went across for the service and she said to me, "I cut your picture out of the paper now you're famous." She pointed to a frame on the mantle and it was Charles Hawtrey. She had spent all those years with that image in her mind and completely forgot what I looked like.' He shook his head resignedly. Michael tried to imagine what he must be thinking. And what it must be like to have a mother.

'I really, really wish I'd just had that one chance to hug my mother. Even if I never saw her again, just that one moment that I could take with me and remember. Did you ever hug your mother, Tit?'

'Ooh no, no, no. That's not the way our family did things.'

228

'Connie doesn't seem the type to want to hug her mother, does she?'

'She'd need a shovel, they buried her six years ago!'

With a smile, Michael stood from his chair. 'I'll get that drink in, what do you want?'

'I'll have a pint of Fosters, thanks Lu.'

As Michael left for the bar, Connie came out of the toilet, flitting across the dance floor to Chastity with a big grin on his face.

'Oh, you've finally come up for air, then? Lulu's gone for drinks. Do you want a pint?'

'No thanks, just had one!' said Connie, wiping the edge of his lipstick. Chastity heaved.

'Ooh, you filthy whore!'

'What time does the kickboxing display start?'

'There isn't one, I was lying to make sure you came.'

Connie shrugged. 'Oh, well. I've had a good innings. And outings. And innings...' Chastity smacked his arm.

'You've been gone ages and we need to go soon. You know how stressed Lulu is.'

'I was doing it for Lulu! If they're all de-spunked they're not going to bother her, are they?' Chastity shook his head in despair.

Michael was pleased there was no queue at the bar. The quicker he got the drinks and got back to the table, the quicker they could all drink up and leave.

'Two pints of Fosters please,' he said softly, holding out a twenty pound note.

'It's all on a tab, sweetheart,' the barman replied. Michael shoved the note back into his Gaffa tape-enhanced cleavage. But he could smell something odd. He wasn't sure at first what it was, though it made him uncomfortable. In a moment he realise it was Knuckles. As he turned, they were practically nose-to-nose.

'So, that's one for you and one for me is it, Lulu baby?' he said tenderly.

'I will order you a pint if you drink it somewhere else,' said Michael tetchily, moving away further along the bar. Knuckles followed.

'You're gorgeous. I like them young,' he said looking down at the tip of the twenty pound note.

'Can you not find someone from your own species?'

'In fact, the younger the better. I bet you'd look really sexy in a school uniform.' Michael couldn't believe this was happening again. He was further angered knowing this thug pervert would approve of sex with a girl in a school uniform while at the same time accusing anyone gay of being sick in the head.

'Just go away! Do you always talk this much? Breaking in a new tongue?'

'You should get to know my tongue better, Lulu baby. It's like a spaceship.'

'Your tongue's like a spaceship?'

'Yeah, 'cause it can take you to Heaven and back!'

'Christ! Is this what women have to put up with?' said Michael under his breath, picking up the two pints to return to his table. Knuckles grabbed his arm.

'You don't mind daddy talking dirty to you, do you baby?' Michael struggled to pull away without spilling the drinks.

230

'Look, just piss off will you? It's like having a pint with Gary Glitter!' His fellow bridesmaids had seen this happening and had raced across the dance floor to his rescue. Chastity removed Knuckles' hand from Michael's arm.

'Are you having trouble, Lulu?'

'Can you not sense my animal magnetism?' said Knuckles, undeterred. Connie pushed his way between them.

'She knows all about the animals you hang around with. She just prefers men a little higher on the food chain!'

'You're not her type, Knuckles,' Chastity growled. 'And I can say with some authority that she's certainly not yours!'

There was a brief moment's silence as everyone suddenly realised what had been said. Knuckles grabbed Chastity's wrist tightly, as he wriggled to get away.

'How did you know my name's Knuckles? Here, hold on a minute. Is that a wig?' He yanked Chastity's hairpiece from his head.' You're a bloke! He pulled off Michael's wig too and held it aloft for everyone to see. 'They're all fucking blokes!' he shouted to the other men. The room fell silent.

'Give me back my wig, Knuckles!' screamed Michael. 'It's from the Dolly Parton catalogue!'

'Hold on, I know you... Michael! You're Michael!' Michael was mortified. Standing wigless with a pint of beer in each hand, he hesitated not knowing which way to turn. He threw both pints in Knuckles' face and, grabbing his wig, grasped Chastity's other wrist to run. But Knuckles' grasp was strong and he had no intention of letting go.

Chastity gasped for breath, stretched to capacity like a tug of war rope.

At the other end of the hall, realisation drifted into focus through a mist of alcohol, as the kickboxing team suddenly recognised they all been given head in the toilet cubicle by a bloke in a frock. Shaun, who'd been dancing with Frenchie, was the first to react. As he moved to run across the dance floor, she swung him round by his arm and pushed him into his crowd of friends. They all fell like a group of inebriated skittles. Then with a scream that lasted the full length of the hall, she ran at Knuckles at the bar, her enormous bulk accelerating towards him like a locomotive. He gasped with horror as she launched herself into the air from a few feet away and smashed into him at full force. With the excruciating sound of wood scraping against wood, the entire counter slid back three feet before tipping over and crashing against the back wall. Emptied of all air, Knuckles landed on his back with Frenchie on top of him under a shower of broken glass and booze.

Free from entrapment, Chastity snatched his wig from the floor. 'Leg it!' he yelled, grabbing the back of Connie and Michael's frocks and running them to the exit.

'What about our other costumes?' cried Connie. Chastity ignored him, throwing him and Michael through the swing doors to the entrance lobby. He paused briefly and looked back for his dear friend Frenchie. The whole event had turned into a drunken brawl, as the men now appeared to be fighting each other. Frenchie was back on her feet and in the middle of the throng, laughing loudly and thumping anything that came near her. Seeing Chastity at the exit, she assured him with a wink and blew a big kiss before turning to throw her next punch.

Outside in the darkened street, Chastity, Connie and Michael ran as fast as they could, stilettos permitting. Even though they were in a North London street at night in full drag, Michael felt safer than he had all day. They stopped for a moment to catch their breath.

'I think I'm going to be sick!' Connie retched.

'I'm not surprised, the amount you've swallowed tonight!'

'Hold my hair!' he cried, leaning forward to throw up. Chastity grabbed the back of his wig and ripped it clean off his head, holding it aloft like a dead pheasant before handing it to Michael.

'Hold this for her, I'll try and get us a cab.'

Meanwhile back inside the Community Centre, a bruised and battered Knuckles was making a call on his mobile.

'Oi, Billy. I've found Michael. He's turned queer, disguising himself as a girl. Yeah, a girl! He tried to get off with me, fuckin' sicko! He goes under the name Lulu. Yeah, he's a drag queen. We've got him now!' With a deep and vulgar cigarette-stained laugh, he slammed his phone shut.

CHAPTER TWENTY THREE

After the initial trauma of escaping Knuckles and the kickboxing team and then having to get home from North London in full drag, reality was beginning to sink in. At Connie's, Edith was trying her best to console a tearful Michael. Daisy was doing the best he could to cry and eat a family sized bag of crisp at the same time. And Chastity knew that Connie was stressed because he was uncharacteristically cleaning his lounge.

'Well, God alone knows what's going to happen now,' said Chastity. 'Knuckles will have got straight on the phone to Billy-no-nut. He will soon find Lulu now her cover's blown.'

'Oh, I can't bear it! I can't bear it!' shrieked Daisy. Michael was inconsolable.

'That's it now. It's all over! There's no way I'm going to get the money in time to pay him off.'

'There there, me darling. Come to Edith.'

'And when he finds Lulu and discovers we've been hiding her, what's he going to do to us? I mean, Anne Frank for fuck's sake!' said Connie, waving his feather duster in the air.

'I've got no choice. I'll have to sell the shares to Fifi after all.'

'Oh, that's the fucking cherry on the bastard cake!' Connie launched his duster through the air at Michael, missing his head by inches.

'Ah! Now, err... let's not rush things. I'm sure we will think of something.' Chastity's words were of no comfort to Michael.

'But there's a legend that Billy drugs you, ties you to a chair then cuts off all your fingers, one by one.'

'Bloody hell, I've just had my nails done!' said Connie, holding his hands up for all to see.

'It's true. They say he's got a load of dismembered fingers in a Primark box under his bed!' Chastity was horrified.

'No? Surely it can't be true? Primark? The shame of it all! Connie, we need a plan. We've got to buy more time.'

Connie thought for a moment. 'The posters! Lulu's all over the posters outside.' Chastity leapt to his feet.

'That's right! Daisy, go downstairs and take down the posters out front. Everything with Lulu on. And Connie, run around Soho and tell everyone to say Lulu's not in the show anymore.' As Daisy and Connie ran for the front door, Chastity clasped his hands to his face. 'I only hope it's not too late!'

At Sugar Sugar's front entrance, Daisy grappled nervously with a big bunch of keys, trying to find the one to unlock the poster cabinets.

'Right, start with the big posters Daisy. And don't forget the ones around the side,' said Connie, buttoning up the front of his jersey against the cooler weather.

'What about the front lobby?'

236

'Yes, all of them! I'm going to run around Brewer Street and Old Compton and spread the word while everyone's still open.'

Just a few metres away under shelter of darkness, Billy sat beside Knuckles in the Daimler, puffing on a cigar. They watched Connie run off up the street as Daisy opened a poster cabinet by the front entrance.

'Taking the posters down, faggot? Smart. But not smart enough. Cause I already know!' laughed Billy. Knuckles smirked as he dialled a number on his mobile and handed it to him. 'Hello Vince. No, just shut your mouth and listen! Forget about that. I've got a way for you to pay off what you owe me for the drugs. I've got a little job for you. I want you to deliver something to someone else that's really pissed me off! Soho. Tomorrow night. Sweet.' He handed the phone back to Knuckles, who put it back in his pocket and pulled the car away from the kerb.

At that moment, Madame Fifi arrived at the club. 'Daisy! What are you doing with my posters?' she screamed. 'Put them back this instant!'

'But it's Lulu! Billy knows who she is so we've got to hide her,' Daisy gushed tearfully. 'He's got dismembered fingers in a Primark box.' Fifi drew a deep breath.

'Primark? This is more serious than I thought! Regardless, I'm running a business here, not a sanctuary for wayward drag queens. Put my posters back up. Immediately!' Shoving her hand against the glass door she stormed inside.

Halfway down the stairs, she paused for a moment. 'It would seem that there is more to this than meets my eye,' she pondered to herself. 'This Billy has lost his pride, as well as his ten thousand pounds and a bollock. That puts the price on Michael's head a little higher, would you not say? Hmm.'

She continued to the bottom of the stairs, the seed of an idea germinating in her twisted mind. Perhaps she had at last found a solution to her own dilemma. 'I will not be further humiliated. If Michael will not sell the remaining shares of my club to me, I will sell him to Billy and take them for myself!'

Reaching her office, she threw her coat into the chair and picked up the phone. 'Enquiries? Give me the number for Billy's Bar. Southend-on-Sea in Essex. HURRY UP!'

The following night in the dressing room, Michael was getting his makeup all wrong. He had not long learnt how to apply it to his own face, and although the more he did it the better it got, tonight his hands were shaking too much.

'This is a really stupid idea,' he moaned, slamming his eye pencil onto the dressing room table. 'Billy probably knows exactly where I am by now and you're expecting me to do a fucking show? I should be putting on a ferry to France, not putting on lipstick!'

'If you're hitch-hiking every big butch lorry driver from here to Dover, how are we going to keep an eye on you?' said Connie.

'Keep an eye on your shares, you mean!'

'Now, you're gettin' yourself in a two and eight. Take a chill pill, duck,' said Edith, patting Michael on the shoulder.

'Don't you think Billy would have the ports and airports covered by now?' Chastity said. 'Don't underestimate how much you've pissed him off by pissing off.'

'Him and everyone else, Dolly!'

'Look, the safest place you can be is on stage. What's he going to do in front of two hundred people? He can't shoot you now, can he?' Chastity continued applying lip-gloss. Michael slumped back in his chair and sighed.

'God, I need a drink!'

The door from the customer area opened and in walked a woman Michael hadn't seen before.

'Ooh, atmosphere!' she said, waving her hands in front of her face as though she were describing a pungent smell. 'I'm not interrupting anything sinister and twisted, am I?'

'Fanny? Darling!' Chastity jumped to his feet and pulled her into a hug. 'No, we were just talking.'

'Pity. Oh well, I'm here now!'

Having seen the woman's reflection in the mirror, Michael turned in his chair to take a closer look. The first thing he noticed was how tall she was. Her age was hard to distinguish, though she wasn't a spring chicken. Long russet hair bounced in giant curls across quite broad shoulders, and as her hands stretched around Chastity's back, her long and perfectly manicured glitter fingernails sparkled.

'I heard about Lettie,' she said solemnly. 'I'm sorry for your loss.' She removed her coat to reveal a short black sequinned cocktail dress showing ample cleavage and long legs.

'Yes, well let's not discuss that Jewish bitch at the moment. You know Edith don't you?'

'Yes we know each other, don't we Edith? You're adorable! How are you dear?'

'Well, you know,' said Edith bashfully, shrugging her shoulders and grinning.

'Lulu, this is Fanny. Fanny the Tranny, queen of the transvestites,' said Chastity dramatically, as though introducing the next act on stage.

'Not anymore,' she added. 'I've been to the butcher in Istanbul. Had my pork chopped.' Connie had initially appeared relatively uninterested by her arrival, but she had got his attention now.

'No? So you're a real woman now, then?' he said, taking a sip of bottled water and looking her up and down.

'Connie darling, I've always been a real woman! But now I have all the matching accessories. I'm like the Venus De Milo, still gorgeous but with a couple of bits missing! I'll show you. See?' Fanny lifted up the front of her skirt and pulled her knickers down around her knees. With a nervous cough, Michael swiftly turned back to his makeup. Having only met Fanny a few seconds ago, it seemed intrusive to be staring at her vagina quite so soon.

'Well, would you be looking at that?' said Chastity with wonderment.

'Looks like a real clack, doesn't it darling?' asked Fanny proudly. Away from his field of expertise, Connie had already lost interest.

'Why would I know?' he said, taking another swig of Evian.

'Isn't that what happened to that little blonde boy?' Edith asked Chastity.

'No that was a different thing altogether. She's talking about Scott - the one who got drunk and pissed up an electric fence? He's called Sally now.'

240

Stooping down, Edith moved in for a closer look. She screwed up her face and squinted.

'Is it supposed to be all puffy and wet like that?' she said, pointing.

'Ah! No that's just a bit of seepage around my vulva.'

'My neighbour's boy had one of them.'

'No Edith, that was a Volvo,' Chastity corrected.

'Weren't you born with one of these, Edith darling?' Fanny asked, amused by the look of deep concentration on Edith's face.

'I don't think so, duck. There's just a kind of flap.'

Connie spat his water across the makeup table, coughing and spluttering. 'Can we just stop talking about clacks, flaps and Volvo's for a minute?' he shouted, dabbing his chin dry with a towel. 'Don't forget we've got a show to do.'

As Fanny pulled up her knickers, one of Sugar Sugar's bar men entered carrying a tray of drinks.

'What's this?' asked Chastity.

'One of the punters has bought you all a bevvy,' he said handing the tray to Edith. Alcohol was just what Michael needed. On stage probably was the safest place for him to be now that Billy knew he was a drag queen. But he was still stressed, what with that and all this alien genitalia being waved about in the room. He grabbed at a drink.

'Oh fantastic. Cheers!' he said, drinking it down in one.

'Ooh, golly wars!' laughed Edith. 'You must've been thirsty.'

'I think it's got more to do with nerves,' said Chastity. 'Anyway, whilst we've all got a drink, let's make a toast to your new clack.'

'Yes. To Fanny's new fanny! Here you are, everyone,' said Edith offering the tray, but as she did it tipped forward, pouring everything down the front of Chastity's costume.

'Ooh, sorry duck. Aw, it's gone all over your frock! I hope that's not a bad omen.'

'Oh for feck's sake!' said Chastity grabbing the towel from Connie's hand. 'I'll have to change. Lulu, you open the show instead. At least then you can tell us if there's anyone from Billy's Bar you recognise in the audience.'

Despite knowing Michael would be nervous just being the first on stage, let alone under the circumstances, Connie leaned forward and whispered cattily in his ear, 'But if you see a gun Dolly, run like bugger!'

After a brash five minute theatrical overture, Michael took to the dry-ice covered stage. Wearing a beige trench coat and dark glasses, a single spotlight followed him suspiciously darting about like a film noir spy in hiding. He sang with a slight Dietrich lilt to match the German parlour-music backing track.

'I know there's someone after me. He's counting every breath I breathe. Whenever I go out, he follows me about. I cannot hide!'

He was trying to look at every face in the audience to see if he recognised any of Billy's mobsters. But with about two hundred people in the auditorium, it wasn't easy through dark glasses. He removed them and put them in his pocket.

'He watches through my bedroom window, each time my head lies on the pillow. It's not an easy chore, I'm on the second floor. This man is mad!'

So far, he couldn't see anyone he recognised from Southend. Though unusually, his eyes did feel a little blurry. Perhaps it was the dry ice he thought, blinking heavily.

'I wish he'd go away and let me be, but everything I do he wants to see. So every time I turn around, he's there - biting my tail. Biting my tail.'

Without warning, a sharp pain shot through his stomach. He winced. The audience laughed believing it to be a part of his act, but it wasn't. More worrying, the sound of their laughter seemed to reverberate through his head as though it had taken on an echo.

'I know he photographs my bits. He's really giving me the shits. God knows what kind of tool, lurks under his cagoule, to spy on me?'

The pain in his abdomen accelerated, burning like fire. His head started pounding. His convulsions brought yet more laughter from the audience, though to Michael it was sounding more and more distant.

'I wish he'd... I'm... err... I'm...'

Everything went black and he collapsed unconscious, disappearing from view into the dry-ice. The audience were on their feet applauding the drama of it all. However, Chastity and Connie knew this wasn't what had been rehearsed. Confused, they looked at each other. As Fanny zipped Chastity into his next costume, Connie glanced around the door onto the stage. He grasped his chest with horror as he saw Michael's lifeless body lying face down on the boards.

'What's happening out there?' Chastity had seen Connie's face and ran to look.

'Oh my God,' gasped Connie. 'She's been shot!'

CHAPTER TWENTY FOUR

Connie slipped a rolled-up dressing gown under Michael's head as he laid rambling and slurring semi-conscious on the dressing room floor. Fanny held on to a tearful Edith as Chastity loosened his costume and searched his body for evidence of wounds.

'I can't see any blood. I think she's just collapsed. It's probably the stress and gulping that drink down.'

'That's it! Lulu's drink,' said Connie. 'She said that Billy-no-nut drugs them before he cuts off their fingers.'

'Sorry darling, am I missing something here?' Fanny hadn't been expecting such drama.

'Do you think we need an ambulance?' said Chastity.

'No, she's conscious now. But she'll need watching, especially as we don't know what she's taken. She was the only one who drank from the tray before it went over. Do you suppose all of those drinks were drugged? How would they know which one he would drink?' Connie shuddered at the thought.

'We need to get her away from Soho immediately, before anyone arrives to kidnap her,' said Chastity.

'Get her away from the poisoned dwarf in this state before she gives her our shares!' added Connie.

Chastity had to think fast. They had called an interval in the show, but too long a gap would create too much attention after only one song.

'Connie, we need a plan.'

'What about Edith?' he replied.

'Yes! Edith, can you take Lulu home with you? We'll have to get her makeup off, get her dressed and then put her in that yashmak, so you can get her to the bus stop. No on second thoughts, take a cab. Connie hand me my purse. Edith, go and get your coat on, love.' Edith took a twenty-pound note from him and ran off to the kitchen.

'There is something sinister going on, isn't there?' asked Fanny suspiciously, helping them lift Michael into a chair. 'Is this to do with Lettie?' Chastity grasped her hand despairingly.

'Oh, Fanny, love! It's all going tits upwards.'

Chastity was about to explain what had happened, but he was interrupted by Madame Fifi storming into the room.

'What is the meaning of this?' she screamed. 'And what is this boy doing in my club masquerading as a drag queen? Since his arrival it has been one humiliation after another. This is the doings of Lettie! Why? Why? He is a messenger of doom, I tell you, DOOM!'

'Oh why don't you shut the fuck up!' spat Connie. 'I've just about had enough of all this. She's slumped here half dead with the Essex drug Mafia after her and all you can worry about is your fucking club. "Doom, I tell you, DOOM!"' he said, dramatically mimicking her accent.

'If it wasn't for me, you charlatans would both be on the streets!' Fifi retaliated.

246

'If it wasn't for you killing Lettie, we wouldn't be in this fuckin' mess in the first place! So why don't you take your fake tits and your deformed penis and fuck yourself right up your own fat arse!' snarled Connie, looking to Chastity for approval. Fifi had steam coming from her ears.

'What did you say? You twisted, evil little cockroach! Do you know who you're talking to? I've never been so insulted in all my life!'

'Remember back that far, can you? Never insulted? Can you hear this? She's got a face like an horse with lipstick. Do me a favour!'

'STOP IT!' Chastity shouted. 'Stop it both of you. Fifi, you're in this up to your neck as much as the rest of us. If Billy-no-nut and his men descend on Sugar Sugar, do you really think they're going to tidy up and put a quiche in the oven on their way out?' He had got Fifi's attention. 'Someone working for Billy has drugged Lulu's drink. We need to smuggle Lulu out of here, get the show started again to avoid suspicion, then find this drug dealer. Otherwise it won't just be Lulu wearing fingerless gloves. It will be all of us!'

While Fifi investigated who had paid for the tray of drinks, Fanny helped Chastity get Michael ready to leave. Pulling him to his feet, they led him out to the entrance lobby. His legs were very wobbly but he could walk and talk, though his perception was marred.

'Come on then, Lulu love. That's it,' Chastity comforted as they approached Edith by the exit.

'Ooh, he looks like death!' she said.

'It's a yashmak darling,' smiled Fanny. 'They're all the rage this season!'

Michael raised his head and grinned at Edith. His eyesight was a little out of focus, but he could distinctly see two of her. He squinted and tried to readjust, but try as he may he could still only see two Ediths.

'I'm seeing double!' he giggled. Chastity looked then did a double-take. To his surprise, he could see two Ediths as well.

'Buggeration, I'm seeing double too!' Edith looked at her double and laughed out loud.

'No, silly arse, this is my sister Ethel.' Ethel giggled too.

'Silly arse!' she repeated, like a parrot. Chastity was gobsmacked.

'You're a dark horse, Edith. In all these years you never told me you had a sister!'

'Well. I can't tell a lie... I forgot!' She looked away, smiling with embarrassment.

For feck's sake, how can you forget you had a sister?'

'Well I don't see her that often. She lives up The Institute. She ain't all that cum-piss-monty.'

'Compos mentis?' suggested Fanny, more bemused than ever.

'She's stayin' with me for a few weeks while they rebuild it. Some nut case burnt it to the ground.'

'I want to see a solicitor,' shouted Ethel, shaking a finger in Chastity's face.

'Don't be rude now Ethel,' said Edith calmly. 'She's got psychotic leanings. Or is it psychopathic? Oh, I always get them two mixed up!' She laughed, as did Ethel and Michael. Chastity was open-mouthed.

Fanny bit her lip in contemplation for a moment before turning to him and saying, 'Chastity darling, are you sure this is a good idea?'

'I don't see we have any choice. Right, off you go then,' he handed Michael by the elbows to Edith. She looped his arm through hers, telling Ethel to do the same on the other side.

'Come on then duck,' she said pushing the glass door open.

'Phone me, Lulu. Anytime,' Chastity called after them up the street. 'Jesus, I hope I've done the right thing! Anyway Fanny, look. Can you cover for Lulu for a day or two?'

'Of course, darling! I had a feeling you might need a little support. I'm glad I'm here for you. And it would be nice to get up there and perform again after all these years. I'm up for the craic.'

'I know. We've all just seen it!' Chastity laughed. They looped arms and walked back downstairs to the customer area.

It had been some time since Fanny had performed on stage at Sugar Sugar. She had never been part of the residential team but had made guest appearances now and again. In fact, some of the older clientele had recognised her when she first arrived. And the timing of her surprise arrival couldn't have been better. Aside from being able to cover for Michael, she also got on quite well with Fifi. If Billy was now attacking Sugar Sugar, the Sisterhood would have to side with her, and Fanny being neutral could make this connection a little easier.

It didn't take long for Chastity to find Fanny's old backing tracks. The frock she arrived in was already glamorous enough for the stage, so she offered to do a spot while they waited for news from Fifi about Billy's drug dealer.

'I like this one,' said Chastity pointing to a song on Fanny's list. 'Do you think you'll remember all those words?'

It will be like riding a bike,' smirked Fanny, 'though perhaps with a different saddle!'

Throwing a waist-length set of silver beads around her neck by way of something to play with, she ran to a microphone centre stage under the proscenium and launched into her legendary masterpiece.

'*I met a man some time ago, his name was Doctor Sin. He said, "now what's the trouble," I said, "where do I begin?" He moved my world in such a way, that there's no turning back. He doctored my appendage, then he cut off all the slack!*

'*If you are looking for something special, perhaps a different view of life? A little relish on your frank-furter? Then I could be your perfect wife.*'

She span her beads with her hand like a second world war propeller.

'*They call me Fanny, Fanny the tranny. Nice to meet you, how'd you do? They call me Fanny, Fanny the tranny. And I could be the girl for you.*'

'Sit on this then, baby!' yelled a drunk from the audience.

'Twenty pounds an hour, extra for children and animals!' she shouted back unabated.

'*Some find it freaky, or maybe kinky. Perhaps a little avante garde. But if you're in the mood, for trying something new, I guarantee I'll get you hard! They call me Fanny, Fanny the tranny, Nice to meet you, how'd you do? They call me Fanny, Fanny the tranny. And I could be the girl for you.'*

From her vantage point slightly above the heads of the audience, she could see the barman who had delivered the drugged drinks pointing someone out to Fifi, though it was hard to tell who he meant. Taking the microphone from its stand, she continued with her song, parading from one side of the stage to the other kicking a leg back dramatically with every step.

'I know I'm not made from the mould that God had first intended. But just like News at Ten, I can be specially extended. I'm every inch a woman, not a fella in a frock. And up my skirt's all Fanny, there's no sign of any cock!'

As her anthem neared its conclusion, she could see Fifi pushing her way at speed through the audience towards the dressing room. Perhaps she had discovered the perpetrator of this chaos? The entire crowd joined in the last chorus.

'They call me Fanny, Fanny the tranny. Nice to meet you, how'd you do? They call me Fanny, Fanny the tranny. And I could be the girl for you!'

The auditorium shook with rapturous applause. After taking a curtsey, Fanny looked over to the butch girl on the sound system and dragged one finger across her neck in a cut-throat motion. Message received, the stage lights dimmed and cabaret was replaced with kicking dance music.

'She's found him!' Chastity said to Fanny as she re-joined them in the dressing room. 'Come on.' They both followed Connie and Madame Fifi in the customer area.

'That's him,' said Fifi, pointing to a shifty looking lad wearing a football shirt and a baseball cap.

Holding his bottle of beer under his arm, he was selling pills to two bodybuilders in the middle of the busy dance floor. 'He must have tampered with the drinks before having them sent over. Let's go teach him a lesson he will never forget!'

Chastity and Connie followed as Fifi and Fanny pushed through the crowd towards him. Grabbing an arm each, they tipped him backwards off balance, knocking his bottle smashing to the floor. Without stopping, they dragged him towards Fifi's office - the rubber heels of his trainers leaving wavy black trails on the wooden floor.

'What the fuck?' he shouted, taken off-guard.

'You drugged our drinks, you chavvy low-life scum,' growled Chastity.

'And you're going to pay, Dolly. Big time!'

'You what? Get your fucking hands off me, you queer perverts!' he yelled, kicking and struggling. In the dim light of the bar, the two women had at first appeared no threat to him. But he hadn't anticipated them both having quite as much testosterone.

'We have ways of making naughty boys pay,' said Fifi. 'And you, young man, have been a very naughty boy!'

'Argh!' he cried, looking in horror first at Fanny and then at Fifi. 'Get them... him... what are they, a he or a she?'

'Well, that's a bit of a long story actually!' said Chastity.

'Take him to... THE SAFE ROOM!' Fifi commanded theatrically. Unable to break free, he was getting a little freaked.

'What? No! Let me go, you fucking faggots! Let me go! I'll get the gavvers on to you.'

252

'Our Chief Inspector's having a whiskey at the bar,' laughed Fifi. 'Shall I extend an invitation? He simply adores cheeky little boys like you.' His eyes flashed like a trapped animal, feet kicking desperately at the door and doorframe of Fifi's office, trying anything to break loose.

'You're a sicko! You're all fucking sickos!'

'I know, darling. Isn't it delicious?' smirked Fanny, deepening her voice for dramatic effect. The dealer was dribbling at the mouth with fear, gasping and spluttering as they dragged him through into the next room.

'You can't do this! Nooooo!' His scream muffled as Chastity closed the door to the safe room behind them and joined Connie at the bank of closed-circuit television sets in Fifi's office.

CHAPTER TWENTY FIVE

It was all Edith and Ethel could do to stop Michael falling from the taxi straight into the gutter. He tried to make sense of his surroundings but sound, sight and touch were all drifting in and out of focus at the same time. There was a very strange bubbling in his stomach and he felt nauseous. He could see that they were standing in front of a terrace of small Victorian houses, though it was quite dark. He had the sensation of being about to drop from a precipice.

'Here we are then,' sighed Edith, giving him a little hug. 'It not much, but it's home.'

'I feel giddy. I've got vertigo,' he mumbled.

'No, you ain't got far to go, duck. We've already got 'ere!'

'Are we by the sea? I can hear seagulls.'

'Aw, you soppy date, that's a car alarm,' she laughed, handing Ethel a key. 'Open the door, dear.'

'You soppy date,' echoed Ethel. As they stepped up to the portico, a nearby dog began howling protectively. Michael gasped and jumped back with horror.

'It's a wolf! I'm not going in there, you've got a wolf. He will eat us all alive!' he cried.

'That's next door's Afghan hound,' laughed Edith, pulling him through the door into the hall. 'They lock him out in the back garden at night. Come on, in you get.' The narrow hallway appeared to be revolving right in front of Michael's eyes.

'We're in a tunnel. The tunnel of no return. We're all gonna die! We're all gonna die!' He cried loudly.

'Shh!' said Ethel, putting her hand over his mouth. 'This ain't no tunnel. It's Edith's back passage.'

'I don't want to be up Edith's back passage!' he spat through her hand.

With a struggle, they moved him through to a small dark room at the back of the house. As Edith switched on the overhead light, his eyes were flooded with colour from an array of mismatched ornaments and an oddment of framed pictures dotted around the room. It was too much for him to focus on all at once. Right now he just needed to lie down and close his eyes.

'Do the tea, Ethel,' said Edith, taking Michael from her and sitting him on a long tatty overstuffed settee to one wall. 'Now this is me parlour, duck. You can sleep it off on this day bed.' As she let go of his arm, he slumped to one side against a pile of threadbare cushions. Edith lifted a blanket across his legs and sat beside him, smiling and brushing the hair from his eyes. 'You'll be safe here you know, dear.'

'I feel really sick!' he said, rubbing his tummy.

'I'll bring you one of me china pos. The toilet's down the bottom of the garden with the fairies. Bit like Ethel, she's off with the fairies an' all!' she laughed. Michael wasn't sure what a china po was.

'Down the garden?' He was trying to understand, but it was so difficult with the room spinning and every word echoing. The only thing of clarity to him was Edith's kindness.

'It's not easy to get down there at the moment. It's all overgrown with stinging nettles since my Bert died. Ooh, he did love his garden. It used to be beautiful,' she remembered with a happy grin. 'We had an apple tree, a pear tree and a country cottage border right round the outside. I hardly ever saw him, he'd spend so long out there! Till he wanted his dinner, that is. Gave him a ferocious appetite being out there in the fresh air all day. Anyway, aside from that I think there's a storm coming. I can feel it up me waters.' She leaned and pulled forward a small round table, straightening the doyley as Ethel returned with a tray. Putting it gently down she stood on tiptoe, placing her hand delicately over her mouth and coughing to draw attention.

'Tea up, everyone! How many lumps do you want? Cream or lemon, Mrs Farquar?' she said softly, picking up an imaginary milk jug and pouring nothing into the three teacups. Edith raised her eyes to the ceiling.

'That was bloody quick!' she said, lifting the teapot lid and glancing inside. 'Oh, you've filled up the teapot from the hot water tap again haven't you, you silly old moo.'

'Silly old moo!' Ethel repeated.

'Yes, you! I told you, cold water in the kettle, then on the stove till it whistles.' Ethel whistled like a steaming kettle. 'That's it. Oh, I'll go and do it. You keep an eye on Lulu. She can't help it,' she said, patting Michael's hand. 'It was all them bombings during the war. Sent her loop-de-dish and a dog end!'

As Edith stood and carried the tray back out to the kitchen, Ethel sat in her place, staring intensely at Michael. Even in his surreal state of mind he could sense there was something scarily unhinged about Edith's secret sister.

'I've got a condition, you know,' she said.

'Eh?'

'They won't let me have a fork or knife. I have to use plastic.'

Michael fidgeted nervously. 'Oh my God!' he said, backing himself up into the corner of the day bed.

'I'll look after you. I'm your number one fan. I was going to be a nurse. But that was before the incident. And now, there's no tellings what I might do.' She slowly reached out a long bony hand towards him.

'Edith? EDITH?' he cried out for help, pulling the blanket over his head.

Back in Madame Fifi's office, Chastity and Connie were at the closed-circuit television screens intently watching the drug dealer's demise at the hands of Fifi and Fanny.

'What you going to do? Keep away from me!' he screamed from the monitor.

'Sell drugs in my club, would you?' bellowed Fifi. 'If drugs are to be purchased, it will be from me.'

Connie lit a cigarette. 'Ooh, nasty underpants. And they should have took his chaddy socks off before they strapped him down,' he said, pointing at the screen. 'You know, lit a few candles... it's not been thought about. Still, he's quite fit. I like them feral. I'd love one of these monitors in my bedroom. What does that tattoo above his arse say?'

Chastity strained his eyes to see on such a small monitor. 'I think it says no entry. He'll be sorry he

258

put that invitation across his back. Still, naughty boys have to be punished.'

'Listen to Miss No Sex Unless We're Married talking,' smirked Connie. 'Chaste by name and by nature. It's about time you took that wedding ring off now. Nicky won't be coming back you know. How many years has it been?' Chastity adjusted the modest gold band, spinning the tiny diamond back to the front.

'Four,' he said with a smile, remembering the day his ex had first put it on his finger. 'I do take it off now and again. When I shave my fingers. Anyway, I thought you said you liked this ring?'

'It takes the emphasis off your liver spots,' said Connie, flicking his cigarette ash on the floor. Chastity didn't really want to talk about his past right now. Luckily, there was plenty to distract Connie from the subject.

'Ooh look, Fanny's got that long pole with the hook on the end!' he laughed. The dealer however didn't find this at all funny.

'Huh!! What the fuck are you going to do with that?' he cried out, struggling to break free of his tethers.

'Open the air vent, darling.' Fanny smiled up at the camera and winked mischievously. Connie squealed with delight.

'Now, that's just fucking evil!' But this was nothing compared to what was coming. From a cardboard box in a large metal cupboard, Fifi took an enormous black dildo and waved it in front of the dealer's face.

'And what's that? Oh, fuck off no! You're having a laugh, ain't ya?' He began thrashing madly, desperate to escape.

'Would you be looking at the size of that?' said Chastity in awe. 'That can't be for use, it must be Display Only.'

'Hmm. Though I do enjoy a challenge myself!' Connie licked his lips. Fifi took a large handful of Crisco from a big can in the cupboard and began lubricating the monster member.

'This is going to hurt you more than it hurts me,' said Fifi with fake compassion. 'Darling, meet Hercules!' The defenceless chav was hysterical.

'Please! I'm begging you! Noooo!'

'You know, I could sit in her office and watch this all day,' said Connie casually. 'We should have brought sandwiches! And put a tape in to record it. There's queens up Compton Street that would pay shit loads to see this.'

Put a tape in? The coin dropped and lights began flashing in Chastity's head. 'Of course! BRILLIANT! What a way for Fifi to finally put that willy of hers to good use.'

'Eh? No, I'm sorry Dolly, you've completely lost me now.'

'A cunning stunt.'

'What, as well as her willy?'

'I have a plan to top all plans!' Chastity flapped excitedly. 'It's going to be bye-bye concrete sling-backs, bye-bye Billy-no-nut and hello Sugar Sugar shares. Connie love, this is it. All our troubles are finally over!'

Michael's night was restless and disturbing. His dreams were erratic and speeded up in parts like a Harold Lloyd film. And outside the window, a powerful electric storm seemed to rock the house with every clap of thunder. It kept waking him and made Edith's parlour appear like something from a Hammer Horror B-movie.

At one point he dreamt he was entering a small chapel of rest. As the huge wooden door swung slowly open with a deep dark creak, he was looking up the aisle towards a coffin on a stand at the altar. He could see a man standing looking into the casket and several people sat in pews at the front, though he couldn't make out who they were. As he effortlessly glided slowly forwards, the man turned and walked in his direction. It was Billy. Blood-stained cash notes rained on him from above as he swaggered straight past Michael and out of the chapel without even noticing his presence. At the front sobbing loudly, he could now see Connie and Chastity in full mourning drag, Frenchie in her wedding dress and Daisy on the end of the pew eating a pasty with his arm around Edith. The only one not sobbing was Madame Fifi, who kept glancing at her watch impatiently. A Rabbi in a black gown and hat surreally floated up from behind the coffin grasping a leather-bound book to his chest. Spelt out on the front in big gold letters it said, The Drag Scripture. Then looking directly at him, the priest began to laugh hysterically. It was Lettie, with a full face of drag makeup framed by payot ringlets and a long grey beard. Michael did everything he could to stop moving closer to the coffin, but had no control. Lifting off the floor and rising to hover just inches above it, he looked down to see that the corpse was his own. To his horror the black piercing eyes opened, staring menacingly straight back at him.

He awoke with a start to see his own face right in front of him. As he screamed in fear, so did the face. He then realised it was Ethel, sitting astride his chest and holding a large mirror to his mouth.

'Ethel, what are you doing?'

'I was checking if you was still breathing,' she said, climbing down and teetering off into the darkness. The parlour appeared to be pulsating around him as moonlight shadows from trees outside the window darted here and there. He closed his eyes and drifted back off to sleep.

As his next dream flooded into focus, he realised he was on a hospital gurney being wheeled along a barren corridor by Connie and Chastity dressed as nurses. 'She's going to turn you into the perfect drag queen!' said Nurse Connie, as Nurse Chastity nodded in agreement. The trolley stopped in an operating theatre. A green smocked, rubber-gloved surgeon turned to face him. It was Lettie again, fully made up holding a horrifyingly large scalpel.

'Hello gorgeous!' cried Surgeon Lettie with a loud evil cackle, moving the razor sharp blade closer to his face.

'Don't! Don't...' Michael could hear himself pleading, struggling desperately to take control of this
262

hideous situation. As he leapt from the trolley, he realised he was wearing an orange layered going away dress with a matching jacket, fur hat and muff. Suddenly, he was Barbra Streisand as Fanny Brice in the movie Funny Girl.

'...Don't tell me not to live,' he belted, pushing past his deranged medical team and running back out into the corridor. He could feel cold air biting against his vulnerable naked body through the back of the dress - open and tied with strings like a hospital gown. '...To rain on my parade.' The music slowly echoed away into the distance, replaced by the sound of his own pounding heartbeat as an intern grabbed him and wrestled him to the floor. It was Stud Muffin. Suddenly Michael was dressed as a girl in Frenchie's bridesmaid frock. Sitting astride him, the stripper ripped off his gleaming white smock to reveal his naked muscled torso and pinned Michael down by each arm, moving in as though to kiss.

A deafening thunderclap shook him out of his nightmare. He sat bolt upright and looked around Edith's parlour, sweating and panting. Though the spinning of the room seemed to have subsided a little, his head was pounding. 'Arrgh! Oh my God, my brain!' He said cupping his forehead. His mouth was dry and gluey. He reached and took a swig of cold tea left over from earlier. As he leaned forward, his stomach gargled loudly. 'Oh my God, my gut!' As he sat back upright, he let out a long, awfully loud and really rather wet fart. 'Oh my God, my arse!'

Jumping to his feet, he grabbed for the chamber pot on the floor, but in his haste he kicked it. It shot way back under the day bed out of reach, taking one of his shoes with it. He desperately looked around the room for an alternative, but it was hard to see in the dim light with so much clutter. He looked for a light switch to no avail. Although he now only had the option of one shoe, he was still fully clothed from the night before. It was clear the only chance he had was to make a run for the toilet at the bottom of the garden.

In mostly pitch black other than hints of moonlight through the window and frequent blinding flashes of lightning, he made his way to the back of the house. At the end of the hall was a small old-fashioned scullery with a Belfast sink, scrubbing board and mangle. He turned the giant key in the back door and twisted the handle. The door blew swiftly open on a gust of rain-soaked wind. He could see the dark outline of a small shed at the end of a long path through a swathe of violently swaying nettles. A judder ran through his body - a primal fear of the unknown magnifying the remnants of the drug still racing through his veins. As he stepped out onto a little paved area, he could feel the cold rainwater seeping through his socks. The nettles were chest high. As they were tossed by the fierce wind, little patches of the concrete path ahead became visible in the moonlight for a brief moment, before disappearing once more beneath the sea of foliage. The wind whistling through the trees seemed to be speaking in voices of the long dead. He took a deep breath and gulped as best he could with an ever increasingly dry throat. He was terrified, but comforted by the thought that the journey back would be easier. He couldn't hold on any longer, he would have to make a run for it.

To a deafening clap of thunder, he put his head down and ran towards the shed. Unlike his dreams, everything seemed to be in slow motion. He missed the path several times, his already wet socks sinking into mushy clinging soil. He lifted his legs high as he ran, trying to combat the waves of nettles pushing him back.

Then suddenly to his absolute horror, out of the corner of one eye he could see a white shrouded figure, glowing in the intermittent moonlight. He turned to face his nemesis, staring straight at him over the fence from the next garden. The ghoulish creature opened its enormous mouth and let out a long blood curdling moan.

'Wooh, wooh, wooh, wooh, wooh!' Michael was mortified. He screamed and fell backwards, disappearing into a sodden grave of nettles as his bowels finally emptied into his pants. He jumped back to his feet before the monster could reach him and tear him limb from limb, only to realise that it was next door's Afghan Hound with its front paws up on the fence.

'Oh God, I wish I could die!' he moaned. 'And when I get to Heaven, I'm going to punch Lettie so hard in the mouth her teeth will fly out of her arse!' He was relieved that it was only a dog and not the Mummy of Death after all, but horrified that he had emptied his bowels in the middle of Edith's garden. He threw the handful of soil he'd scooped in panic at the dog, which yelped and jumped back down out of sight. Then he painstakingly made his way slowly back towards the house, trying desperately not to make a bad situation any worse.

Back in the scullery, Michael closed and locked the back door. He looked down at himself, soaking wet and smeared with mud with bits of nettle sticking out of every part of his clothing. He figured the best thing to do was to clean himself up as best he could in the sink. His only saving grace was that there was no one there to see him in this embarrassing state. He undid his button fly and slowly pulled off his jeans, dropping them into the sink. Then he bent forward to remove his loaded underpants.

As he stood back up, a flash of lighting revealed a twelve-inch kitchen knife pointing directly into his face. He screamed and jumped back, pants flying from his hand and sticking to the tiled wall behind the back door. It was Ethel.

'I thought you was a burglar,' she said coldly. Standing naked from the waist down, he tried to speak but nothing came out at first. He looked behind him at the pants sliding slowly down the tiles leaving a trail, then back at Ethel, still pointing the knife at his head.

'Ethel, what the fuck... it's me, Michael! Put the knife down now, there's a good girl.'

'I don't know anyone called Michael,' she said tightening her grip on the knife.

'I mean Lulu! It's me, Lulu! Just go back to bed.'

'I can't. My bed's wet,' she said quickly shifting the point of the knife from his face down to his naked penis.

'Oh, that doesn't matter,' he gasped desperately. 'We all have accidents now and again. Look at me. I've just shit myself!'

'My bed's under the window. The rain's coming in.'

'Oh. I see what you mean, I thought you meant... Just put the knife down then move your bed away from the window. There, you see! Problem solved.' Ethel thought for a moment.

'I'll make a wish and twist the bed-knob. Then I'll be Angela Lansbury and it'll fly me to Portabello Road, won't it?' Michael had no idea what this psychotic old lady was talking about, but did believe she was capable of castration in an instant. He could hear his own heartbeat and beads of sweat began to form on his already sodden forehead.

'Eh? Oh, yes... anything you like. Just put... the knife... down!'

At that moment, the overhead light switched on. 'I heard a scream, what's goin' on?' said Edith, looking at Michael open-mouthed. Ethel hid the knife behind her back as though Edith standing behind her wouldn't see it. Michael quickly covered his manhood with both hands. 'Give me that thing here,' said Edith, taking the knife from Ethel's hand. 'Why are you naked? And what's that up my wall?' she said, pointing at his slithering pants. Michael's embarrassment and shame was overwhelming. His eyes welled with tears.

'I tried to get to the toilet, but I had an accident. Next door's dog...'

'Oh don't worry duck,' she said, putting down the knife and handing him a towel to wrap around. 'We'll soon have you sorted out. Look at you, poor love, covered in weeds.' She pushed back his fringe and removed a small sprig of leaves from his hair. As she held it up to look at it, Michael froze. He'd seen this distinctive plant somewhere before.

'Edith?' he said, taking it from her. 'No wonder your Bert spent all his time in the garden and had such a ferocious appetite. He was probably stoned. It's

267

weed alright, but it's not stinging nettle. You've got a garden full of cannabis!'

In Billy's Bar, Tamara watched nervously as Billy paced up and down waiting to hear from Vince the drug dealer. The phone ringing made her jump. 'Hello Billy's Bar, Tamara speaking. How can I help you?' she said, glancing at Billy as she picked up the receiver. He stopped and looked at her hold the phone away from her ear to protect it from the shouts of the caller. 'What's the matter with you, you little toss bag?' she shouted back impatiently. This was the call Billy had been waiting for. He stormed across and snatched the phone out of her hand.

'About fucking time!' he growled. 'You're supposed to drug Michael and bring him here! If you're telling me...' He paused, having trouble understanding what Vince was trying to tell him. 'Slow down you nonce, I can't hear you!'

Tamara was just as keen to hear what Vince had to say. She knew that Michael was with friends looking out for him, but she also knew how cunning Billy was. But she smiled when she saw the look of discontent on Billy's face.

'Dildo like a fat bloke's arm? Hercules? What the fuck are you on tonight? You've let me down Vince. I want my money by Friday. You won't be such a wanker with no fingers, will ya!' Slamming down the phone, he grappled desperately for cigarettes from his back pocket, accidentally dropping his lighter on the floor in the process. It spun across the wooden planks and out of reach under one of the display fridges beneath the phone. With a loud scream of

268

frustration, he slammed his fist down in anger on the back counter.

'Now Michael's really pissing me off!'

'Oh, erm... why don't you give him another couple of weeks to get your money? Please Billy?' said Tamara desperately, taking a lighter from her pocket and trying to light Billy's cigarette for him. 'I know Michael. He won't let you down, I promise he won't!' Billy snatched the lighter from her petite hand and pushed her backwards along behind the counter.

'Oh no, it's gone way past that now. Fucking amateurs. Why do I surround myself with such idiots?' he yelled, running his arm the length of the counter, knocking glasses and beer bottles smashing in all directions. 'I'll have to go get him myself. But when I've got him, my God is he going to pay!'

The following afternoon, Chastity, Connie and Daisy sat around a table in the empty customer area at Sugar Sugar waiting for Michael's return. Madame Fifi paced the floor in front of them, increasingly frustrated that Billy had not returned her secret call. She had done everything she could to persuade Michael to part with the shares, and all attempts to find out who he really was and why Lettie had left him such a legacy had failed. Maybe Chastity and Connie knew more about what was going on than she did. If she could get them on side, they may divulge that piece of the puzzle to help her get the shares, or at least assist her in achieving her goal.

'So which one do you piddle out of then?' asked Daisy quite innocently, breaking the silence.

'Stop this at once!' screamed Fifi, slamming her hand on the table. 'Up with this humiliation I will not put. You speak as though I am some kind of circus freak! It is how I was born. You wouldn't treat me this way if I were in a wheelchair!'

'But ya are, Blanche, ya are!' bitched Connie sarcastically, in her best Bette Davis accent.

'No, stop it now. She's right,' defended Chastity.

'I'm not the outsider in this camp,' said Fifi. 'You are not thinking! This Michael arrives out of nowhere pretending to be a poor and innocent child with no family. And yet Lettie has left her fortune to him and not you, her dearest friends. What is he doing here? Do you still believe this is all such a big surprise to him?' Connie and Chastity looked at each other as doubt began to creep in - their trust in Michael blurred by a desire for it all to make sense.

'You mean, you think she arranged all this with Lettie before she died?' asked Connie.

'Or was it... before he killed her?' nodded Fifi knowingly.

'No! He couldn't have killed her. Could he? He doesn't have it in him,' said Chastity. 'Besides, Lettie was run over and Lulu hasn't got a car.'

'Hasn't he? How do you know?' smiled Fifi cunningly. Chastity didn't have an answer. 'And why is he hounded by this wicked baron, who has drugged him and wants to cut off his digits? And forcing my darlings Chastity, Connie and Daisy to hide him.'

'He wouldn't, would he?' said Daisy, tears welling in his eyes.

'He owes so much money. Desperate men do desperate things. Who knows what else he has done?' She moved in closer. 'Do you know how many years in prison you would get for hiding a wanted criminal?
270

That's if this Billy-nut-crunchy doesn't get you first!'
Daisy began to cry hysterically.

'I don't want to go in prison! Don't let them cut my fingers off!' he bawled. Chastity was very uncomfortable.

'Ooh, I feel like Cloris Leachman in Kiss Me Deadly!'

Connie was unsettled too. 'Now I'm really getting scared. I told you he would be trouble, didn't I? I knew it the minute I saw him.'

'It's all so hard to believe. He's somehow blackmailed Lettie into leaving everything to him? Then he's killed her and made us believe he's naive so that he can case the joint before he takes over?' said Chastity, shaking his head.

'He has infiltrated our lives and turned my precious children against me by promising them shares in my club,' said Fifi dramatically. 'What kind of evil lives amongst us?'

At that moment her mobile phone rang. 'Yes? This is Fifi. Ahh, Billy darling. We speak at last!'

CHAPTER TWENTY SEVEN

Chastity and Connie were utterly shocked that Billy would be phoning Fifi.

'Vince? Was that his name? Yes that was amusing,' she said into the phone, as she walked away from the group attempting to keep her conversation private. But they were hot on her heels listening. 'In that case, you should have returned my call earlier! Michael? Yes, I'm sure we can come to some mutual arrangement. But I need him to sign something before you... relocate his fingers.' Chastity and Connie looked at each other in profound disbelief at what they were hearing. 'Tomorrow afternoon? Yes, I will be waiting for you. Now ciao.'

As she snapped her phone shut, Chastity grabbed her by the shoulder and spun her round. 'Hold on a minute. Returned my call earlier? You had this all planned!' he shouted in her face. 'You're prepared to give Lulu a death sentence just to get her shares? Without even trying to find out the real truth? What kind of evil lives amongst us, you said? We're looking at it!'

'This has nothing to do with you. It's business!' she snapped in her own defence.

'It wasn't nothing to do with us just now when you wanted us on side!' spat Connie. 'You've tried to turn us against our sister just so you can hand her over to Billy-no-nut.'

'Connie, how can you trust that imposter?' pleaded Fifi.

'I trust her more than I fucking trust you, you deceitful old pug! And if you're prepared to kill for those shares, who's to say that you didn't murder Lettie?'

Daisy was beside himself with grief. 'Oh, I can't cope with this anymore! It's like being on Eastenders,' he snivelled, taking a hanky to his nose and blowing.

'Because Creighton Cross left it all to her and not you,' said Chastity. 'Yet you thought it would automatically revert to you if Lettie suddenly died. But in the meantime, she left it all to Lulu. And that's why you want rid of her too!'

'Fools! FOOLS!' Fifi threw her arms into the air and turned away before they had a chance to back her into a corner. 'You think you have it all worked out. There is no clue in your empty heads of this enormity. You think you know everything, but you know jack!'

'Now I'm really confused,' gasped Daisy through tears. 'Who the fuck's Jack?'

'You're deformed with bitterness, evil and revenge, you spiteful twisted old moose,' said Connie, following Fifi across the room. 'I've known some mooses in my time, but you're the moose to top all mooses.' He turned to Chastity. 'What's the plural of moose, is it mooses or moosi?' Chastity shrugged. Connie continued unabated. 'You shouldn't have been a club hostess, you should have been a bloody traffic warden! Your willy's not the only thing that's not right about you!'

Fifi stopped and turned to respond, but seeing the woman who had just arrived by surprise at the bottom of the stairs topped any level of harassment Connie could possibly throw at her. Grabbing at her chest she shrieked a deep intake of breath, stumbling back against one of the tables. Chastity and Connie stopped in their tracks with shock and gazed at her clinging on to the table-top - eyes wide and staring, lips peeled back as though the very sight of the woman had poisoned her like a shot of strychnine.

'Is she having a heart attack?' said Chastity, grabbing Connie's hand. Fifi responded by stretching out her arm and pointing a long immaculately manicured finger to the figure at the bottom of the stairs.

'Verity... Van... Cougar!' she gasped.

'Ain't you had that little thing removed yet, honey?' asked Verity in a New York Manhattan drawl, removing her tan leather Chanel gloves. Chastity and Connie span to see who had so devastated the indestructible Madame Fifi.

She was a tall curvaceous woman, draped in a figure hugging beige and leopard skin ensemble with matching booties and hat. Immaculately turned out, she wore little jewellery other than a massive killer-diamond on a broach fastening a cream cashmere throw draping her shoulders. In style and demeanour, she easily matched Fifi pound for glamorous pound. And the way she had floored her without batting a single eyelash made it clear she was a perfect adversary. Chastity and Connie looked at her in awe and then at each other. This was going to be good!

Fifi pulled herself to her feet and tried to recoup any ounce of dignity she may still have.

'Verity Van Cougar! My God, she breathes? I thought you were dead! What are you doing here? You are not welcome. I want you to leave... IMMEDIATELY!' she scowled across the room at her.

Verity looked a little taken aback by this unexpected welcome. 'You invited me... didn't you? I got a phone call?'

'Don't be absurd! Why would I invite my past to haunt me? Those days are over. I have a new life now, and you are no part of it. Go, go now!'

Verity laughed as she walked further into the room. 'Oh girlfriend, you haven't changed a bit. Still the acid temper, still the delusions of grandeur. And still wearing the gowns from the old show, I see.'

'You too, but at least mine still fit!' returned Fifi.

'Oh yes, that's you alright. Still the same old Lettie!'

'LETTIE?' screamed Connie, Chastity and Daisy.

'Hmm. What name is she using this time? Oh, of course. That's you over the door, isn't it honey? What did it say... Madame Foofoo?' Fifi ran at Verity, pointing a threatening finger in her face.

'Don't do this, Van Cougar. I'm warning you.' Totally unaffected, Verity turned from her and sat at the table opposite Daisy.

'Well, this is a bar isn't it? Isn't someone going to offer me a drink?' she said, tapping her perfect fingernails impatiently on the table.

'Daisy love, get Miss Van Cougar here a drink,' said Chastity. 'And while you're at it, you had better

get the rest of us a brandy. Make Foofoo's a double.'
Fifi shot him an acid glance.

Daisy stood. 'What drink do you want, then?'
he asked Verity.

'Grand Marnier in a tall glass over crushed ice
with a twist of lime, a sprig of mint and a climax of
chilled mineral water.'

'Don't push it love, we're not even open!' said
Daisy coldly. She smiled and squeezed his hand
warmly.

'In that case, I'll just have what everyone else is
having thank you, sweetie.' A little taken aback by
her friendly response, Daisy smiled and went for the
drinks as she turned to face Chastity and Connie.

'Well, people. Allow me to introduce us both.
I'm Verity. The great Verity Van Cougar, cabaret
supremo and jazz singer extraordinaire. And this here
is Letitia, my former stage partner and the most
outrageous burlesque star that Berlin has ever known.
And Interpol's favourite pin up girl. I give you the
fabulous, the outrageous, the irrepressible and most
notorious showgirl of them all... Letitia Von
Schabernaket!' Chastity and Connie gasped with
shock.

'NOOOO!'   screamed Fifi despairingly,
collapsing into a chair.

'I'm sorry to interrupt you both tiptoeing down
old Memory Lane,' said Chastity scratching his head,
'but you see, we're all a bit confused here. You say
Fifi's real name is Letitia Von Schabernaket?'

'Chastity, keep out of this!' screamed Fifi.

'Don't tell us to keep out of it, you deceitful old
crow,' said Connie, banging his hand on the table in
front of her. 'We're up to our neck in it, what with

Lettie, Lulu and Billy-no-nut. We have a right to know what's going on.'

'Yeah, especially since you killing Lettie started all this in the first place,' said Chastity. Verity put her hands on her hips and laughed.

'My oh my! You have been busy girlfriend!'

'Lies! Lies! It's all vicious, twisted lies! Why are you doing this to me?'

'Doing it to you?' Connie snatched a cigarette from his packet. 'Five minutes ago you were prepared to sell our Lulu to the highest bidder, and now you're upset 'cause your actions have backfired? If you hadn't killed her...'

Fifi jumped to her feet and threw her arms into the air. 'For the last time, I DID NOT KILL LETTIE!'

Meanwhile, in Edith's parlour, Michael was drinking a cup of tea. Though still not the full ticket, the worst of his ordeal was over. After throwing a bit of bleach around her scullery, Edith had baked a sultana cake to try and cheer him up. Her advice to have a just little something to eat rather than a big meal was wise.

'How you feelin' duck, now you've had a good night's sleep?' she said, offering him a second piece of cake.

'Much better thank you Edie, although I do still feel a bit sick. And my head's pounding.' He shuffled in his seat, scratching his buttock. 'And I've come out in a rash right around my private bits. It's so itchy, it's driving me insane.'

'Well I expect that's 'cause you've had the thru'penny bits. You've got nappy rash, that's all. Oh

278

you have been through the wars duck, what with Ethel putting the frighteners on ya, the silly old hoof.'

'Silly old hoof,' repeated Ethel, spitting some of her cake down the front of her pinny.

'Yes, you! And fancy all that mippy-ja-rannie being out the garden. Bert use to sit there for hours on end with his roll ups. I didn't know it was special toots he was smoking. Suppose that's why they call it Flower Power,' she said, slapping her leg and laughing.

'Thank you so much for letting me have it all.' Michael reached across and squeezed her hand. 'It's going to make a big difference.'

'Well it's not any use to me now, is it duck? And if it's gonna help you pay off this Billy and cheer you up then take as much as you want. And it'll be easier to get to me loo, won't it?'

'That's true. Now don't forget. Don't tell anyone 'cause it's illegal and you'll go in prison if they know you're growing it. It's our big secret Ethel, isn't it?' Michael pointed a commanding finger.

'Secret. The mippy-not-narny up the garden,' she said, lifting out her top plate of teeth to remove a trapped sultana. Michael looked away politely, but then his mobile rang.

'Hello? Oh, hi Tamara. Yes sorry I had it switched off for a while. I've not been too well.' Edith sat forward in her chair as the expression on his face turned to horror. 'Oh God, no! Look, I've got another way to pay him off. Well a start, anyway. I'll make my way up there tonight. Thanks sweetheart. I still owe you.' He stood and put his phone in his back pocket. 'I'm going to have to start bagging some of that up, Edith. Billy's meeting with Fifi tomorrow

279

afternoon at Sugar Sugar, so I need to get back before then and find out what's going on.'

'We'll help you, come on,' said Edith nudging Ethel to her feet and putting the empty tea things back on the tray. Michael smiled. Such kindness was something he wasn't used to. Although he'd only known Edith for a few weeks, he somehow felt as though she'd been a part of his whole life. He felt at home.

'I only hope this down payment of grass will be enough to save my neck!'

The atmosphere back at Sugar Sugar was stifling. Madame Fifi was close to foaming at the mouth. Though Chastity, Connie and Daisy had often been on tenterhooks when it came to Fifi and her lack of personal anger management, they'd never seen her quite like this before. To Verity however this was a person she knew from old, whatever she may be calling herself nowadays.

'You're expecting us to believe you didn't kill her?' shouted Connie.

'I should have killed her. In fact I wish I had. She was a spiteful, greedy queen. She had no life of her own, so she wanted mine! And she was prepared to go to any length to get it.'

'Wanted your life? Blimey, she must have been desperate!' Connie was finding it hard to tell fact from fiction with her now.

'She craved to be me! To take everything I have and destroy my soul. When she discovered that Creighton Cross owned this building and still had fifty per cent shares in my club, she move in on him and manipulated him into giving it all to her. Before you
280

came here, she changed her name to mine and began to dress like me.'

'Well, there's no accounting for taste!' Connie shrugged at Chastity, hoping for a clue as to how much of this was believable, but he was just as baffled.

'The stupid old fool fell for her masquerade. She chewed him up, got everything she wanted and then she spat him out. You didn't think he had thrown himself out of that third floor window, did you?'

'What, Lettie?' asked Daisy, taking a therapeutic Mars bar from his jacket pocket. 'That's not very nice is it?'

As much as Chastity wanted to punch Fifi right now, he could see logic in what she was telling them.

'So you think Lettie killed him?'

'Of course she did. He wasn't of any use to her once she had forced him to re-write his will in her favour.'

'But she was a drag queen, a man. Why would Creighton be interested in her?'

'Creighton was bi-sexual,' said Verity. 'I discovered that when I had an affair with him in the eighties. Hell, we all did! But then he fell for Lettie, or perhaps I should say Fifi. With her, he had the best of both worlds. It was a match made in Heaven and he was in awe of her.'

Fifi looked at Verity. Though they'd gone their separate ways a long time ago, she realised that she was actually quite comforted to see her. Someone who'd been through what she had and shared the same struggles. She pulled a chair up closer and sat down.

'And he was the love of my life,' she said. 'But I was young and headstrong and wanted to be independent. By this time I'd earned plenty of my own cash, so he gave me half of this club and the apartment upstairs. That way, I could leave my old cruel life behind.'

'What was your old cruel life?' asked Connie with glee, getting comfortable in a chair and lighting another cigarette. Verity looked at Fifi as if to get approval to finally tell all. Fifi shrugged and handed her the story.

'There were three of us. Me - Verity Van Cougar, Lettie Von Schabernacket and Greta Vin Derbar. And we were the talk of Berlin! Our burlesque show at The Vindergurderbreurgenshaften-shitz club was second to none.'

'Vindergurderbreurgenshaftenshitz?' questioned Chastity.

'That's what she said, Vindergurderbreurgen-shaftenshitz!' nodded Connie.

'People flocked from miles around to see us!' Verity rose to her feet to walk the story through. 'I could sing. And Greta could do some amazing things with a variety of fresh vegetables and small animals. Stupid bitch overdosed in eighty-two. But the real star of the show was Fifi. Our very own Letitia Von Schabernacket. She was spectacular!'

'What did she do?' Chastity had waited years to find out about Fifi's mysterious secret past.

'She had va-va-voom. Pure class. And fabulous tits! Beautiful with it, too. All she had to do was stand there and the guys would all go nuts, some of the girls too. But it was more than that. She was an enigma. People had been defecting to Berlin to escape Soviet rule since the sixties. We take freedom for granted in the west now, but then it was precious and
282

celebrated. The place was alive with performers, artistes and some of the eastern block's greatest minds. They called it the Brain Drain, many of the clever ones got out early. Everyone was reading Herbert Marcuse and quoting tolerance versus oppression. It was Jim Morrison, it was Rock n Roll.

'Creighton had some kind of immunity, though we never really knew why or how. He crossed the checkpoints whenever he wanted. He had quite a healthy black market business back then. Many years earlier, he'd managed to smuggle Fifi to the west across the Spree Canal in a boat full of crabs.'

'Hard smell to get rid of, that!' bitched Connie, flicking her ash on the floor. Fifi was too busy reminiscing to deign response.

'So you see, to everyone who celebrated freedom she became a symbol, a success story. And it was at our club they celebrated. It was all such a long time ago, but I remember it like it was just yesterday.'

She described a large but rather tatty underground hall, constantly filled with a haze of cigarette smoke and the smell of beer and sweat. A long dark wooden cocktail bar ran the entire length of the rear wall. A couple of dozen round tables overloaded with chairs filled every possible piece of sticky carpet and several smaller more private alcoves lined each side.

'These were ideal for the wheelers and dealers because they were lined with mirrors,' said Verity lighting a Sobranie. 'You could see who was entering and leaving the club from anywhere you sat. Every contract, deal and escape mission in town was dreamt up in one of those booths!'

The ceiling was adorned with faded mirror balls left over from the thirties, and through a hole in the wall you could see an unexploded bomb from the war. 'Well, that's what we were told by Heinz who owned the club. I don't know if it was a real. But it gave the club an edge, you know, made you appreciate every moment you had left,' she laughed.

'Oh my life, I could put up with that with my nerves, couldn't I?' said Daisy, opening a second Mars bar. Verity continued.

'And then there was the stage running out through the centre of the tables. It was magnificent. And that was where we did our thang!'

'What sort of thang did you do then?' asked Chastity excitedly, moving his chair closer.

'Once all the support acts had finished, me and Greta opened our part of the show. We were so sassy, and gorgeous!' She described the two of them dressed in matching mother of pearl beaded flapper dresses, with co-ordinating skullcaps and long swinging beads. 'We ran to the front and span around and around,' she demonstrated their famous routine. 'Then the band struck up a ragtime number and we sang!

'Hello and welcome, it's showtime. Let's raise a glass of good cheer. Sing hallelujah, it's showtime. We're glad that some fucker's here!

'Put on the lights and the make-up. We'll entertain you, no fear. We're both happy to be slappy, show our tits and our ass. And if you're lucky, we'll share a bubbly glass... of champagne.'

Chastity could picture every moment of Verity's story as though he himself had a ringside seat to Berlin's most outrageous show. The two young girls on stage Charleston'd their legs and arms in the air,
284

spinning and jumping and squealing with delight at the electric response from their audience. Specs of glittering lights from the mirror balls floated around the room, lighting up swathes of cigarette smoke curling up towards the ceiling. The tiny jazz band swung in every direction to their own choreography as the girls continued singing.

'Hello and welcome, it's showtime. And we're about to begin. We'll get things rolling in no time. We're the original sin.'

'She's like a ray of spring sunshine,' sang Greta.

'And she was never that bright!' responded Verity.

'But there's no use in elocution, when you're flat on your back. We're only temping while other work is slack!' They span into a hammy tap routine, wiggling their bums and tits to the whooping of the crowd.

'This speak-easy's nice and sleazy, prohibition is dead. Let's entertain you, there's nothing more to be said!'

To rapturous applause, they ran off into the wings. Then came a drumroll. THE drumroll. The audience were on their feet as the pace changed and the band swung into an outrageously over the top anthem to jazz camp, a lush flourish of brass and double bass that would have made Mae West proud.

Suddenly the curtain rose and there she was. The one, the only... the ORIGINAL Leitita Von Schabernacket! Head to foot in glittering sugar pink diamante, dazzling eye and mind into believing she was allowing each and every person more of her flesh and her soul than she'd ever revealed before. They were desperate to see her, to touch her, to hang on her every word. Chastity imagined the absolute thrill of being unable to move in the presence of her genius as she just stood - power in the posture of her stillness. The room fell silent. Then she sang.

'I'm a working girl, I work the streets. You're the kind of guy, I'd like to meet. Come back with me, I'll give ya action. But when I'm through, you're gonna need traction!' The room exploded with the screams and cheers of her adoring public, as she took four slow but pronounced steps closer to the baying pack.

'Give me a dollar. Give me a dime. Come up and see me, we'll have a good time. I'll show ya love. I'll show ya endurance. But before you call, take out insurance!' She twisted her knees to one side, bending them to allow a large heart-shaped diamond in her ample breast to capture a clear, pure jet of light from a single overhead spot. Slowly moving her torso from side to side, she reflected the beam back out to individual men in the audience. One by one they appeared to orgasm, as it touched them and joined them directly to the bosom of their goddess.

'I'll give ya honey, I'll give ya spice. Come play with me, I'm awful nice. I'll treat ya good. I'll treat ya mean. And with me on top, no one will hear you scream!' She ripped the torso of her costume from her body to reveal a diamond in her navel. Tossing the shred of garment into the crowd, she thrust her hips violently, throwing her arms into the air and her head back and forth, from side to side in theatrical spasms of ecstasy.

'So take my number, give me a call. Take some advice, you'll have a ball. Anytime you need sugar, come to my door. My name's Lettie. What's yours?'

286

She span on her heels, scraping varnish from the boards and marched indifferently up stage away from her acolytes. Turning to face them for one final glance, she purred, 'Now ciao!' The curtain dropped, and as quickly as she had arrived, the divine diva was gone.

CHAPTER TWENTY EIGHT

It had all been a lot to take in. Chastity, Connie and Daisy were worn out with all the excitement about Madame Fifi and her secret past, yet at the same time impressed with what Verity had told them about her. They had a much clearer understanding of what had made her so tough and desperate to remain in control, and from where the experience came to make Sugar Sugar so successful. They had even gained a small insight into another side of Lettie, but there were still unanswered questions.

Chastity looked at Fifi. She was much calmer now and seemed almost relieved to have the burden of such secrets off her shoulders. His phone rang.

'Are you OK, Lulu love? Good. I'm pleased you're feeling better, we were all worried about you. Really? Yes, alright love, I'll see you tonight. Take care. Bye now.'

'Is she alright?' asked Daisy.

'Yes, she's on the bus. She'll be back for tonight's show. Poor cow. The things she's been through the past few weeks. I don't believe for one minute that she killed Lettie. So if it wasn't you Fifi, then who was it?'

'Well, the more we learn about Lettie the more it's clear she's the villain here,' said Connie. 'Who else did she upset? It could have been anybody.'

'But she left everything to Lulu,' Chastity mused, pacing the floor. 'Could it be something to do with Billy's Bar?'

'She went there to track him down, didn't she?'

'But then why would she want Lulu here at my club? Lettie was un-hinged!' Fifi had spent a long time thinking this may be the case.

'I'm not so sure,' said Verity, lighting another cocktail cigarette. 'This Lettie manipulated Creighton and let me remind you Fifi, he was nobody's fool.'

'Whoever killed her, she knew it was going to happen and she planned accordingly,' said Chastity. 'She set out to destroy you and she's still running circles around you now, even though she's been dead for six weeks. No, she wasn't un-hinged. She had a plan.'

Verity nodded. 'And it's all about this Lulu!'

Later that night, Connie knelt on the dressing room floor peering excitedly into a black bin-bag full to the brim with Edith's garden. 'Of course you do realise this officially makes you my new best friend, Dolly?'

Michael laughed. 'That's nothing. There's another seven bags at Edith's and that's only half the garden. And it's still growing. There's more than enough to pay off Billy.'

'You might not need to Lu, I've got another plan,' smiled Chastity, with his mobile to his ear.

'Eh?'

'Yeah, you still haven't told me yet either, Tit. What is it?' said Connie.

'I will tell you both, but tomorrow because we'll need Fifi's help. And we'll probably need Verity's help to persuade her.'

Connie re-tied the top of the bag and hid it under a pile of costumes. He stood back and stared at the costume rail. Chastity could see a puzzled look on his face reflected in the mirror.

'What's wrong?' he asked, pressing re-dial on his phone.

'There's costumes missing!'

'What? Not my Dusty frock, that's still at the dry cleaners?'

'No, more than that. I'm not sure what, but the rail looks different to me.'

'They've probably just fell down the back. We'll have a closer look, but later. We're running out of time, come and get ready for the show.' Connie shrugged and began to outline his lips in the mirror. 'Anyway Lu, you were saying?'

'It was a fucking great kitchen knife!'

'A kitchen knife? Jesus H Christ, she's worse than I thought.'

'And then she said she was going to turn the knob on her bed and be Angela Lansbury. What does it all mean?'

'Bedknobs And Broomsticks. It's a Disney film about witchcraft.'

'Fifi weren't in it, was she?' laughed Connie.

'Oh, I'm really worried about Edith now!' Chastity chewed on his bottom lip. 'No... I'm just being silly. She knows Ethel better than anybody. Maybe she's not come in tonight because she's unwell and gone to bed early.' He snapped his phone shut. 'I'm just panicking unnecessarily. She'll be in tomorrow afternoon as usual, I know she will.'

'Ow! Ow! Oh God, it's getting worse!' cried Michael suddenly, jumping to his feet and scratching his crotch.

'My God Lulu love, that rash is terrible! How on earth did you get that?' said Chastity, looking at the marks spreading into the small of his back.

'Looks like the clap to me,' said Connie, clapping his hands in an impromptu flamenco routine. 'Mind you, you need a shag to get that.'

'It's not, it's...' Michael looked at them both pausing and staring at him, waiting for an analysis. 'It's nappy rash.' He put his head in his hands with embarrassment as they both burst into laughter. 'It was the drugs! I had a bit of an accident.'

'Oh, you poor love,' said Chastity through giggles. 'Do you remember when Lettie had that stomach bug, Connie? Oh, it was awful. Every time she put on a frock, she parked her breakfast in it. Ran down her legs like gravy browning it did.'

'Yeah, I remember alright,' said Connie, applying his false eyelashes. 'The dressing room stank like an old people's home.'

'We just couldn't get those stains out of the costumes, Lu. Tried bleach and everything. We had to throw three of them away.' Michael wasn't amused.

'It's not funny. It's really sore and itchy.'

'At least you don't stink. Much,' Connie bitched with a wink.

'Anyway I was in the middle of telling you,' Chastity continued from earlier. 'Verity had the same frock on as Fifi, but in leopard skin with these beige bits. You could see they were from the same show. And the look on Fifi's face when she walked in!'

'Like Medusa, hissing snakes and everything, Dolly.'

'What with Lettie giving the shares to you and then Verity turning up spitting all Fifi's secret past, she's really had the rug pulled away from under her.'

'And she's shit scared of you!' added Connie.

Michael hadn't expected to hear this. 'Fifi is? Of me? Why?'

'Cause she believes that Lettie is trying to destroy her,' Chastity answered. 'But she can't figure out why she wanted you here. She's afraid of what's coming next.'

Michael had until this point believed that the grass from Edith's garden would be enough to get Billy off his back. But his confidence sapped as he remembered that this lunatic would arrive on his own doorstep the very next day. Suppose it wasn't enough to buy his freedom? And what if Chastity's secret plan didn't work either?

'Oh my God! What IS coming next?'

'That's the Fifty-per-cent Shares and Half-a-Million dollar question,' sighed Connie. 'And stop scratching your bollocks! You'll make it worse.'

'We need to find out more about Creighton Cross at the meeting with Fifi and Verity tomorrow before Billy gets here. Lettie had a reason for all of this, and tomorrow we might just find out what it is!'

An hour later, Michael's rash still didn't feel any better. He had smeared the whole area with an ointment that Edith had given him, but it just made him feel greasy. And as if it wasn't enough just to suffer, he'd been bullied into performing a particular song to emphasise his humiliation. Connie's reasoning of art imitating life was of no comfort as Michael stood on stage to perform.

'*There's a scab on my snatch and it's weeping, my knickers are sticking like glue. It's a bit hit and miss when I go for a piss, and I haven't a clue what to do!*' he sang, dancing round in a circle to the oboe accompaniment while scratching at his undercarriage.

'*I've tried rubbing round with carbolic, and scraping it off with a stick. I've got a sore quim from squatting in Vim, and I can't even reach of a lick!*' The packed house roared its approval.

'*I got a new cream from The Chemist. It was something he kept out the back. It was lovely on toast with butter and jam, but no fuckin' use on me crack!*'

The one advantage was that nobody questioned him scratching, believing it all to be part of his character's performance.

'*So now the 'festation is spreading. It's making a mess of my thatch. But try as I may, it just won't go away, I'm stuck with a scab on my snatch!*'

The following afternoon, Michael was exhausted. He hadn't slept all night worrying about Billy's impending visit to Sugar Sugar. As if that wasn't enough, Edith still hadn't turned up for work. Daisy and Verity watched Fifi pace the floor of the customer area while Chastity once again attempted to reach her on the phone.

'It's no good, I still can't get an answer. You don't suppose she's forgotten about the clocks going back, do you?'

'I don't know why they still do that. I hate it when they go forward and you lose an hour. It's like

294

alien abduction! Here, let me have a go,' said Connie, snatching the phone from him and redialling.

'Are you sure you've got the correct number?' said Fifi, wringing her hands.

'Worried you'll have to mop your own floors, are you?' Connie snapped.

'But she's normally here by now!' It was odd to see Fifi appear so concerned about anyone other than herself.

'Stop oozing emotion, Dolly. It's like that tired haggard old face of yours, it doesn't suit you. Anyway, listen up. Chastity's got a plan.'

'Oh Yes, I have! Fifi you've invited Billy here this afternoon. There's a way that you can get rid of him once and for all. If it works, Lulu will be safe and wouldn't have to pay him a penny.'

'I am not getting involved in your petty schemes and tribulations. This is not my problem!' she replied, throwing her arms into the air.

'But all you have to do is entice Billy into the safe room, like you did that drug dealer. Then we'll put a tape in the CCTV machine and film him with you and your knob out.'

'Blackmail? What a blinding idea! Would you do it? Please?' Michael pleaded.

'No. Absolutely not.'

'Hold on a minute...' Chastity began.

'Hold on to yourself for a minute. I have better things to do.'

'But if we've got film of him with a drag queen, we've got him,' said Connie. 'He's terminally straight, he can't afford to let anyone see a film of that!'

'A drag queen?' snarled Fifi. 'How dare you! Do it yourself.'

'We can't do it because we're not women, he won't fall for it. But he will know you're a woman,' continued Chastity.

'Probably,' shrugged Connie. 'We'll draw the curtains. Put a lower wattage light bulb in.' Verity's amusement only served to make Fifi more incensed.

'This is an outrage!'

'But you did it for Lulu with that dealer,' said Daisy.

'What I did to him I did because he was dealing in my club behind my back. I'm the only dealer here!'

'Oh, help the poor boy, honey!' Verity could see the sense in what they were asking. 'You know all the old tricks. Blackmail used to be your speciality. You were an expert. Even Interpol thought that. You were Miss November on their calendar in nineteen-seventy-eight.'

'Very cold, bitter month November, don't you think?' glared Connie.

'It was a winter wonderland shot, in the woods. With squirrels, rabbits and that big fat beaver.'

'What if I told you I could get you marijuana?' asked Michael hopefully. 'You can deal it here yourself. I won't ask anything for it.'

'Ah, it all becomes crystal clear now!' she yelled. 'This is why Billy-nut-sundae is after you, boy. You are responsible for this trail of devastation and humiliating destruction taking over my club! A tornado of terror strife and horror...' Then stopping suddenly in her thoughts and raising an eyebrow, she asked calmly, 'How much can you get?'

'Shed loads. If you help me, I will help you.
But first I need some information. We've got to work
out why I'm here. So tell us about this Creighton
Cross.' He turned to Verity. 'Chastity said you both
had an affair with him?'

'Yes, in the mid-eighties. He liked to flash his
money around. And he had plenty! This place was
already running as a gay discotheque and there were
several other buildings and clubs around Soho.'

'And you two liked the money, I suppose?' said
Chastity.

'What girl doesn't? But it was Fifi who really
caught his eye. It was that trick with the coke bottle...
can you still do that, honey?' she winked.

'Shut up, Van Cougar!'

'Let's just say we never needed a bottle opener!
But people move on, you know. I fell pregnant and
Creighton thought it was his.'

'I'm warning you! They don't need to know all
this nonsense,' Fifi shouted, coming back up to the
boil.

'He thought it was? You mean it wasn't his?'
Chastity leaned in closer.

'Hell no, though I didn't tell him. None of us
could cope with a child back then. We had careers
and he had his empire. It wasn't a place for a baby.
So I had to leave the show and move away until it was
born.'

'Where's the baby now?' asked Michael.

'Damned if I know. I've often wondered, poor
little thing.'

'Well, what happened to it?' said Connie
lighting another cigarette.

'I had to have him adopted. Berlin was over, they were already talking about pulling down the wall. I got a contract to work in New York and then go on tour. The road's no place for a baby. Mickey I named him. Poor little Mickey.'

There was a moment's silence. Everyone was stunned at where this could be leading, nobody more so than Fifi herself.

Chastity took Connie's cigarette from his mouth and began smoking it himself. 'Mother, Mary of the blessed drag queen! Connie love, are you thinking what I'm thinking?'

'Oh my life! So he was... what - Mickey Van Cougar?'

'No,' said Verity not quite sure where this was leading. 'Van Cougar's just a stage name. My real name's Violet. Violet Small.' Michael jumped to his feet.

'Oh my God! Oh my God! No. It can't be, can it?' he gulped.

'What is it, honey? What's the matter?'

'That's me! I'm Michael Small. And I'm adopted. That's why Lettie wanted me here. To meet you!' He took a step closer to her, apprehensive as to whether or not he would be welcomed. 'Mum?'

298

CHAPTER TWENTY NINE

Grasping at her throat and gasping for air, Madame Fifi collapsed into a devastated heap on the floor. Chastity and Daisy ran to pick her up.

'My God!' she said under her breath, knees struggling to support her. Verity was equally shocked at the revelation that after all these years her long lost son was standing right in front of her.

'Mickey? Is that you, honey? Heavens to Betsy, this is more serious than I thought.'

'I'm not listening to a moment more of this pointless folly!' screamed Fifi gruffly, attempting to walk away. Daisy and Chastity caught her as her legs gave way once more.

'So that's where Lulu's singing voice came from,' said Connie excitedly. 'It's in her fucking blood!' Fifi was thrashing about close to hysteria trying to escape the room.

'Fifi, come back here and sit your ass down!' Verity commanded, directing Chastity and Daisy to put her in a chair and hold her.

'So if Creighton Cross wasn't my father, who is?'

'Don't do this, Van Cougar! I'm warning you...' Fifi struggled. But it was too late.

'You're looking at him!' There was another moment of stunned silence as all eyes fell on a mortified Madame Fifi. Michael dropped into a chair with disbelief. Connie on the other hand fell into fits of loud hysterical laughter. Fifi turned to Michael. It was now her who was pleading.

'Don't listen to her, please. She's deranged! Too many years on the road... she's confused... she's got it all wrong!'

'Oh my God, it can't be! Can it?' Chastity was baffled. 'But you... I mean, if you... but how?'

'Fifi came on tour with me in the States before she came to London and took over this place. It was boring on the road,' began Verity. 'We got drunk on Champagne and... boy, were we drunk! Well, you know how it is... let's see if this little thing works, shall we?' Fifi's eyes were red with rage.

'Van Cougar, I will kill you for this!' Jumping from her chair, she ran at Verity punching, clawing and kicking. They fell to the ground, rolling and grasping each other's hair. Connie was rolling on the floor beside them, holding his stomach with uncontrollable hysterical laughter. Daisy on the other hand began to sob.

'Stop it! Stop it!' Chastity ran to break it up. 'Ladies... I mean, man and lady... well, maybe not lady, but …'

'STOP!' Michael threw the table aside, drinks and all. The room fell deathly silent as he walked slowly across the room to the two women, still holding onto each other on the floor. 'You're my mother? And you're my father? And neither of you wanted me? I'm going to be sick...' He turned and walked towards the dressing room. Fifi let go of Verity and crawled on her hands and knees behind him, trying to catch him up.

'Lulu? I... I mean Michael?' She grabbed Michael's leg. He stopped as she pulled herself up on
300

him until they were face to face. 'We were young, we had careers. I didn't know this was going to happen. Can you imagine me with a baby? Can you? The great Madame Fifi? It's preposterous!' Then with a sigh, she looked down at the floor with shame. 'I'm... err... I'm so sorry,' she said quietly, taking his hand.

'Bloody hell! There's a word I never thought I'd hear her say. She must be in shock,' Connie said to Chastity.

It was almost too much for Michael to bear. Tears welled in his eyes. Covering his face with his arm, he turned and began to cry. Fifi reached out wanting to hold him but couldn't bring herself to visit such alien emotion. Instead her emotions turned to anger. She spun on her heels.

'Look what you've done, Van Cougar!'

'Don't you blame me girlfriend! If you want to point your finger at someone, blame this Lettie.' Michael turned back.

'All these years I've had to fend for myself,' he sobbed. 'And all because you both abandoned me. Life on the road might not be the best place for a child, but what about life in an orphanage? And on the street? Feeling abandoned and unwanted?' Chastity had a tear in his eye too.

'All he's ever wanted his whole life is a family, bless his heart,' he said grabbing Connie's hand. 'Ooh, I feel like Lillian Gish in Orphans of the Storm!'

'I feel like Valium!' Connie sighed.

'How did Lettie find out about all this?' said Chastity.

'I don't know,' Connie replied. 'But she sure as hell knew Fifi wouldn't want all this family shit to surface. You know how cold-blooded Fifi is. She even looks like a reptile!'

'Do you mind?' defended Michael. 'She may act like a lizard in a Chanel twin-set with matching shoes, but she's still my father!'

'Oh yes. So she is. Sorry!' Connie apologised dryly. Chastity took a deep breath and wiped the tears from his cheeks.

'Let me try Edith's number again. I hope she's sitting down. She's not going to believe all this!'

'Chastity, don't tell her about this, please don't tell her! It's very important. She must not know!' cried Fifi.

It was Ethel who finally answered Chastity's call. Looking at herself in Edith's hall mirror, she removed her headscarf and dabbed sweat from her forehead, checking she looked nice enough before picking up the phone. She spoke slowly and clearly.

'Hello? Pennsylvania-six-five-thousand? No, I'm afraid Edith's no longer with us. The angels have taken her. All dressed in white they were. She's gone to a much better place. She'll be happy now. Thank you for calling, I'll note your interest on my little pad and send it up to People's Friend. Goodbye!' Gently replacing the handset, she glanced fervently at the ground around her feet. 'Now where's that crocodile got to? I need a new pair of shoes. Here croccy-croc! Here croccy-croc! Come to Ethel!'

Back at the club, the colour drained from Chastity's face as his hand went limp and his mobile fell to the floor. 'Oh my God! It can't be true!' he gasped, staring into the distance.

'What? What is it?' Connie grabbed him by the front of his jumper.

'It's Ethel. The senile, deranged old bint. I think she's killed Edith!' The entire room fell into further disbelief as Fifi walked cautiously closer to Chastity.

'What...? What did you say?'

'She's killed her!'

'Oh God, no?' Michael ran at the wall, hammering his hands against the red flock paper. 'It's all my fault! I knew Ethel had squirrels in the attic. I never should have left her alone with Edith.'

'No! This can't be happening!' cried Fifi, dropping to her knees at Chastity and Connie's feet. 'Please no, why did it have to be her and not me?'

'Eh?' said Connie exchanging glances with an equally dumbfounded Chastity. 'What's come over you? I can't handle this! I liked you better as a controlling unfeeling bitch. This isn't normal.'

Fifi threw her arms into the air and screamed at the top of her voice, 'SHE'S MY MOTHER!'

'I can't take much more of this,' sobbed Daisy. 'I wish I'd gone to bingo with Mandy now!'

'Eh?' said Michael walking across and lifting Fifi to her feet. 'Your mother?'

'Connie love, do they sell those Valium you wanted at that chemist on the corner?' asked Chastity, wiping his brow with the sleeve of his jumper.

'Hold on a minute,' said Michael. 'If she's your mother, and you're my father... that means that Edith...'

'And loopy Ethel's your Great Aunt,' said Connie, laughing. 'You want to watch it. These things run in the family, you know!'

'Wait a minute.' Chastity scratched his head with frustration. 'How can she be your mother? She told us her baby died.'

'It was her husband, my father. He saw my anatomy and took me away from her. She was so young. These things weren't done in those days,' said Fifi, turning to Michael. 'I too went to an orphanage but in Eastern Europe. I too had to fend for myself.'

'But you knew you had a mother,' he said. 'At least you had choices.'

'I didn't know until Interpol investigated me. Once I'd tracked her down, the best I could do after all that time was to watch over her, make sure she was alright.' She put her hand on his shoulder supportively. 'Don't tell Edith. She mustn't know all these horrors. She is old and set in her way, her heart would not survive the shock.'

'Oh I can't bear it! I can't bear it!' Daisy cried inconsolably, running away and up the stairs towards the entrance lobby.

'It may be too late anyway. We've got to get over there now. Snap out of it everyone!' Chastity took charge. 'Come on Connie. And you Lulu love. Verity, get Mister Fifi Von Schabernacket here a brandy. Let's go!'

'Phone me as soon as you get there!' said Fifi after them as they ran to the stairs. Three steps up, they were met by Daisy storming back down at breakneck speed. Unable to stop his enormous mass, he ran straight into them like skittles at a bowling alley. They all landed in a mass of twisted bodies at the bottom.

'He's here! He's only bloody here, ain't he?' Daisy panted hysterically.

304

'Who?'

'Billy!'

'Jesus H Christ, he's fecking here!' gasped Chastity, pushing himself up from the floor on Connie's head. 'Quick, we've got to hide. Get behind that bar you two,' he pushed Connie and Michael in the right direction. 'Daisy, get into the dressing room and stay there till I call you. Bite on something to keep you quiet. And Fifi,' he said turning to face her. 'You know what to do. He's your son, for God's sake! If you two hadn't abandoned him in the first place, he wouldn't be in this fecking mess now!' He nodded to Verity for support then ran as fast as his legs would carry him to join Michael and Connie behind the counter. 'And in the name of all that's holy, don't let him down...'

Fifi was a little too shaken to concentrate. Verity lifted her chin and looked her in the eye, putting a hand on each shoulder.

'Focus! It's our boy. We owe him this much don't we? So pull yourself together girlfriend, we've got a show to perform!'

Suddenly Billy was at the foot of the stairs. In an instant, Fifi and Verity assumed perfect posture and composure. Billy was a little taken aback by the two devastatingly turned-out women awaiting him. This was not what he had expected. Smiling and straightening his tie, he stepped deeper in the lioness' lair, unaware of the plan that had been devised to ensnare him.

'So, which one of you lovely ladies is Madame Fifi?' he said, bowing his head with a sly grin. Verity nudged Fifi out of her hesitation with an elbow in the ribcage.

'Ah, you must be Billy. My, how handsome you are? I'm so pleased it's me! Fifi, I mean. I mean, Fifi... I'm Fifi.'

'Hold it together, girlfriend!' whispered Verity through a fixed smile. Fifi glided effortlessly forward, hand outstretched.

'Hello Fifi. You're gorgeous!' he gushed, kissing her hand. 'Pleased to meet you, darling.'

'Likewise, I'm sure. And this is my sister, Verity.'

'Verity Van Cougar, at your every service,' she purred. 'My oh my, you're a big boy aren't you? My sister here likes that in a man.'

'Verity's heart's in the right place, even if most of her face isn't,' Fifi vamped cattily. 'Billy, dahhling! It is such a delicious pleasure to meet you. I feel I can relate to you, we have so much in common.'

'More than you could ever dream,' Verity batted back. 'Isn't that right, Fifi sugar?' Billy laughed to himself, not quite able to believe he had two such goddesses fighting over him. But these two sensational sirens had drawn much bigger men than Billy to his demise a hundred times before.

'So, where's Michael?' he said, looking at Fifi's enormous cleavage. 'I thought we could negotiate a little deal, you and me.'

'Well he's not down there, sweetie!' she said, giving them a little wiggle. Billy licked his lips and swallowed. She lifted his chin to make eye contact once more. 'He will be here soon. I thought we would... surprise him! But we have plenty of time. Plenty of time.' She took him by the hand and led him slowly towards the office. 'Come into my safe room,
306

Billy my darling. Perhaps a drink? Loosen up a little. Get to know each other.' Billy gave Verity a little apologetic shrug as they passed.

'Don't mind me, go ahead,' she smiled. 'Take a couple of beers. You'll not need a bottle opener!' Fifi returned the compliment with a smile - the plan was working.

'Come! Come! Tell me all about yourself, Billy. A man of such power. I find you so fascinating and exciting and... stimulating!' Gushing and giggling, fiddling with her hair like a naughty schoolgirl, she pulled him willingly into the office and closed the door.

After a few seconds, Verity called out to the three drags. 'OK, the coast is clear. You can come out now.' Jumping up from behind the bar counter, they tiptoed cautiously over to join her.

'Excellent,' Chastity said, clasping his hands together with delight. 'Part one of our plan is underway.'

'You know, she's good isn't she?' Connie nudged Michael. 'You can tell she's done this countless times before, can't you Lu?'

'Do you mind?' frowned Michael. 'I don't really want to be thinking about my parents having sex!'

'Right,' said Chastity. 'Verity, you go into Fifi's office and put in the videotape to record them. We've got to get over to Edith's as soon as we can. We'll get a cab.'

'I'm sorry honey, but I don't know how to work these things!'

'That's a good point. How does it work?' said Connie.

Michael glanced at his watch. He'd been the last one to see Edith and that had been some considerable time ago.

'Look, you three stay here and figure out how to get the vital evidence. I'll go to Edith's. I feel responsible for this. And she is my grandmother, after all. Anyway, there's less risk of Billy seeing me this way. I'll call you as soon as I know anything.

'OK, love,' Chastity nodded. 'Don't mention to anyone about Fifi being your dad and Edith your grandmother till we figure out what's going on. And be careful of that Ethel, there's no knowing what she's capable of. Come on girls, to the office!' Grasping each other's hands, they tiptoed to the CCTV bank. Michael grabbed his jacket from the back of the chair and ran up the stairs.

'Hold on Edith, I'm coming!' he said, as he pushed the glass entrance door open and stepped out onto the pavement. But as he turned, someone grabbed the back of his jacket. Spinning back, to his horror he found himself nose to nose with Knuckles.

'And where do you think you're going, you little faggot freak?' he snarled, tightening his hand around Michael's throat.

'Kn-knuckles! I err... let me go!' Michael stuttered. 'I've got to go somewhere. My grandmother! She's...'

'Billy's very upset with you,' he growled menacingly in his ear. 'Do you know how much trouble you've caused him? Oh, you've really pissed him off!'

He dragged Michael kicking and struggling to the Daimler. An enormous ugly monster of a man
308

with a shaved head and tattooed face stepped from the back of the car and took him from Knuckles' grasp, holding both his arms from behind with huge black gloved hands. Michael was terrified for his life and shaking with fear.

'I... I've got drugs for him,' he gasped desperately, eyes welling with tears. 'Grass. Loads of it! I'll pay him everything I owe him. Just let me get to my grandmother's house.'

Knuckles laughed. 'Do you hear this? The poof's got to get to grandma's house? Thinks she's Little Red Riding Hood now, does she?' he teased sarcastically. 'And what will she do? Look at me with those big eyes and bite me with her big teeth? And...' He paused for a moment, thinking. 'Oh fuck, what was the other one?'

'Ears, boss,' said the henchman, kissing Michael menacingly on the ear.

'That's it, ears. I always forget that one!' Michael could almost hear the remaining seconds of his life ticking away in the grip of these two deranged thugs.

'Knuckles, let me go!' he cried, kicking at him.

'Oh, no,' he said, moving in close and putting his hand once more around his throat. 'You slipped through my hands last time. When you were dressed as a girl trying to touch me up.'

'Eh? Me trying to touch you up? You think a lot of yourself, don't ya?'

'Oh yeah?' He tightened his grip. 'You won't be so cocky with your face cut, will you darling?' Michael's eyes widened as a tear dropped from his lashes.

'But it's a matter of life and death...'

'That's right. Yours!' Without warning, Michael took the full force of his strong clenched fist to his stomach. He buckled under the impact as every drop of air was forced from his body. He gasped for breath, but before he could fill his lungs there came another punch and then another. Doubled over, he could see his own feet hanging from his aching torso. As he lifted his head, Knuckles' fist hit the side of his face like a block of iron. A searing pain spread in what seemed slow motion through his head, like water bursting through a dam and flooding his senses. The din of Soho dulled, becoming a single whistling tone in his ears as light faded to darkness and he shifted into a different level of consciousness.

'Put him in the car, and keep him there.' He could hear Knuckles' voice muffled somewhere in the distance. There was a taste of blood in his mouth and a feeling of being pulled backwards. A sharp pain on the back of his head as it hit the car doorframe snapped him back into the real world. He was being forced into the rear of Billy's Daimler. Like a wild animal in a trap, he thrashed around kicking and fighting, anything he could do to resist.

'Let me go! Let me go! No! Please, I'm begging you...' he screamed desperately through tears. With one final push on the face he was in the car and his fate was sealed. As the henchman let go of his arms and climbed in next to him him, he raced for the door at the other end of the back seat, but a third diabolical monster was blocking his escape. Knuckles shut the door behind them, closing Michael off from the outside world. Then, sitting in the driver's seat, he turned to make eye contact.

'Billy's got a little adventure planned,' he laughed. Michael made one final lunge for the door but it was no use.

'Feisty little fucker, ain't she?' said one of the henchmen.

Knuckles smiled. 'Don't let her scratch your eyes out - while she's still got all her fingers!'

Sandwiched between two thugs bent on his painful demise, he could see his life flashing before him. Every moment of loneliness, yearning and despair was culminating in this one final journey towards his painful execution.

CHAPTER THIRTY

In the office, Chastity was flicking frantically through the small instruction booklet of the CCTV system.

'Here it is – record... page sixty two.'

'Be quick!' whispered Connie. 'I wish we could tell her to tread water for a bit while we figure out how this fucking thing works.'

'Fifi's not stupid, she knows,' smiled Verity, remembering how they had learnt to play these games together back in Berlin.

'Here it is - so press record and the red light should flash. That's it!'

'How do you get the volume up?' asked Connie, lighting a cigarette. With a turn of a knob, they could hear Fifi and Billy from the safe room.

'That's it... shhh!'

'...And all those tattoos, Billy? What a man! Let me see now. A skull and crossbones - my little pirate! A heart with an arrow through it - did someone break your heart, my poor darling? And... what's that?'

'That's my mother,' smiled Billy, proudly.

'My God! What happened to her head?'

'There's nothing wrong with my mother's head! Just, the tattoo went a bit wrong.'

'Oh well, at least she will not be watching us from that angle! Now, undo my zip darling.'

They watched the monitor intently as Billy slowly undid the back of Fifi's dress, kissing her neck gently as he lifted the straps from her shoulders. He quickly took off his own shirt and threw it aside before hastily dropping his trousers to the floor. In just her matching designer knickers and a bra, she turned to face him.

'She's definitely had those tits done,' observed Connie quietly.

'Good for her,' Chastity whispered. 'If I won the lottery tomorrow, I'd have everything done.'

'It'd have to be a roll-over then, Dolly!'

'That's right, darling,' continued Fifi. 'Look at those big strong hands! Now, kneel in front of me.' She pushed Billy down by the shoulders. 'No, over a bit.' She shuffled him to one side to make the most of the secret camera angle. 'That's a good boy. Now close your eyes. I've got something very special for you!' Billy closed his eyes with a grin. Fifi leaned forward, and with a quick resigning glance up at the camera, dropped her knickers to the floor.

'That's the little fella!' laughed Verity. Connie put his hand over his mouth.

'I think I'm going to be sick!' he retched. But that was nothing compared to Billy's reaction when he opened his eyes. His face just inches from Fifi's manhood, he gasped as the enormity of such a little thing sank into his thick skull.

'Errgh!' he gagged, mortified by what hung before him. Then his horror turned to rage. 'What the fuck? Oh, you're having a fucking laugh, ain't ya? Get away from me you filthy freak.' With a cough, he spun on his knees and emptied the contents of his fat gut into a metal waste paper bin.

Chastity, Connie and Verity jumped up and down hugging each other with glee.

314

'We've got it! That's the money shot. We've got it! Ha ha!'

The safe room door's hinges groaned under the strain of Billy tearing it open. He stopped for a moment in disbelief, watching their excitement. Then he drew breath in horror when he noticed the image of Fifi on the monitor. He looked up to see the camera for himself, suspended from the ceiling just inside the door a few feet above his head. A locomotive of anger rose from his stomach. He looked at Fifi stepping back into her dress and then at the excitement from the office.

'What? You've all been watching this? You've tried to make an idiot out of me and I'm not fucking having it!'

'You might like to just slip some clothes back on before you FUCK OFF, Dolly!' laughed Connie, pointing at Billy's underpants.

'You're sick! You're all fucking sick in the head, you perverts! I ought to smack you right in the mouth!' He drew back his fist but Connie didn't even flinch. Chastity just laughed.

'Connie getting knocked about by a naked man covered in tattoos? That's just foreplay for her!'

'You've not heard the fucking last of this! By the time I've finished with you, you're going to wish you were never born!' growled Billy viciously, pulling up his trousers and staggering out towards the stairs. Chastity and Connie chased after him with mocking laughter.

'Yeah go on, get out. And take your deformed Mother with you!' Connie yelled after him. 'If she'd only held out a bit longer in there, we could have copped a look at his missing bollock.'

'How can you cop a look at a bollock if it's missing?' Chastity giggled.

As Fifi quietly stepped from the safe room, she turned for Verity to zip up her dress. 'Did you get it all on film?' she sighed. Verity patted her shoulder proudly.

'You did good, girlfriend.'

As Billy ran up the steps towards the entrance lobby Daisy passed him on the way down, jumping out of his way with a yelp.

'Daisy! I thought I told you to stay in the dressing room?' shouted Chastity angrily.

'I needed a Mars bar from my bag upstairs. I was desperate! You told me to bite on something. But come quick, they've got our Lulu prisoner in the car outside!' Fifi and Verity were right behind, as Chastity and Connie followed him back up the stairs in Billy's wake.

Knuckles leapt from the car when he saw Billy run from the front entrance, harassed and still buttoning the front of his shirt. 'Alright Billy?' he asked, holding the door open for him.

'No, I'm not alright! Start the fucking car.'

'I've got a surprise for you. Look what we found trying to escape.' He gestured proudly in through the window at Michael struggling in the back, but Billy appeared preoccupied. 'You look fuckin' awful boss, what's happened?'

Billy turned back to face him and threw up over his shiny black shoes. He looked first at Billy wiping his mouth with his sleeve and then down at his shoes, swimming in sticky lumpy sick. Billy jumped into the passenger seat.

316

'Just start the fucking car, will you?' he coughed, taking a piece of window rag from the glove compartment and mopping his face. Knuckles shook the liquid from his feet and ran round to the driver's side.

'But we've got Michael. He's in the back.' Suddenly realising what he was being told, he span in his chair to face the captive.

'Billy, please don't do this,' pleaded Michael desperately through tears. 'I've got grass, loads of it. And there's loads more where that came from. I can pay you back everything I owe you with interest. There's a whole bag full of it in the club now as a down payment, if you don't believe me. Please Billy, I'm begging you, please?'

'Oh, you're going to fucking pay alright. For what you've done and the rest of the bastard freak show.'

'Not so fast, Billy nut-nut!' shouted Madame Fifi from across the street as they exited the club. A collective gasp of excitement rang out from a small effervescent crowd that had started to form around the car. 'You dare crawl from under your rock on Southend beach and try to intimidate me? The great Madame Fifi?' As she threw her arms dramatically into the air, her audience applauded knowingly. 'You have no idea who you are dealing with,' she threatened, reaching Billy's car window. 'This is my town! You are insignificant here. So take your sad, badly tattooed arse and your little group of amateur thug gremlins and get out of my face!'

'Fifi!' Michael screamed from the back seat. 'I'm here in the car. They've got me. Help me, please help me. He's going to kill me!'

Without breaking her acid glare from Billy, she leaned confidently into his window. 'But first, let Michael go.'

'Oh no,' Billy growled back. 'We've got unfinished business. This is Michael's last day. 'Cause tonight you see, I'm going to cut his throat!'

'Don't be a fool, Billy! I can have the film of our little playtime right across the internet within one hour. There will be a copy at my security firm's office. You will never be able to return home again.' Billy was horrified.

'You filmed it? You bitch!'

'Oh, you've heard?' smiled Connie.

'Filmed what?' asked Knuckles confused at what he'd missed.

'Shut it! And get Michael out of the car.'

'But Billy, I've just...'

'Just do it!' He slammed his hand on the dashboard. Knuckles nodded back at the thugs to let him out of the car. Freed from captivity, Michael ran across the road into Verity's outstretched arms.

'Sweet Jesus, what have they done to the poor child?' she said pushing back his damp fringe. 'His face is bleeding.'

'You've not heard the last of this, you perverted slut!' Billy spat.

'Do your worst, darling. And then, I will eat you for breakfast!' Fifi responded casually. 'Now ciao!'

Hands defiantly on hips, she span on her heels and paraded back to the group. The back wheels of the Daimler sent up a cloud of burning rubber as it tore away from the kerb, only to stall moments later from Knuckles' slippery sick-soaked shoes sliding

318

around on the pedals. A loud scream of frustration from Billy echoed up the street. But it was drowned by the laughter and rapturous applause from the crowd of onlookers as the car re-started and finally sped into the distance.

Leaving Verity's arms, Michael ran to hug Fifi. 'Dad. You saved my life!'

'Don't call me that! I'm far too fabulous to be anyone's father.'

'Well I have to say I'm impressed,' gushed Connie. 'You annihilated him!'

'Right on the nose, girlfriend!' Verity agreed.

'Yes. I was rather spectacular, wasn't I?' However a greater emergency was on her mind. 'Right, get over to Edith's house and call me as soon as you have news. Here, take this and get a taxi.' She handed Connie a handful of cash notes from inside her bra. He nodded and ran up to the crossroads.

Chastity put his arm around Michael. 'Are you OK, Lulu?' He was still shaking but, like Fifi, his mind was on a more pressing issue.

'Yes. Yes, let's just go.' As they turned to join Connie waiting for a cab, Verity put her hand on Michael's shoulder.

'Mickey, honey? I'm afraid this is where I say goodbye.' He drew in a deep breath as his eyes once again welled with tears.

'But Verity? Mum? We've only just met. I haven't even had a chance to get to know you yet.' His voice wobbled as his rib cage shook from his sobbing.

'Ahh!' sighed the crowd of onlookers collectively.

'You have your new family here. I've got work commitments and... err... I think Fifi here needs to get back to work without me breathing down her neck.' She returned Fifi's smile. 'We have an understanding that goes way back.'

'But... will I ever see you again?' Michael grabbed at her arm for an extra moment before she walked away.

'Of course! Now we've met, I'm not letting you go again, honey. I'll be back from time to time. Fifi has my number.' He began sobbing as she pulled him into a long hug and kissed his forehead. He breathed in deeply, determined to remember his Mother's scent, trying to make every last second count. Pulling gently away, she looked him fondly in the eyes. 'My little Mickey,' she said softly, pushing away his fringe kissing his forehead once more.

She turned to Fifi. 'Well, bye again, you old hag. It's been good catching up. You've got a nice thing going here.'

'Do you think? Really?' Fifi was keen for her old friend's approval of what she had done with her life since they had parted. 'Goodbye again, you old lush. Take care of yourself. Until next time.' They air kissed affectionately before Verity turned back to Michael.

'And Mickey, honey. I'm so proud of you!' With a wave to the onlookers, she walked elegantly up the street to their rapturous applause.

'Bye, Mum,' he called after her. 'I... I love you.' And then turning the corner, she was gone.

Michael stood watching the space in which he'd last seen her. His heart lifted fleetingly as a familiar face ran back around the corner towards him, but it was only Connie.

'There's a cab coming,' he said, a little out of breath. 'Verity just blew me a kiss and waved goodbye. Where's she gone?' Michael couldn't speak.

'She'll be back,' said Chastity, squeezing Michael's hand. A black London cab pulled around the corner and stopped in front of them. 'Anyway on another subject, I do hope Ethel hasn't realised it's Halloween tomorrow. I dread to think what she's done with Edith!'

CHAPTER THIRTY ONE

Michael phoned Tamara from the taxi to warn her that Billy was on his way back. He was relieved to hear she'd anticipated the danger and absconded to her sister's in Bishops Stortford. With only a day or so to go before receiving his inheritance from Lettie, he wanted to be excited and make plans. But the only thing he could focus on right now was Edith.

As the cab pulled up outside her house, Michael leapt out and ran for the front door, hammering on the knocker incessantly. Chastity ducked his head into the driver's window.

'Can you wait here please? You might have to take us to Guy's Hospital.'

'Right you are, mate,' replied the cabbie.

Connie was banging his hand on Edith's front window. 'Ethel! Ethel! Open the bloody door, mad woman! Oh, there's going to be bits of Edith strewn all over the house, I just know there is!'

'Oh, please don't say that,' said Michael.

'Yes, shut up Connie!' agreed Chastity.

Trying to see through the net curtains into the darkened room, Connie was interrupted by a tugging at the back of his jacket. He turned to see three little children staring hopefully back up at him. One dressed as a ghost, one as a witch and one as Madonna.

'Trick or treat, mister?' said Madonna, holding out a plastic bucket.

'Fuck off, you little brat. Before I rip out your eyes and eat them!' shouted Connie aggressively. The kids ran away up the street, screaming and crying.

'That wasn't very nice,' said Michael.

'It's Halloween, it's not supposed to be fucking nice!' snapped Connie.

'Ethel!' Chastity called through the letterbox. Suddenly the door opened and there she was, drying her hands on a tea towel.

'Ooh, hello!' She smiled. 'I was just straining me greens, I didn't know I had visitors.'

'What have you done with the body?' growled Connie, grabbing the front of her wrap-around pinny. Her happy smile turned to a frown as her eyes widened with fear. Michael pushed past her and ran to search the house.

'Ooh, don't push! I've got a condition. What are you talking about? What body?'

'You should never have been let out of your cage, you crazy deranged nutter!' continued Connie.

'What have you done with Edith? Where is she?' Chastity shouted. As she looked back at him, her bottom lip began to wobble and she burst into tears.

'I haven't done nothing. She's my sister. I'd never hurt our Edith.'

'Then where the fuck is she?' said Connie pulling her out of the door into the street.

'She's up The Institute,' she sobbed, dropping her tea towel on the pavement. 'They asked her if she wanted to see it. Then she never came home again. I didn't know what to do. I'm not used to being on my own.'

'She's not here,' called Michael from the top of the stairs. Chastity and Connie looked at each other, a little shamed by their spiteful outburst against this small, vulnerable elderly woman. Connie let go of his grasp, gently smoothing the crumpled fabric flat. Chastity put his arms around her.

'Oh, come here darling and give me a hug. Don't go getting yourself all upset now, silly girl. We're sorry we shouted, really we are. Jumping to conclusions. We were just worried about your sister. You look so alike, they've taken her instead of you.'

'Well, I've had my turn. Now it's her turn. We've always shared everything.'

'I know, love. There, there.'

As Michael joined them on the doorstep, Chastity noticed the way he was looking at Ethel. He stepped back and let Michael take her hug from him. As his arms closed around her back, a warm glow spread throughout his whole body. As deranged as this tiny wrinkled old lady was, she was his flesh and blood. His very own family. He felt very protective. Chastity knew exactly what was going through his mind and he himself felt a little tearful. However, they needed to get Edith.

'Connie love, upstairs on top of Edith's wardrobe is a Huntley and Palmers tin. Fetch it down, it's got some of her old photos and her birth and marriage documents in it. And try the back parlour for any photos you can find too, it's like a boot fair in there.' Connie nodded and ran up the hall. 'And check Ethel's not left any gas on or fires burning. Check the kitchen... and lock the back door,' he called after him. 'Now Ethel dear, where is this place?'

'What, the Institute? It's by a big wall. You can see it from the cafe, they take us there now and again.'

'A wall by a cafe? Anything else?'

'Yes, it's very wet,' she said, dabbing her eyes on her pinny.

'What, rising damp?'

'Yes, and when it rises, it goes up. Then it comes down again. Like Noah's Arc in Woolworth's.'

'Woolworth's?' Chastity and Michael looked at each other baffled.

'Sound like the Thames Barrier, mate. Up Woolwich,' chipped in the taxi driver.

'That's what I said, Woolworth's.'

'Right, get her in the car Lu, I'll get her hat and coat. We'll figure out whereabouts it is when we get to Woolwich. It's such a relief to know Edith's OK. But whether we can convince the Institute they've taken the wrong woman or not and get her back out is another ball of wool altogether!'

Though newly rebuilt and refitted, Ethel's Institute was still a cold and cavernous place. White walls, ceilings and gloss floor tiles with an array of matching wipe-clean tables and plastic chairs and sofas, all glamorously lit by dozens of strip fluorescent lighting hung by chains from the ceiling. Over the din of activity from a vast array of extremities of the mind, Edith sat with another white-gowned elderly lady at a table talking.

'Well I never did! Who'd have thought?' she said, taking a sip of tepid tea from a plastic beaker.

'And do you know, from that day on Margaret always put a little bleach in her tea to keep her teeth nice and white?' said the woman, patting her arm.

'I'll have to try that one!' Edith smiled.

From the other side of the room, the Warden pointed Edith out to Chastity. With a huge sigh of relief, he ran with Michael across the highly polished floor towards her. For Connie however, running on a shiny surface was a little more of a challenge in his leather-soled brogues. He grabbed Edith's table with both hands to stop himself from sliding any further.

'Bloody hell, that floor's a death trap in these shoes! It's like Streatham Ice Rink in here. I'm like Jane Torvill, only thin.'

'Oh Edith, am I pleased to see you?' said Chastity, grasping her hand to his chest.

'Oh, hello duck! This is my friend Pat,' she replied. Chastity looked her over sympathetically. A moss-green plastic pearl necklace with just one matching earring set off her tea-stained white gown, and her mounds of grey-rooted black hair was piled atop her head and held in place with Sellotape.

'She was just tellin' me how she helped Margaret Lockwood with her manky gums,' continued Edith. 'Ain't she clever?'

'I doubt it,' Chastity replied cynically.

'Word of advice,' interrupted Connie. 'Don't ever watch a Margaret Lockwood film when you're off your face. That fucking mole! If I got up to swat that fly off the TV screen once, I did it a thousand times.'

Michael stooped and gave his new-found grandmother a small peck on the cheek. She smiled back up at him, eyes twinkling, and he realised for the first time that his eyes were exactly the same colour.

'Ooh,' she continued, 'And Pat made all those lovely frocks for Marilyn Monroe an' all. She did that white one that goes up in the air. I was telling her about your frocks, Connie.'

'That's not Connie Francis!' pointed Pat.

'No, you daft apeth. This is me daughter Connie, who makes all the costumes. She's doo-lally-tat, this one!' Edith laughed, slapping her hands on her legs.

'You can say that again,' Chastity agreed.

'She's doo-lally-tat, this one!' Edith said again.

Connie patted Chastity on the shoulder. 'Are you sure Edith's not better off here?'

Chastity looked at Michael, then Connie and then back at Edith. 'Ooh, I feel like Teresa Wright in Shadow of Doubt!'

'Edith, what on earth happened?' said Michael, squatting to eye-level. As Edith spoke, he could now see through her soft downy wrinkles that she had the same nose as him, and the same chin. He had never seen this in Madame Fifi. After so much cosmetic work, all family resemblance was long since gone.

'Oh, you'll laugh you will! They came in the van and asked me if I wanted to see the new Institute since the fire. Lovely, ain't it?'

'Ooh, I remember that fire. September nineteen-forty-five,' said Pat, grasping at the pearls nervously.

'But Edith, they thought you were Ethel. Why didn't you say anything?'

'Well, they told me I had a nice cup of tea and some dinner waiting. Then I told 'em I had to go to work, and they gave me this basket to weave.' She
328

held aloft a big knot of screwed-up wicker. 'Well, I can't get the hang of the fuckin' thing!' Michael took it from her and put it back on the table.

'But didn't they realise you weren't Ethel?'

'Well, it's all new nurses since the fire. They had a photo of Ethel, but it was from nineteen-sixty-eight and it looked like me. Oh, we did laugh, didn't we Pat?' The two old ladies giggled mischievously. Chastity took her arm and lifted her from her chair.

'Come on Edith love, it's all sorted out and it's time to go home. They've shown Ethel to her room and she's having a bath and a cup of tea. They said to let her settle then we can visit her in a couple of days.'

'Is she alright then?'

'Yes, she's fine. I think she's glad to be back.' He patted her hand reassuringly. 'Anyway, we've got a cab waiting. Feck only knows what that will have on the clock by now!'

'I'll get me coat then,' said Pat, rising to her feet.

'No Pat, you've got to stay here,' said Michael gently pushing her back into the chair by her shoulders.

'Why?' she frowned.

'Because... because Dorothy Squires has had a costume malfunction. The marabou feathers keep sticking to her lipstick and need lowering into the cleavage. She needs your help.' Pat clasped her hands together excitedly.

Chastity smiled. 'Spoken like a true drag queen!' he said, exchanging a knowing glance with Connie.

'Weren't it Dorothy Squires that kicked that cab driver in the face?' said Connie. 'If she was coming with us, it wouldn't matter what was on the clock!'

'See you again then Pat,' Edith waved. 'I'll come visit you. Bye then. Be lucky!'

'Can we just hurry up now?' twitched Connie impatiently. 'It's creepy being locked inside an asylum over Halloween.'

'Yes, come on Edith hurry along now. I never thought I'd hear myself say this, but after the past couple of days it's going to be good to get back to work and some sort of normality.'

'As normal as a man can be in a bra and high heels,' said Connie putting a cigarette in his mouth ready for lighting. Michael was suddenly flooded by a wave of sadness.

'You say that, but me and Nigel might be leaving tomorrow.' He dipped his head to the floor.

'Eh?' said Connie.

'Six weeks. Tomorrow is six weeks to the day since Lettie's wake. Anything could happen. Tomorrow night could be my last show!'

CHAPTER THIRTY TWO

In dramatic contrast to the Halloween celebrations filling Soho and Sugar Sugar, the dressing room had an eerie quiet. As Michael applied his makeup in the mirror, he was painfully aware that it could be for the last time. It had only been six weeks since he'd worn it for the very first time and so much had happened since then. Despite the horror of that first night, he'd actually begun to enjoy his new job and the people he shared it with. But there would be no point in continuing after receiving so much money from Lettie, though he had every intention of remaining around his new family.

He stopped for a moment and looked at Chastity sitting beside him applying eyeliner. He could see Connie in the mirror already fully made up, hand-sewing the finishing touches to a large black costume. It was going to be odd not being here with them every night.

'What a week!' sighed Connie, breaking the silence. 'First Fifi's knob, then Ethel, then Verity, then Billy-no-nut and then Edith. And that asylum! My hands are still shaking,' he exaggerated, holding one up to demonstrate.

'Don't waste it,' said Chastity dryly. 'Give her a scrubbing brush someone, this floor needs doing.'

'Oh, welcome to the fucking slave ship! Just strap me to an oar.'

'Anyone we know?' Michael laughed.

Connie walked over to take a peek out through the door to the customer area. 'It's packed out there tonight. Everyone's in costume. It's gonna be fab! Talking of which...' He bit off the last of the sewing thread. 'Ta da! Here you are Lu, the replacement costume.'

'Thank you,' said Michael, taking it from him and holding it up. 'I wonder what happened to the other one?'

'I told you there were some missing, didn't I? Anyway it's probably for the best. Lettie had her scabby armpits in the old one. And she was fatter than you.'

'I am grateful you made it. It's a lot of work for just one Halloween show.'

'Well, whoever takes over from you can wear it next year. Unless they're gargantuan like Lettie, in which case I've kept these spare bits for dart inserts,' laughed Connie, holding up the offcuts.

Chastity smiled at his completed face in the mirror's reflection then turned to Michael.

'Right Lulu, are you ready to be The Phantom Hooker Of Olde Soho? Now, don't worry if you fuck it up, love.'

'We probably all will 'cause we only do it once a year,' supported Connie.

'The audience will just think we've changed it a bit. So have fun with it, Lu.' Michael put down the costume and sat looking at the floor. 'What's wrong, you're very quiet?'

'It's kind of freaky playing the Phantom part knowing Lettie always used to play it, especially being Halloween and all. It all seems a bit surreal, like stepping on her grave. If it wasn't for all of you, I'd probably be dead myself by now.'

'With your dismembered fingers trying to claw their way out of that Primark box under his bed,' growled Connie comically, with an evil Panto laugh.

'Well, yeah. And the last six weeks. What a roller-coaster ride! It's going to seem odd now not being here doing the show with you both.'

Connie put his arms around him and kissed him on the cheek. 'Despite everything Dolly, I actually think I'm gonna miss you.'

'I'm going to miss you too,' agreed Chastity.

'But just think about all that gorgeous, delicious cash you're going to get.'

'And the shares for you two,' said Michael.

Connie walked back to his chair and sat with a deep sigh. 'Well, on that subject,' he said, rubbing his hands together nervously. 'I didn't think I'd hear myself saying this Dolly, but... let me have a swig of that gin first.' He reached tetchily out to Chastity for his drink. Taking a long mouthful and gulping it back, he placed the glass back on the table and took a deep breath. 'Alright, here goes. Hold my hand, Tit. Here it is... I think you should give the shares to Fifi.'

'Really?' This was the last thing Michael ever thought he'd hear Connie of all people say.

'Well, she did save your neck. And we've still got our jobs. And after today, getting back at Fifi doesn't seem so important somehow.'

'That's true,' agreed Chastity. 'And at least she'd know what to do with them.'

'Yeah. And what are we going to do, anyway? Stick them in a drawer?' smiled Connie. 'Perhaps just buy us something nice instead. Like a cake? Or some leather bondage porn?'

'Ooh,' remembered Chastity. 'I've seen a lovely new knee-length platinum blonde wig in Berwick Street. It's a Lady Godiva. Comes with a matching muff and earrings.'

At that moment, the room was flooded with noise from the busy customer area as Daisy and Edith ran in, quickly closing the door behind them.

'Don't panic, we're here,' gushed Daisy.

'Right Edith, you remember how to work the smoke machine?' said Chastity, taking her by the hands to help her focus.

'Yes duck. Press the red button on the top and count to three.'

'Good girl. And Daisy, you work the front and back tabs and the trap door for Lulu's entrance.'

'OK. It's left for up and right for down, isn't it? Or is it right for up and left for down?' Daisy took an emergency Mars bar from him pocket to help him concentrate.

'Do your best, love. You look terrified, Lulu.' Chastity patted Michael's hand supportively. 'Don't be nervous. If it all goes wrong it will make the show funnier. And don't forget to put on your mask just before you spring up on the trap door.'

'And watch your fingers as that trap comes up or you'll lose them. Then you'll have to spend some of that delicious fortune on shoes from Primark so you've got a box to keep them in!' laughed Connie.

'I'm not nervous about tonight, I'm nervous about tomorrow. How do I get all the money? How does it arrive?'

If I know our Lettie, there will certainly be drama. So the only advice I can give you love, is this - in the name of Mary, Mother of the blessed drag queen and everything else that's holy, for feck's sake brace yourself!'

Sugar Sugar was packed to the brim with excited customers of all shapes, sizes and costumes for its now legendary annual Halloween Special. A cheer of anticipation went up as the wall lights slowly dimmed to pitch black. Following a drumroll, they listened silently in the darkness as they were transported back to a bleak and dangerous Edwardian Soho. They could hear horses hooves on cobbles, long dead drunks laughing and shouting, a ghostly organ grinder twinkling out a merry waltz - all painting a picture in their minds of the macabre performance to come. As the show lighting lifted, a spooky mist drifted across the boards and billowed down over the front edge of the stage towards the awe struck onlookers.

Another cheer lifted as Connie and Chastity walked flirtatiously onto the stage dressed as Edwardian prostitutes, complete with long bustle-backed skirts and bonnets, and enormous life-like rubber cleavages.

'Not much trade tonight, is there?' said Connie, sounding surprisingly more common than he did in real life.

'You wanna try washing that clack of yours a bit more often!' came Chastity's bitchy reply.

The audience roared with approval. A barrel organ waltz rang out and swaying from side to side with the music, they began to sing.

'We're just a couple of Olde Soho tarts, we're scarlet women of the night.'

'Give us a shilling, you'll find me quite willing,' sang Chastity.

'A florin gets the works!' added Connie.

'Oh, everybody loves a prostitute. A hooker, a molly, a whore. We're working the street just to service your meat. Yes, everybody loves a prostitute!'

Michael meanwhile, clambered down a stepladder from behind the backdrop to the large cavity beneath the stage. A damp musty smell filled his nostrils as he descended into the creepy dankness. As he stepped from the bottom rung, the ladder fell sideways, sliding across the bare brick wall and smashing a solitary light bulb. Eyes adjusting to the sudden darkness, he could see light from the performance above slithering through the gap around the edge of the trap door. Three stories below street level and in near darkness, visions of the real Edwardian Soho flashed through his head, and a chill ran down his spine at the thought of the hideous carryings on that may have taken place on the very spot he was standing. He began to feel claustrophobic and wasn't sure he could cope with waiting there for the song to end before his big entrance. If only he could find the fallen ladder.

Unaware of Michael's fear just a few feet below them, Connie and Chastity continued giving it their all.

'Her name is Shirley, she goes out quite early to taverns as the boys go in,' Chastity pointed at Connie, while scratching at his crotch and sniffing his fingers.

'Her name is Ada, she goes out much later when they come out again!' Connie retorted, cupping his breasts.

'Yes, everybody loves a prostitute. A hooker, a molly, a whore. Once you've shown us your cash, you can give us a bash. Oh everybody loves a prostitute!'

They swayed their ample skirts from side to side into the refrain.

'A fallen girl or two, can make your dreams come true.'

'A farthing and maybe I'll show you me ha'penny,' Connie sang, lifting the front of his skirt and pointing to his crotch.

'Me thrup'penny bits, an' all!' Chastity wobbled his tits.

'Oh, everybody loves a prostitute. A hooker, a molly, a whore. And when you've had your share, there's another one there, 'cause everybody loves a prostitute!'

Daisy signalled across the stage to Edith in the opposite wing. With a thumbs-up, she pressed the smoke machine button and counted to three. As further mist billowed about Connie and Chastity's feet, they huddled together in theatrical fear downstage of the trap door.

'There's just one thing alone, that chills us to the bone. A spooky old spectre. We always expect her, to creep up behind us and steal our vaginas. The Phantom Hooker of Olde Soho!'

Dramatic, deranged church-organ music rattled the room. 'Ooh!' cooed the audience. Just as Daisy was about to open the trap door for Michael, he noticed through a slit in the curtain that the audience were parting for The Phantom to enter from the back

337

of the room. Through a corridor of mock booing and hissing, he swayed his long black cloak from side to side, reaching murderously out at people here and there, as if to grab by the throat and strangle. Chastity nudged Connie.

'Look! Lulu's coming up through the audience,' he whispered.

'I thought she was coming up through the trap door?' Connie replied quietly.

'Shows initiative, you see. Fabulous teachers, that's what we are.'

'Aren't we marvellous!' They stepped back, allowing The Phantom to take centre stage, spinning to face the audience and sing in a warped theatrical voice.

'I've come to haunt you! Back from the grave. Who will I slaughter? Who will I save? I'm the Phantom Hooker of Olde Soho. Forever you'll be in my grasp. I'm the Phantom Hooker of Olde Soho!'

'You know, Lulu's very good isn't she?' whispered Connie.

'Hmm. A bit too good. Something's not right here!' frowned Chastity. The Phantom continued.

'Don't be mistaken, I won't be forsaken. You're leaving your old life behind. No misunderstanding, I'll now be commanding your body, your soul and your mind. I'm the Phantom Drag Queen of Olde Soho!'

'Drag Queen? That's not in the script!' said Connie.

'I've got a horrible feeling about this.' Chastity gulped, stepping forward into character. 'Oh Phantom Hooker of Olde Soho. Pray reveal to us all at last your true identity!'

338

To a deep drum roll, the creature finally ripped off its grotesque mask and threw it high into the air. Chastity's suspicions were confirmed. This wasn't Michael giving the performance of his life.

CHAPTER THIRTY THREE

'Hello gorgeous!' yelled the unmasked Phantom with excited glee.

'LETTIE?!' Connie and Chastity were mortified, though the audience cheered and applauded their approval. This sudden return from the dead was a surprise nobody had expected. Daisy ran from the wings and screamed.

'Arrgh! It's a ghost! It's a ghost!' Edith was equally shocked.

'Well, bugger me sideways!' she said, clasping her face in her hands. Chastity and Connie looked at each other in utter disbelief, then back at Lettie. They'd seen him in drag hundreds of times but now he looked different somehow. The hooked nose was gone, as was the turkey neck. There were no bags under his eyes and not a wrinkle in sight.

'Your face,' gasped Chastity. 'My God, you look so... different.'

'I've had it all done dear,' said Lettie, tipping back his head for dramatic effect. 'The only things that are real are these babies.' He pulled open the top of his cloak to reveal a huge sparkling diamond and ruby necklace. He ran his fingers across it, red talons clicking over the rocks. 'Six weeks of pain and discomfort just to look as fabulous as this. Was it worth it?' he shouted out, turning to the audience. They screamed their support.

'Six Weeks? SIX WEEKS!' It was all beginning to make sense to Chastity. 'What the feck have you done with our Lulu?'

'Nothing, my darling. Why, what did you have in mind?'

'She... she's still down there,' stuttered Daisy, snapping out of his mortification. 'I didn't pull the lever. I thought that was her coming a different way.'

'Well pull the bloody lever, woman!' Chastity snapped. Running back behind the tab curtain, he yanked the handle. With a loud snap the trap door opened and catapulted a shocked Michael into the air. Everybody watched as he dropped back to the floor with a loud painful thud, crying out in pain. The audience laughed. Jumping quickly to his feet he turned to find himself face to face with Lettie. He started backwards with horror.

'You?!' In the darkness beneath the stage he'd heard some sort of commotion, but it was a little muffled and he couldn't really make out what was going on. But of all things imaginable, the last he expected was this. He could feel his blood pressure rising as his breathing quickened. All he could think was that he wanted to punch his nemesis in that newly created face. He lunged forward ready to strike but Chastity held him back.

'You know, we'll have to get that trap door seen to!' said Lettie casually. Chastity could feel his skull pounding under the pressure of his brain trying to comprehend exactly what was going on.

'Trap... what the bugger are you doing here?' he screamed. 'The coffin... we saw you in the coffin! How can you be here?'

'But darling, I own the place!' Lettie giggled.

342

'WHAT?!' everyone gasped collectively. The audience squealed with delight.

'Daisy, go get Fifi,' Chastity ordered. 'And hurry.' The crowd rapidly parted as Daisy thundered through in the direction of the office.

Connie glared acidly. 'You've got a fucking nerve showing your plastic face here after all you've put us through, you manipulative, deceitful old whelk!'

'You evil, evil queen!' added Michael, shaking with anger.

'But the funeral. You had a funeral!' Chastity was quivering too.

Lettie laughed. 'My dear, dear Chastity. After all these years, don't you know a cabaret show when you see one? That was my twin brother Brian in the casket. Didn't he look fabulous in my makeup?'

'Twin brother?'

'Oh excuse me,' said Connie sarcastically. 'I must have smacked the wrong corpse!' He reached forward and slapped Lettie hard across the face. Lettie slapped him back, so he slapped him again. Once more Lettie returned, as did Connie and then once again Lettie. The roar of the audience grew louder and louder with each attack. Finally Lettie was bored.

'Oh, enough of this nonsense!' he said impatiently, pulling a long, glistening sword from a scabbard inside his cloak. Everyone gasped, taking a step backwards. The audience applauded enthusiastically.

'This is better than last year, ain't it?' said one skinny queen at the front.

'Shh!' scolded his entranced friend.

'Oh my God, she... she's got a machete!' cried Michael, standing protectively in front of his grandmother.

'Now listen up!' Lettie pointed the sword around the gathering. He turned to shout at the sound technician. 'Oi, dyke? It's time. Press play.' The girl at the DJ desk nervously pushed the button. Silly jazz music blasted through the speakers. 'Not that, you dozy slag! Track five,' Lettie screamed, swinging his weapon around above his head. Everyone took a step further back. The girl's shaking fingers fumbled the song forward to a theatrical Jewish violin lament. Lettie lifted his eyebrows and took a deep breath, nostalgically holding his hand over his heart.

'It's been six weeks, but finally now Creighton's probate is up.' His eyes widened psychotically as he giggled through his words. 'I own this club, Connie's flat, the whole building. In fact, I own half of Soho! So now you all work for me.' His deranged laughter echoed around the room.

Meanwhile, Daisy slammed through Madame Fifi's office door just as she took a sip from her whiskey. Nearly choking, she jumped to her feet.

'Fifi, come quick! Come quick!' he cried, panicking through tears.

'Daisy! How many times have I told you? Don't run. You're too big. You will have the plaster off the walls!'

'It's Lettie. She's back from the dead. She's gone mad. And she's up on stage and she's got one of them machete things!'

'WHAT?' she frowned through Botox. Slamming her glass down onto the desk. With a determined scowl, she unlocked the top door of her filing cabinet and took out a revolver.

'Aw my Gawd!' sobbed Daisy, running back out while grappling in his pocket for his last remaining emergency Mars bar.

Back on stage, Michael was trying to understand Lettie's diabolical master plan.

'But what about the half-a-million? And the shares you promised me?'

'Don't be ridiculous! As if I'm going to give all that to someone I'd only known a month,' he laughed insultingly.

Michael had fire burning in his chest. 'You've fucking used me!' he growled, moving closer and pointing a finger in Lettie's unperturbed face. 'It's abuse, that's what it is. If you had any idea of what the past six weeks has been like for me...'

'Oh, calm yourself, love.' He pushed Michael's finger away. 'You've got a job, haven't you? At least I got you away from that hideous psycho Billy. He's out of your life once and for all.'

'No thanks to you!' Michael scowled.

'And I taught you a song, didn't I? Gave you your big break? Lulu L'Amour, Soho's new darling? As soon as I discovered Verity was your mother, I knew you'd be a singer. And what a fabulous voice it turned out to be!' Chastity was shocked.

'You've... huh...' He was having trouble concentrating over the Jewish violin. Turning to the girl on the DJ desk he shouted, 'Turn that bloody music off, you stupid fat moosh-malt!' The crowd laughed as the violin ground to an abrupt halt.

'You've heard Lulu sing?' he continued. 'Where exactly? Surely not here?'

'I've been around, popped in from time to time. Just to check you're not screwing up my inheritance.'

Daisy reached the stage somewhat out of breath. 'I didn't see her pop in! Honest Chastity, I didn't,' he panted. 'And you know me, I'm sharp as a fox with a Stanley knife.'

Fifi could hear the whole conversation from the back of the hall. She watched with contempt as she loaded six fresh new bullets into the revolver.

'It was you I saw in the street?' said Michael. 'With your face all bandaged up like the Elephant Man?'

'Not quite the analogy I would have used,' Lettie frowned.

'Sounds spot on to me!' snapped Connie. 'And you stole that Phantom Hooker costume too. And to think I used to like you.'

'Yes.' Chastity stepped forward. 'We thought you were our friend. We loved you. But you've turned everyone's world upside-down and now here you are, back from the grave without a care in the world for Lulu or any of us, dripping in diamonds, rubbing everybody's faces in it. We're supposed to be part of the same team. What about the Sisterhood?'

'Oh, you and that bloody Sisterhood! Chastity darling, that old diamante tat you're wearing is like your face. Worn, tired and ready for re-mounting!'

'She has got a point,' smiled Connie unsympathetically.

'Whereas these sparkling little babies are for real! *And unlike love, they lustre on!*' he sang, to the delight of the crowd.

346

'Oh, for feck's sake!' Chastity cursed.

Michael's whole body was aching with hurt and betrayal. 'Oh God, this is insane!'

'I know, darling. But isn't insanity delicious?' Lettie turned to see Fifi climbing the stairs to the stage, revolver pointed at his face. 'Oops! Look out, your father's here.'

'Lettie! You're alive?' she hissed.

'Ta da!' He threw his hands into the air and curtsied.

'But you should be extinct!'

'I know that was your plan, you diabolical murderess. But you see Fifi darling, you ran over the wrong Cohen brother.' She tightened her grip and squeezed her finger a little on the trigger.

'Don't be absurd! I didn't run over anybody. Get out of my club this instant. Up with this charade I will not put!'

'Actually, this is my club. Creighton Cross, remember? Or is it the dreaded Alzheimer's? You are knocking on a bit now, darling.'

'You twisted, bitter, deranged little skunk! I still own fifty per-cent of the shares.'

'Oh, Fifi, Fifi, Madame fucking Fifi! Read your contract, sweetie. You only own fifty per cent if you're a free woman... man... thing. But if you're in that awful Cell Block H, your shares revert to the owner of the remaining shares. And that's me!' Fifi lowered the gun momentarily.

'What do you mean, Cell Block H?' Lettie laughed at her sarcastically. She raised the gun once more.

'This is her boys,' Lettie shouted. Without warning, two policemen leapt from the wings and pulled Fifi's arms behind her back. The revolver was ripped from her hand as cold hard cuffs snapped tightly shut around her wrists. 'Take the old trout away. And throw away the key!'

Edith ran forward and grabbed Fifi around the waist, burying her head against her chest. 'Ooh, golly wars! A diabolical murderess? Not Mrs F? It can't be true.' One of the coppers pushed her off.

'Madame Fifi?' he said. 'I'm arresting you for the murder of Brian Cohen, possession of an assumed illegal firearm and the subsequent attempted murder of Bernard Cohen. You do not have to say anything, but it may harm your defence if you do not mention when questioned, something which you will later rely on in court. Anything you do say will be taken down and may be given in evidence.'

'Knickers!' laughed Lettie. 'Take her scabby drawers down and give them as evidence!'

Fifi was horrified. 'What did you say? Scabby drawers? How dare you? My knickers are top of the range designer.'

'Oh, got a label have they? What's that then, drip dry?' Lettie giggled. 'On second thoughts, they must be from the Kylie range. How else would they fit that big arse? Get her out of my sight. And take her gargantuan buttocks with you!' The policeman looked at Lettie's sword. 'Stage prop!' he grinned mischievously, sliding it back into its scabbard.

Fifi struggled as they aggressively led her down the stairs and through the audience. 'Now ciao!' Lettie waved after them. The audience booed and hissed in full pantomime mood as their cabaret baddie was carried away to pretend prison forever. But to those in the know, reality was of course far more sinister.

'But I'm... I'm innocent!' Fifi screamed, feet dragging behind her on the woodblock. 'I have killed no one! Unhand me, this instant! You have not heard the last of this! Let me go. I know your superiors. Do you know who I am? Let go of me! LET ME GO!' Edith ran into Michael's arms.

'Fifi? Dad?' he cried. 'Oh my God. Chastity, do something. Please, do something!'

'Is this all part of your dastardly masquerade, or are they real police?' asked Chastity.

'Real? Abso-fucking-lutely!' Lettie replied sharply.

'I'm so sorry, Lulu love,' Chastity said to Michael, bowing his head.

Edith turned in anger and punched Lettie on the arm. 'You spiteful little bleeder! I ought to slap your legs.'

'What do you do for an encore, bite the head off a kitten?' chipped in Connie angrily.

Ignoring them both, Lettie turned to address his audience. 'At last, the evil old hag is totally destroyed! I love it when a plan comes together.' As the crowd erupted with applause he sang, '*Ding, dong, the witch is dead. Wicked witch, the witch is dead!*'

He stood at the front of the stage with his arms in the air, milking adoration like a megalomaniac Emperor believing his own God status.

'She's totally lost it, hasn't she?' said Connie, open-mouthed in disbelief. 'Eva Peron comes to Soho. Don't cry for me, Sugar Sugar.'

'We've lost a bitch and gained a monster!' Chastity sighed, wiping away a tear.

'We thought Ethel was a feather short of a hat. But she is definitely not right in the fucking head!'

Michael's anger was like a knot of steel pounding in his stomach. 'Fifi didn't kill Brian Cohen. I'm sure of it. I can feel it in me prostate. I think she killed her own brother, and Creighton Cross. We can't let her get away with this. We've got to do something!'

'We will,' Chastity took Michael by the hands. 'By feck, we will! But don't do anything rash, we need to talk it through. In private. You're the heir to this throne, not her. My God, if it takes me to my last breath, she's going to pay for this!' They started back with a gasp as Lettie spun viciously to face them.

'What are you all whispering about? There's a show to finish. And if you don't, you'll all be on the street. Tonight,' he sneered. 'And that includes Edith and Daisy. So get to work! I'm going to my new office. Now ciao.' He descended the stairs, accepting worship from his subjects on the way through.

'Daisy, take Edith. And change the backdrop on your way past,' ordered Chastity. Daisy gently guided her away by the shoulders, both sobbing uncontrollably. As they stepped down into the dressing room, Daisy pulled the backdrop handle. The entire back of the stage was suddenly an enormous sequinned rainbow flag, shards of multi-coloured light reflecting to every corner of the club. Chastity turned solemnly to Michael.

'Well, Lulu. It looks like you're stuck with us now, I'm afraid.'

'I suppose that makes you a fully-fledged drag queen,' added Connie, patting him on the shoulder.

'Congratulations, Dolly. Sorry it didn't work out the way you wanted.'

'Don't apologise. As it happens, I'm exactly where I want to be. Doing exactly what I want to do. I'm Lulu L'Amore! And The Sisterhood will prevail. Come on girls, we've got a song to do!'

To an enormous cheer from the audience, they ripped open the Velcro on their costumes to each reveal a sequinned jump suit with flared sleeves and bellbottom trousers. Connie's was pink, Chastity's yellow and Michael's a vivid royal blue. As a giant glam rock anthem began blasting from the speakers, Michael sang defiantly through tears, channelling every ounce of anger from every cell in his body, every nerve and every fibre. He was strong and he'd earned his badge of attitude, now nothing and no one could stand in his way. He was a drag queen!

'When I was young, my life had no meaning. My emotions were numb, devoid of all feeling. I was distraught, life brought me to my knees, without a thought, for a person like me.

'Then something that, I wasn't expecting, came right out of the blue, and changed my direction. Now here I stand, right where I want to be, Heaven on Earth, for a person like me.

'Unlike before, I have clarity, and that means a lot, for a person like me. I've seen the light, rainbows across the sky. I'm where I belong, till the day that I die.'

www.ingramcontent.com/pod-product-compliance
Lightning Source LLC
Chambersburg PA
CBHW072201130726
47910CB00011B/1771